INUKSUK

Gregory Spatz

BELLEVUE LITERARY PRESS
New York

First published in the United States in 2012 by
Bellevue Literary Press, New York

for information, address:
Bellevue Literary Press
NYU School of Medicine
550 First Avenue
OBV A612
New York, NY 10016

James Wright, excerpt from "Lying in a Hammock at William Duffy's Farm in Pine Island,
Minnesota," from *The Branch Will Not Break,* © 1963, by James Wright. Reprinted
by permission of Wesleyan University Press. Heather McHugh, excerpt from
"What He Thought," from *Hinge & Sign,* © 1994, by Heather McHugh. Reprinted
by permission of Wesleyan University Press.

Bellevue Literary Press would like to thank all its generous
donors—individuals and foundations—for their support.

  This project is supported in part by an award
ART WORKS. from the National Endowment for the Arts.

Library of Congress Cataloging-in-Publication Data
Spatz, Gregory, 1964-
Inukshuk / Gregory Spatz. -- 1st ed.
   p. cm.
ISBN 978-1-934137-42-0 (pbk.)
I. Title.
PS3569.P377I58 2012
813'.54--dc23
                                        2012008326

Book design and type formatting by Mulberry Tree Press, Inc.
Manufactured in the United States of America
first edition
10 9 8 7 6 5 4 3 2 1
ISBN 978-1-934137-42-0 pb

INUKSHUK

For Caridwen

INUKSHUK

1

CHINOOK

H E WAS ON LUNCH DUTY when it happened, jacketless because of the Chinook wind and composing in his head a line or two about the color of the sky reflected in the wet school-yard pavement, the ice-rimmed, quickly vanishing puddles, clouds whipping past upside down . . . *sun oil water*. If he had a minute before class, he'd jot some notes to remind himself, and tonight or tomorrow, the weekend maybe, craft the lines. Meanwhile, these gusting, transitory moments of pleasure verging on epiphany, ears full of word sounds not quite articulable. He told himself he was lucky: The reward was having such feelings at all, being a man attuned to his surroundings enough to experience the old spine tingle beholding a thing of beauty, not in mining his particular sensitivities for a poem. In the midst of this, something else, too—a push, a seismic shift in the surrounding school-yard energy that put him on the alert, making him momentarily more enthralled by the windblown colors and reflections as he tore his attention from them back to the here and now— and then it was in their voices, too, and he knew, because he'd been in the job long enough to recognize all the signs. There was a fight. He would now be called upon to do something. Act. These were old-enough kids, grades nine and ten, no one would come running for him; no more grade-school, middle-school tattletales ("Fight! Fight! Mr. Franklin—quick!"), those simpler, earlier years of his teaching career long gone, like so many other things. They'd flock around, these kids, oversize strangers, cheering maybe or just silently longing for more, for torture, each one thankful it wasn't him in there getting pummeled, but no one would stop it.

The boys he identified from a distance—not bad kids, really, but ones with a preying instinct and a reputation. Scollard, Martini, two he didn't have names for, and the tall, angular one—the instigator, he guessed—Jeremy Malloy. Pink oxford shirt, dark blond hair, jeans seasoned with pocket whiskers and tears at the knees. Franklin

hadn't been here long enough to say for sure, but he knew the type—
never alone, always mugging it up for a pack of friends, all of his
antics, apparently, to be taken down by some imaginary news crew.

What he neither saw nor identified (and certainly never anticipated), in the less than thirty seconds it took him to lope-stride
across the school-yard, gathering himself, finding the words in
advance, alternating anger, dread, annoyance, disappointment, and
a little excitement at the prospect of exercising his teacherly "authority": his own flesh and blood, his own son the one held down in the
snow crust, underwear pulled to his rib cage, blood flowing from
his nose. "Hey there, hey now, HEY, I said that's enough," he heard
his voice booming while something inside him withdrew and spun
out of control, causing the whole scene to fade and tunnel with pin-
pricks. He was weirdly aware of his teeth clicking together, and then
of the sibilance of breath scratching his throat as he drew more air,
impossibly warm, dry air, to raise the volume of his voice. "Hey! I
said stop that now! That's enough. You boys! Thomas?"

Worse, as Thomas rose and separated from the bunch, stood back,
tugging vainly at the waistband of his underwear with one hand and
with the other dabbing at the blood that ran from his nose—"It's OK,
Dad. I'm OK. You can go now. Really. I'm fine . . ."—Franklin knew
just why they'd done this. No, worse than that, he sympathized. The
kid, his own son, with his remote, demented stare, stiff-legged pirate-
boy walk, perennial sniffling, and all the dietary weirdness—he was
an embarrassment. A nuisance, and an eyesore. The very stubborn
thing, whatever it was lately, that seemed to sit on his soul like a
block, it made you want to shake him, shout at him, hug him, do
something anyway to see if you could get a response. See if Thomas
might be made to realize how his obstinacy and difference and insistence upon never doing anything like other people only provoked
everyone around him.

"I said I'm OK, Dad."

"No! You're not! And you'll come with me now. All of you. This
way. On the double."

Or else?

For a moment, watching their faces, Malloy's especially, hand-some, no-good, winter white with pink spots under the eyes, he felt the question just under the surface, animating their features. *Or what, Franklin? On what authority, old man? We'll take you down, too.* Malloy was a hockey kid—hockey royalty. Team captain? Too young. High scorer? Something special about him, Franklin couldn't remember. With the hockey came certain entitlements: all those 4:00 A.M. mornings, some poor mom dragging him off to practice. He was allowed to act out. Expected to, almost. For split seconds longer, he felt how barely anything here was actually in his command. One boy sniffed and shoved his fists in his pockets, hard, feeling for something in there maybe, and backed up a step. One tossed and smoothed aside the black hair falling over his black eyes. Only Malloy seemed openly unconcerned.

"It'll just get worse, boys. You want a two-day suspension or a four-day suspension? Shall I keep going? Six days? How about detention, in-school suspension, and garbage duty the rest of the year? This way, now."

And then they were marching, past the vanishing puddles that had seemed to him luminous moments ago, windows to another world and full of hidden Sule Skerry poetry (his mind went reflexively back to the words *sun oil water,* but not much beyond that remained), the snowbanks reflected in their surfaces now menacing as teeth, grim and dead and nothing to look at or think twice about. Just ice and bare, wind-whipped ground. Students mostly tried to pretend they didn't notice anything going on, but they all did. They saw. They watched. *There goes the new teacher, Franklin, saving his son. The dork.* They stood back and kept eyes averted. One or two stared, one passed secret hand signals at the boys, and behind him he felt the gathering menace of other hostile gestures. Mockery and rage. Turned once abruptly to catch them at it, but no. Nothing.

Then the exterior double doors and the vestibule going inside, the sequence of things he didn't adequately anticipate. First the bell signaling the end of the period, so classroom doors everywhere inside banged open and students barged out, already laughing, talking; next,

Malloy, seizing the opportunity, throwing back a pair of inner hall-way doors, smashing them into red tiled walls and yelling *"Bullshit!"* under the noise of it as he ducked to the side and started to make a run for it; and last, Franklin, reacting (Overreacting? Later, he couldn't say), grabbing out, catching the kid by the back of his pink shirt collar and, not anticipating anything like the force of his own rage, flinging him back (so much stiffer, lighter, less resistant than he might have expected; a kid, after all) and around and against the wall, forearm across Malloy's chest, lifting and holding him there until the boy's eyes watered and only the wheezing sound of his breath made Franklin realize he'd better stop. Let go. Still he was yelling: "You want to try that again? Wanna piece of me? Any of you others want to make a run for it?" He was not even that mad, that he was aware of anyway, but he was yelling. Something had happened to make him go out of control. What?

Only after he'd released Malloy and gotten the other boys march-ing again on a course straight through the crowded hallway for the principal's office, only then did he realize the one who'd given him the slip: his own son, Thomas, gone.

ON THE BUS RIDE HOME, it started again—the bleeding. Devon, his brother, would understand why it pleased Thomas enough almost to make him laugh out loud, except that the garish bubbling of half-thickened blood in his nostrils stopped him. He didn't want it getting any messier than necessary. Didn't want extra attention. Amendment: Devon would *understand*, but he would not *approve*. He'd know that bleeding made you impervious and repellent. No one gave you shit if you were bleeding. No one gave a shit about you. They gaped and made faces, but they left you alone. More impor-tantly, bleeding proved the experiment might be working. The chew-ing gum had been a setback (Who knew? Actual vitamin C in Juicy Fruit), but he was on track again and soon to be unassailable.

He tilted back his head and pinched the nostrils lightly. Felt blood pooling at the back of his throat, swallowed; felt it seeping along his cheeks and lips, and gazed at the tranquil, seldom-observed ceiling of the bus—domed and riveted and blue-green—fixing his attention inward, on his movie. OK. Frame one, opening shot—*Erebus* and *Terror* at sea. . . . Interesting how the voices of other kids faded, became tinny and inconsequential as soon as he had a picture in mind. Who cared about them? He blinked his eyes shut, sniffed again, and exhaled steadily through his nostrils to keep the blood going. Drew up one knee and propped it against the seat back in front of him.

From the start, then. Frame one:

Opening shot: exterior: the *Erebus* and the *Terror* on a sea more or less the same blue-green as that bus ceiling. No icebergs yet, no sign of land. Low-flying mist, and as the ships come closer, you see men on board, wearing black and wrapped in wool. Cue distant dance music—accordions, mandolin, and piano; mournful, ballad-inflected, but melodic and mostly happy. This is a *good* day, despite the ominous backdrop—a joyous day. Roll-across subtitle: *Day 107 of the Franklin Expedition to navigate the Northwest Passage. Stores just replenished in Greenland and closing in on Lancaster Sound. The true start of the adventure . . . or . . . the beginning of the end?* Period rigging and period ships. Mid-1800s, waddling, flat-bellied bombers refitted for the Arctic, both ships loaded practically to the waterline with coal and provisions. Seagulls—no, strike the seagulls. Two-shot: leaning at the railing of ship number one (*Terror*), a pair of men with pipes, talking, gesturing. Establishment shot of the ship, and panning around it to ship two (*Erebus*) with more sounds. Cut to fight scene on board *Erebus*: sounds of flesh hitting flesh—good amped-up Hollywood fight sounds, wet crackle of breaking tissue, cracking ribs, wheezy, punched-out breaths. POW. THWACK. WHUMP. Close-up of a sailor's bloodied face. Able-bodied Seaman Thomas Work—one of the main characters and among the few men who will make it as far as Starvation Cove with Crozier. Shoulder shot of other sailor's face, both men circling—Pvt. William Braine (dead of mysterious causes in less than a year but now very much alive). Both men are bearded and stripped to the waist, backs steaming in the cold, and ringed around by cheering sailors. Work's been goaded into this fight by insults, but because of a religious upbringing (maybe his inferior rank, as well) limits his responses to self-defense. He won't strike until he has to. All of this you know from his stance: wary, apologetic, fists raised. Braine moves in suddenly for the headlock. Clamps a sweating arm around Work's head and squeezes, pops him a few good ones until Work breaks away again. They separate and circle. Camera dollies back to show the men from a distance, the whole ship deck seen from above again, against a wind-ruffled blue-green backdrop of vast emptiness—a kingdom of emptiness. From here, it appears almost like they're dancing crabs, circling each other and swinging fists, music from ship number one mixing together with the action and the cheering, so, from this perspective, it all has the appearance of fun—brutal, sailor merriment. . . .

Someone had entered Thomas's field of vision and was waving a white handkerchief or wad of Kleenexes at him.

"Dude!" It was the dreadlocked bus driver. Koda? Cody? Dakota? Couldn't be more than four or five years older than the oldest kids on the bus. Always singing and bouncing his head to the music on his earbuds as he hauled around the enormous wheel of the school bus with one hand and banged in and out of gears with the other; always making cryptic, blessinglike remarks at the backs of their heads as they exited down the steps. "Someone got you pretty good there, hey buddy?"

"Got me?"

He remembered: the bloody nose, Martini, Malloy, and the other hockey goons. There he'd been, eating his peanut butter sandwich alone, trying to keep the hair from blowing into his mouth and enjoying the unexpected heat on his skin, not bothering anyone, when suddenly the sandwich went flying out of his hand, across the vanishing ice—bland, stabbing circle of pain in the back of his hand where he was hit, so he knew it was not the wind that had snatched his lunch away and caused it to become airborne. And then the rest of it—being propelled suddenly upward and dropped on the ice and assaulted from all sides, and last, the sudden back-severing pain in his ass crack and the sound of ripping cloth and laughter as they tried to draw the elastic of his underwear over his head. His own words as he went down, jumbled and high-pitched, more petulant than fierce and therefore embarrassing to recollect—something about infantile homosadistic jock rituals—whatever he'd said, he was pretty sure it would have been mostly unintelligible.

"A little school-yard fisticuffs?"

He faked a smile. "Aftershocks of a random beating, more like. Hours ago now."

"Here you go." And before Thomas could stop it, the white cloth was being held to his mouth and nose, smelling vaguely of pot, sweat, licorice, and garlic. The outer fringe of it bumped his eyelashes as he blinked and tried to push Cody/Dakota—whatever his name was—back, but it was no use.

"Yeah. Apply some pressure there, bud; you gotta apply pressure. Now, this is a trick my old lady taught me. Lean forward a little." Thomas seemed to have no real choice here, either. He was tilted out of his seat. Felt fingers prying open the back of his coat collar, shirt collar, deftly peeling one from the other, and then an icy shaft of wet streaked down his back.

"What the hell!" he said. Jerked free. "What are you *doing,* man?"

"Supposed to use cold keys or coins, drop 'em down the back of your shirt like that." The driver laughed peculiarly, a sibilant *see-see-shoo-shoo* sound, like he was some kind of hissing hippy leprechaun, cheeks pinkening under his thin beard. "But I don't got any spares. That was just some ice. Relax man. It's just ice. Water."

"Hell!" Thomas mopped the back of his neck, jerked out the tail of his shirt, and stood, so that whatever had gone down there would fall out. Held the white rag for Cody/Dakota to take back but did not meet eyes with him. "I'm OK now. *Thanks.* Really."

"Lookie there. Dang if that nose didn't quit bleeding. See?"

Thomas ran a finger under his nose. Nothing. A little pinkish mucus. Sniffed once hard to restart it and swallowed the last brackish bit of spit and blood at the back of his throat and sat again.

"My old lady never did tell a lie."

"Lucky you."

"I'm like a friggin' *shaman*." The driver ambled back to the front of the bus, bobbing his head, slapping the backs of seats as he went, one hand raised a moment to give a backward wave. "You can just thank me whenever you feel like it."

"I said *thanks*."

Reseated, Cody/Dakota studied Thomas in his extended-field rearview mirror a moment, nodding his head, grinning. Then he gave Thomas the thumbs-up and held it too long, way too long, staring and still grinning.

"Weirdo."

"You're all right, kid."

"I am not."

More kids tromped on board, and more, no one he knew or cared about. Soon it was a humid racket of kids' voices reflected off the windows and metal ceiling—a continual bombardment as claustrophobic as the hold of his imaginary frozen ship. At last came the motorized wrenching sound of bus diesel starting up, squeal of the door closing, and off they went, bumping out of the snow-scarred lot. Thomas kept his head tilted back and practiced knowing where he was without looking out a window. Like the ice masters on board the *Erebus* and *Terror* maneuvering into Peel Sound and interpreting the forms of ice as they went—pancake, sludge ice, bergy bits, dread screwed pack—each distinguishable from the other by its distinct sonic characteristics as it struck the ships' hulls, he tried to maintain his bearings based on the shifting sheen of light reflected in the ceiling, and all corresponding sounds. The stop at the end of the parking lot beside the school sign and the sound of the turn signal; the surrounding barren, wheat-stubbled, snowy fields, acre upon acre, grain silos and rolled hay bales under tarpaulin, and the freaky caved-in top hat–looking glacial, erratic, bigger than a house; the oil derricks, one close, two farther out, enormous praying mantises, bobbing flat-headed alien life-forms eternally rolling their arms around and sucking the earth of fuel; the Lazy U Ranch; the turn, the dull highway haul of absolutely nothing, more oil derricks, cottonwoods, mud, and sand hiss-slapping in the wheel wells, wind beating the windows, and then the first signs of Houndstitch—clusterings of raised ranchers and just-built brick and glass and shotcrete condo warrens for the new oil people, all with street names meant to evoke nature or native lore despite the surrounding tundralike desolation: Winding Creek estates across from the Blockbuster and Tim Hortons—Roaring Brook, Deer Trail, Eagle Feather Way, Rattler Drive, Harbour Crescent—none of it even here until about a year ago. All of it paid for by oil. In the western distance, always, the Rockies disrupting the horizon like a wall of frozen white waves.

Aside from this, and the story that wouldn't come back yet, two things had his focus now. One was what he'd eat tonight and what he'd have to refuse. No to corn; no on his dad's favorite iceberg salad with vinaigrette and chickpeas and hacked-up bits of carrot and ham and slimy silver-tinged tomatoes; no to juice or fresh fruit or berry tofutti dessert. With this was a memory he could almost stop before it was too late: the pleasure of ripping into a package of fruit leather for his after-school snack (every day of his life, practically, until this year)—how the packaging would peel away and then you'd roll the flattened, sticky, tonguelike fruit thing in your fingertips, apple, cherry orchard, grape-a-licious, mango madness, and bite into it. The sweet, acid-sour, C-saturated taste of it nailing him in the back of the mouth and gumming up his teeth, so good, and then doing it again. *Have as many as you like,* his mother always said. *They're good for you.* Of course he craved it; his whole body wanted vitamin C like nothing he'd ever wished for before, except maybe sex. All the more reason to resist and stick with facts. Foods safe for consumption: bread, crackers, peanut butter, tahini, rice, nuts, canned fish, potatoes, well-done meat. If all else failed, somewhere in the middle of dinner slip into the bathroom, drink water until he vomited; take two aspirin from the gargantuan bottle in the cabinet and an antacid to be double sure.

The other thing was the letter from his mother almost certainly waiting at home. It'd been a few weeks since her last, so one would be due soon. He didn't think of it like that, exactly. He got as far as

picturing himself unlocking the mailbox under the tree, the hollow
tocking sound of the lock opening, and the dread-worry sensations
closing around him as he reached in, and then standing there feeling like the ground had opened under his feet. Again her handwrit-
ing on the envelope. Another fat letter full of nothing—place names
and animals and facts about life up there in the territories and the
latest high and low temperatures, names of people she'd met. *My
mother's in the Arctic, talking to schoolteachers about their problems
and observing the effects of global warming on little towns you've never
heard of and never will and would never care about even if you knew
their names or could say them. Ulukhaktok. Tuktoyaktuk. Because
that's what she does and that's what she cares about. More than anything else.*

"Spaceman," the bus driver was saying. "HEY, spaceman back
there with the bloody nose."

Thomas sat forward. Looked around. Light everywhere. "What?"
He'd been a little off in his calculations. They were not, as he'd
thought, approaching the crazy house of quilted-together RVs and
trailers with the piles of split wood and innumerable junked cars just
past Winding Creek (aka Oil Sands) Estates. "You talking to me?"

"You got a name?"

"No."

Head bobbing, grinning, hissing laughter. "I didn't think so."

"Thomas."

"OK then, Thomas. I got some advice for you."

"What's that." For a moment, he thought this might really be it,
might be just the news he needed today—weird warm Chinook wind
day. Why not? The guy could stop a nosebleed. Maybe he had other
powers.

"Come on up here, so I don't have to shout it."

He studied the driver's shivering image in the rearview mirror.
Watched his nose seem to elongate and shrink again (a warp or divot
in the glass?) as he shoulder-checked and shifted and returned his
gaze to Thomas: Native eyes and eyebrows, everything else about
him Slavic or some other brand of northern European. Viking?

"Come on. Right here in the seat there behind me."

"No thanks."

"You gotta lay off the blow. That's my advice, man. It's a killer. Only thing worse?"

Thomas zoned out the rest. He didn't know why it should surprise him anymore: another so-called grown-up parading around advice that was really just a projection of his own messed-up personal life, personal traumas and experiences. Why were they *all* like that? Was anyone *not* like that? Give the guy two more seconds, he'd probably start talking about sex with underage girls . . . or boys—it was probably the whole reason he'd reached out in the first place.

"Is that a fact?"

"It's my walking-talking paranormal nightmare-testimonial, bro. You lay off the stuff or it'll kill you."

"Sure, but I'm not your *bro*. OK?"

The bus driver kept nodding but didn't look back at Thomas. "You just lay off it, whatever your thing is. That's all I'm saying."

"Whatever. If it makes you happy."

And again as he exited the bus, the words seemingly aimed to pierce the back of Thomas's skull: "I don't care who you are or what you know or how much money you got. It's gonna kill you dead."

THE DAY OF SURPRISES: first the snow-eater winds, then the fight, and the image of his son that kept coming back to him afterward— underwear wrenched from beneath his belt, elastic torn from the briefs, and the briefs themselves, laundered how many hundreds of times by him in the privacy of their own laundry room and never meant to be exposed like this. And the expression on Thomas's face. Beaten, defiant. Unreachable. Had Franklin responded appropriately? Could you be mad, sad, and perplexed in equal measures, all at the same time, and know it? It was a first for him anyway. And then the surprise in the hallway and his own rage, his son's disappearance, and the further surprises in Vice Principal Legere's office.

The thing about living in the north, he'd learned (though few

Canadians, he knew, Jane especially, would call this anything like actual north), day after day he could pass in a state of sleep-stupored, mind-numbing placidity—not a thing happening anywhere, to the point where he hardly knew if he was dead or alive. It wasn't bad really, just weird and tiring. The first light of day seeping up somewhere in the middle of first period and long gone by the time you made your way back across the lot—snow squeaking underfoot, icy air freezer-burning your nose and throat and blasting up your pant legs, so you were horribly awake, dreadfully, surreally awake—to unplug your car's block heater and drive home. And on the drive home, wind making the snow swirl and tunnel along the pavement in your headlights like the vapors of some inhospitable alien planet, frost spreading its crazed lace down the inside of the windshield faster than you could blast at it with the defroster or scrub it away with a mitten. Was any of this real? Some days, it was all he could think of anyway: bed—the smell of bed, the sound of the heater clicking on and off in the dark, the heavy blankets piled just right on top of him, the dark cold in the window and the frigid air standing just in front of each window, the clock humming and hours more of sleep ahead. No Jane.

Then, all of a sudden, a day like this, where nothing went right—everything ran against the grain.

Malloy had not come clean to Legere and apologized for his actions—trying to escape, bullying Thomas, being prime instigator. Instead, seated around the table in the conference room, where hearings of this type always took place, they'd witnessed something like an emotional reversion for Malloy from age fifteen to about ten. He wouldn't stop blubbering, kept looking at Franklin with his eyes streaming, accusing him between hiccupped sobs: "You almost killed me! He tried to kill me! We weren't doing *anything*. I swear! It was a *game*." The other boys said nothing. They sat dumbstruck. Legere, too, twirling a gold ballpoint pen around and around his right index finger and thumb. What did Franklin know about this kid, after all? Almost nothing. He'd never had him in a class but had heard of him from other teachers and witnessed some of his antics. It was a small-enough school that everyone seemed to know everything.

"Look, I saw what happened, OK?" Franklin said. "What you and your friends here were up to, that was not a game. A nosebleed and a wedgie, or whatever you call it . . . So, why don't we start from the beginning and you can explain for Vice Principal Legere here exactly how things got out of hand and exactly how—"

"He was trying to kill me."

"Who—what?"

"You tried to kill me!"

"No, Malloy. The fact is, no, I did not." He tried to keep his voice as level and neutral as possible. Not quite apologetic, but certainly warmer than he felt. "You made an attempt to escape, which I prevented. Now, why don't we . . ."

Malloy lowered his head onto the table. His shoulders shook, but no sounds followed. Franklin couldn't say for sure if he was faking it.

"What?" Franklin began. "For real?"

No response.

"Differing perceptions, *absolutement*," Legere said, patting a hand on the conference table and smiling. Winked once in Franklin's direction, maybe, though it didn't have to mean anything. "I, for one, think we do not gain so much pressing further without parents present. Perhaps we can take five minutes break now, until one or two arrive, yes?" He peered over the top of Franklin's head and seemed to be humming to himself a moment as he sought his next, exact words. "Jeremy can compose himself in the interim and then we talk." Twelve years as vice principal of this new little outpost, composite high school, twenty-plus years in Alberta generally, and still he talked like a displaced Frog. Franklin tried not to picture, as he usually did, Legere standing at a mirror, oiling his hair and pursing his lips at his reflection as he practiced saying things aloud in his *outrageous accent* in order to preserve it.

He nodded. "Sure," he said. He pushed back from the table. "I have class next period."

"This we know, Mr. Franklin."

Outside again by the east entryway closest to Legere's office, he stood rolling in his fingertips the cigarette bummed off Dorrie Weiss there at the reception desk (he wasn't smoking again, not really, just this one to cope, calm the nerves), but not lighting up yet, testing his resolve, eyeing his watch and savoring the last moments before caving into addiction. Ordinarily, fourth period, if he was caught up with everything workwise, he'd be sweating on one of the treadmills or rowing machines at the gym or, weather permitting, jogging around the outside track or on the school cross-country trail. Perfect day for that, he thought, though he was glad, too, for the excuse not to run—considered it, even, according to some inverse logic, exactly the justification for the cigarette he hadn't yet lit: because if you're going to miss a day, may as well *really* miss. He listened to the wind whistling in the eaves and the sounds of traffic out on the main road blown first toward him and then away with the ceaseless clatter and clang of the halyard striking the school flagpole somewhere just out of his sight, the flag itself snapping riotously. Just over fifteen minutes remaining until the start of fifth period and his first of three back-to-back classes: honors ninth, core tenth, and the senior seminar, his plum, Classic Canadian Lit. This week's story, one of his favorites— "The Painted Door": early twentieth-century agrarian prairie life, marriage, betrayal, and death by freezing.

Enter the next surprise of the day. Moira. He hadn't seen her in going on three years and resisted believing, at first, it was really her, not another phantom look-alike approaching from across the lot—scattered-seeming, fast-paced gait, bent forward slightly as if to accommodate for an ungainly height; expression of fixed but unspecified glumness, mostly (he guessed) the unintended consequence of long cheekbones and downward-turning mouth; high-priced, high-end clothing worn as if she'd just flung them on, designer jeans tucked into soft low-heeled boots, candy-cane red sweater, fur cap, and white scarf around her neck. He stood straighter. Felt his skin prickle and his vision sharpen. It was her all right.

"Moira!" He couldn't stop himself—the sound in his voice, already something too deprived and insistent.

"Oh my gosh, John? Is that you really? What are you doing? I mean . . . how . . . what in the world are you doing *here*? Everyone's asked about you; you know, since you quit the group, it's never been the same. Just last week, Ravi was asking if anyone ever saw or heard of you! Oh my gosh! How are you and . . . was it Jane?" She held her palms to her face a moment and looked at him pitifully enough— with sincere-enough seeming pity, that is (or some strong kindred sentiment anyway)—he was reminded all over again how difficult it was ever apprehending what she knew, what she didn't, what she intended. With that, some of the embarrassing things he'd said to her their last afternoon together: . . . *call it a crush. Sure. Devastated infatuation, more like . . . I know people would say it's a matter of transference, projection, what have you, of course, because of my trouble with Jane; still . . . you and I, it's like our souls are mated at some higher ontological plane, like we . . . such longing, it's like. . . .* Had he really said all that? Best not to remember for the moment.

"Jane, yes. She's gone. Been a couple of years."

"Oh, I'm sorry. I *had* heard that I guess, yes. From . . . somewhere, I can't think where. What a mess, those days! All the cheating and lying and everyone's marriages busting up. The horrible zeitgeist of the new millennia. Thank *God* that's over!"

"Yes." He exhaled, shook his head, but said nothing further. *Zeitgeist.* One of those words you didn't hear every day in Central Alberta conversation. He reminded himself how it'd always been this way with her: always the tendency to overemote, always enough real feeling behind the—he didn't want to call it pretentiousness, but it was, almost . . . some form of calculated playacting anyway— he could choose to see past it. "And you! What about—?"

"But you're OK now? Still writing?"

They'd spoken at once.

He nodded, smoothed the cigarette between his fingers. "I'm hanging in. Better than ever, really. And yes, pretty productive. Closing in on a finished manuscript. The old Sule Skerry project; I'm sure you remember." Four, five months ago, he would have boasted to her about the poems that had been taken for publication at an East

Coast quarterly—older ones, completely revised and revamped. But the novelty of publication acceptance had mostly worn off. He was tired of hearing himself find ways to mention it, and then pretending not to have wanted the attention. Besides, she'd know those poems by name—might even quote him a line or two in appreciation. Of all people, she would understand the significance for him, having placed them so well, finally having risen to the rank of most of the rest of the Bowness group, but she'd know, too, they were not exactly new work. Well, it was something to save for later. "Jane and I . . ." He waved a hand. "That was in the pipeline for some time, as you know. I guess you'd say we hit the point where we stopped being able to see the best in each other. Conflicting ideals and priorities—radically conflicting, actually. Maybe that's the long and short of it." He shrugged broadly. "Probably all my fault. No divorce yet. She's north with that CEAP group around Inuvik for now. Part of a nonprofit mission, monitoring climate change and. . . ."

"Yikes. That's . . ."

"Yes. The Arctic. More or less."

"John. What ever did you *do* to that poor woman?"

He laughed. Watched her push back the hair that had blown across her face, strands catching against her mouth. "Would that I could claim that much influence. . . ."

"I'm so sorry."

He shrugged. "All for the best, I'm sure." And like that, he was lying to her—stowing his feelings in a layer of bravado anyway, and posing himself as someone better or more cavalier. More casually self-deprecating. *Pipeline.* A marriage didn't have a pipeline; an oil company did. Jane was gone, plain and simple. *Call it an extended leave of absence*, she'd said. *Call it my pilgrimage to save the world. Call it what you have to.*

He rolled the cigarette a final time between his thumb and fingers and lit up. Drew deeply and waited for the first rush of pleasure to tingle his nerve endings, perk up his blood; sweet momentary lapse of self from self. Closed his eyes and drew again.

"So what brings you out here?" he asked.

"My son."

"Right! I always forget you have kids."

"Kid."

"Right. Sorry. Kid. How old?"

"Fifteen."

And then he knew: bussing in from the Turner Valley. Of course— *Malloy*, that would be her first husband's last name—but the likeness was now unmistakable. Her second husband was Stringer, Springer, something like that—Rick—and her own name she'd preserved for herself through all of that, Moira Francis. Briefly, he tried to remember anything he could about all this—her past, her life story: first husband, high school sweetheart, common-law, never officially married, left her with the two-year-old; second husband, lawyer whose words occasionally crossed with and sparked her own in poems, handsome, doggedly logical, older than she was and loyal to a flaw, but on his own terms. Brought back to mind, as well, the picture of her home life he had formulated based around these and other details. The boy he'd always envisioned (if he pictured him at all) as Devon, younger, dark-haired, with eyes like hers, the unknown portions of his face filled in reflexively from the only guy in his own high school class he knew to have married straight out of school, a wrestler and track jock named Brett. Rick (also more or less reflexively) he'd modeled on the lawyer from *Primal Fear*, always in a dress coat and on his way somewhere, seldom flustered. All of it, he knew now (and had always known, though he'd lacked the specific details by which to correct or amend it), completely wrong.

"Not Jeremy Malloy?" he asked.

She nodded. "Yes. I . . ."

"Listen," he said. "Let's walk."

"Like old times?"

"Sure. Sort of. Old times."

He drew on the cigarette a few more times and flipped away the remaining half of it—there, resisted, mostly—as he crunched his way along next to her across the lot to the football field.

"So, you should know this. I'll just be straight up about it. Jeremy and I had a bit of an altercation today, which began, actually, with other behavior I'll tell you about in just a second here," he said. He kept his gaze from her, staring forward at the half-melted dirty snow crust and bare, sand-patterned pavement, wind pushing back his hair and causing his eyes to water. Like old times, he thought, yes: how they'd walk and walk, never touch; talk about poems and poets, sex, marriage, anything at all really, except the obvious longing between them, and never anything of a too-practical nature from their daily lives that might allow reality (or the truth of their intentions?) to intrude. First only monthly, in connection with the poetry-group meetings in Bowness, and later, more often—weekly, biweekly Sunday afternoons, always the same trails and pathways and the same meeting point, same loop over the footbridges and along the river. How long? Years. Two at least. More. Too jumbled to say. In college, he'd scorned friends of his who'd had these protracted, undefined, semiromantic friendships with women or other men that seemed to go on and on—never understood the necessity of not knowing and deliberately keeping yourself from knowing, month after month, as feelings deepened and turned septic. Tragic. And there he was, letting the same scenario consume his attention, not as a college student, but as a married adult. How foolish was that? The counterpoint of subjects and scenery—wet pines, snowy pines, mud, maples flaming with color, yellow-leafed cottonwoods, ice on the Bow River—and their perfectly matched strides, always moving in a rhythm that felt to him at once specifically theirs alone, and greater than the two of them, so their talk seemed inconsequential, part of some ongoing music sustained by the planet, and yet specifically, privately their own: He wanted that back of course, all of it—the connectedness and ease and the talk, the smell of her, sound of her laugh, sound of her voice addressing him—but felt, too, more or less convinced it was impossible. Wasn't entirely sure how much of it had ever existed. Maybe only in his own head.

"What now? What did Jeremy do?"

"Well, apparently I tried to kill him. That's what he'll tell you anyway. For starters."

"You *what?*"

"He ran. I was escorting him back inside after breaking up a bit of a . . . seems he was instigating a bit of a gang—I don't want to say *beating,* but it was something in that vein—which I happened to catch them in the middle of, but too late to stop anything. . . ."

"I have to say . . . can I just say right now how really *weird* it is you're all of a sudden talking to me about my *son*? I mean, who ever would have thought?"

"Kind of comes with the job description. . . ."

"Why, though . . . I mean—what are you *doing* here? I thought you were so ensconced back at that lovely place—what was it called, your school there in Calgary?"

"It's a longish story."

"Jane?"

"Jane, sure, and about a quarter of a million dollars I thought wouldn't be so bad to cash in on while the oil barons are paying."

"And now here you are in the boonies, dealing with bad boys like my Jeremy, probably wishing you'd never laid eyes on the place."

"It's not so bad." In the middle distance, a raven was hopping foot to foot, whacking its bill at something on the ground. *Tock-tock,* like some kind of demented, stuck clockwork.

"So?"

"So, yes, the fight, or whatever you want to call it. I go have my stern words and so on, break it up, and then I'm escorting them all back into Legere's office, including the kid whose face they bloodied nice and good—who happens, incidentally, to be my son, but never mind that, for the moment—"

"*Your* son? Oh my."

"Yes. And I'm escorting them all back inside, when Jeremy decides to make a run for it. So I stopped him. Maybe a little too harshly. Apparently, yes, a little too forcefully, but he was trying to make a run for it, which . . . boy. . . . So." Picturing it, he still didn't understand the force of what had overcome him, didn't know why the brakes wouldn't have engaged sooner; heard Malloy's back hit the wall and felt the toes of Malloy's boots striking his shins, kicking, the pain in his shinbones somehow not signaling to him soon enough that he should stop, let up, instead fueling his rage and causing him to bear down harder, move his face closer, and yell. "It just pissed me off, highly. So I grabbed him."

"No doubt."

"Well, it might have gone on a little too long."

"Not long enough, alas. He's alive still?" She punched him lightly. "Kidding."

Best not to play along with that one. "Alive and very upset, presently bawling his eyes out in Legere's office. Or was when I left."

"Sounds about right. He was picking on your son—what's his name—?"

"Thomas."

"Well, he was picking on Thomas deliberately to get a rise out of you and test limits. That's what I'd say. That's his thing lately. And then he's always so surprised when the door actually slams on his poor face and people are furious with him. I can't tell you . . . for a bright kid, he can be such a royal dumb ass."

And then he remembered: dumb ass . . . class. He was the dumb ass. Glanced at his watch. First bell in three minutes. "Moira. Shit. I can't be doing this at all right now." He caught her by the wrists and spun her to face him. Her skin was surprisingly warm. "I've got a class in a few minutes."

She gave a crooked smile and nodded. Shivered once and blinked. Was she forgiving him? Understanding her effect on him and forgiving him for that, too? She turned her hands over so they lay palms downward in his. In all their time together, he'd never touched her this openly or long. Their last walk together, the walk of his foolish forthrightness, he'd finished with his arms folded hard across his chest, whether to contain his hurt and embarrassment, to prevent himself from saying more, or to keep himself from touching her, he couldn't have said. Had it always been this easy, and the only thing hanging them up had been his own hesistancy—his own good manners and marriedness?

Part of him stood aside, wondering about this—if it meant

something, anything, nothing … a new permissiveness opening between them, yes, but because of the time apart or something else? And anyway, what did permissiveness signal? Mostly, he enjoyed the pressure of her hands in his, the unexpected weight and warmth.

"Promise?" she said.

"What's that?"

"Promise you won't become a stranger again, stranger?"

"Ha." He laughed falsely. "Doubt there's a remote possibility there, honey. We'll, uh, what do they say in the movies. See you in court?"

"There won't be any court. My son fights his own battles, and he can't afford my husband's fees. His *father's* way of dealing with things would be a little more personal, shall we say. Primal?"

He blinked to bring her better into focus—see if she really meant this or if it was code for some other information. More coyness or flirtation? No. She was serious. You didn't get to look that self-contained and radiant fighting anyone else's battles: She was a one-wick woman, solo candle composed all of self and slowly burning itself out. Not unlike Jane in that way, really. He understood, too, that the person whose attention Jeremy must most want and whose limits he'd been testing (and would likely never find) was her. Of course. All of this made perfect sense for about a millisecond, until he considered his own feelings: how to sort out the distractions and distortions there—what did his desire stir in her or cause him to imagine; how could you ever sort any of it, one thing from the other? No saying. Absolutely no saying or knowing on any of it. A mirage like the illusion of distance on a snowy, sunny day.

"You're a hard one," he said.

"Nowhere near hard enough, I'd say."

"What's that supposed to mean?"

"You don't have time now, remember? Class?"

He groaned. "Here," he said, sliding from his wallet one of the stash of slightly bent business cards he'd been given by the school when he came on board the previous year, and for which he'd never found much use—part of some senior's Print and Media final project, he suspected: cheap paper stock and monster Gothic print that looked as if it might have been lifted from one of his boys' D&D books. "Cell number's there at the bottom. Call. . . ." He went loping back across the lot to the side entryway, past his bent cigarette in the snow, still barely half-smoked. The same stretch of ground crossed once and now hastily jogged back over in the opposite direction—emblematic of absolutely nothing, he knew, and yet in the time between the one trip and the other, everything in his life seemed to have shifted course. Glimpsing his reflection in the upper window of the doorway as he yanked it aside, he wondered, That man, high school teacher and aspiring poet, windblown, shirt collar open in the middle of winter, beaming, desire clanging in his heart like the final rhyming couplet of a sonnet—who was he?

SHE CAUGHT UP WITH HIM just past the turnoff from the main road onto their street. "Thomas Franklin, you could be subtler about being a stalker, you know, hanging around waiting for my bus." She swung out a pace and spun to walk backward, facing him, hands on her hips, wisps of hair swirling around her face; such an abundance of freckles and in such contrast with the paleness of her skin, he had the feeling, as always, looking at her, that she was peering out from behind a puzzle mask or field of static, the red-blue port-wine stain shaped like King William Island creeping from just under her left ear to her jaw and neckline, accentuating this like a hole or tear in the mask. "Ohmygod! Thomas! What happened? Your *face.*"

"That. Oh." He touched his jaw and cheek. "Just some dried blood. It's nothing. From a fight." He shrugged. "We match now."

"We what?"

"Just kidding."

Her mouth fell open. "You are such a *jerk*! I can't believe you just said that to me. Did you really say that? You're *such* a jerk!"

"Come on."

"You *are.*"

Why the pleasure in meanness, he wondered, and then the regret? Idiot. Why had he said that? Irresistible, like tearing at a hangnail. "I was kidding. OK? It was like a joke. Lighten up. Anyway, it's no big thing. Just a bloody nose."

She was beside him again. He watched her boots, black, with fur trim, tick in and out of sight at the corner of his eyes, and waited a little longer before continuing his story. Flat, hard, overcast light; bare tree limbs framing the Rockies in the distance. Every other day for as long as he'd lived here—going on two years since the family breakup, Dad's big real estate cash-in, and the grand exodus from Calgary down Highway 2 south and west all of an hour to nowheres-ville/Houndstitch—they'd been walking home together like this, he and Jill. He'd entertain her with his tales of high school woe, answer her questions about classes and principles of dating, social groups, clothes styles, et cetera, babbling on as if he were an authority on any of it, something like what Devon used to do for him in years past (though he doubted Devon ever fabricated half as much). And more recently, four or five times since the start of the present school year, maybe more, she'd invited him inside with her and they'd ended up on the floor of her basement family room, making out experimen-tally for hours (her word for it—and he had no idea where she got it—*canoodling*) beside the giant muted TV. So her question was a fair one. Had he been stalking? Waiting for the junior high bus in hopes that their paths would cross? Possibly. The prospect of being asked inside was certainly something he'd welcome, if he thought about it—on the floor, her hair tented over him, enclosing them, lips on hers, tongue floating against hers, sweet smells of her saliva and lip gloss and of their shared breath absorbing him, faces so close the shattered mask of her skin disappeared, turned to what it was truly, dots and slashes of pigmentation, nothing hidden, and the port-wine stain . . . exactly the same to touch as any other part of her, though it made her eyes wink shut and the pulse jump in her throat when he did that. Weird. Yes. But he hadn't been thinking about any of this, or of her, he was pretty sure. He'd hung around at the Jerky Shack a few extra minutes, longing for something to eat or drink, anything to take his mind off of whatever—the horrible day, the restrictions on his rations to make the experiment work, the experiment itself, his missing mother, his stupid life—anything *good* that wouldn't just make him feel like barfing later or clawing his skin off; waited until the other bus stop kids had cleared out enough that he could make his way home, alone, without any hassle. Then back out into the wind . . . odd how you still braced yourself, expecting it to suck your breath away like a real frozen winter wind, and when it didn't, how you still couldn't relax.

"These guys tried to steal my lunch. Kids do that, you know, in high school. No one's there to stop them. Some people say it should be like an open campus at lunch, like what they do at some of the bigger schools in Calgary, you know, where you can sign yourself out? Do whatever you want? But I don't know."

Still she said nothing, but he sensed a slowing in her gait, then a quickening to keep up.

"So it turned into, like, an altercation. And everyone got hurt pretty bad."

"Everyone like *who*?"

"Just some guys. The Hazard twins and a couple others. You wouldn't know. Bunch of hockey-jock jerks."

"I should clean you up. We've got just the thing."

"No!" He laughed. "I mean . . . I don't mean *no*. I mean, it's funny. Everyone's trying to help me now, since this fight thing. Even the bus driver decided it'd be cool to drop snow down my back."

"He *what*?"

"It's like an ancient Inuit shaman treatment. I don't know. Worked, though. Stopped the bleeding." He nodded, sniffed.

"I thought it was lunchtime?"

"What?"

"The fight. I thought you said it was at lunchtime?"

"This was after. My nose started bleeding again. Who knows why. On the bus home. I was bleeding all over. Gushing."

They walked a ways farther, not talking, Thomas drawing mouth breaths while things he might say (one of which, stupid or lame or not, he'd eventually have to come out with—he knew himself well enough to expect this) and various ways of arranging the words, pacing his breaths around them for a pause or emphasis, knocked at his skull and throat. *So what was your trick to clean me up? Soap and a good canoodle?* No. Too much like begging. *So what was your idea to clean me up—bum some money off your mom and go back into town for a cheeseburger? Sorry about that, what I said about your face. . . . It wasn't very nice.* He should start there. Yes. Some form of extra apology. *Sorry about that, what I said about your face. About your face, sorry about that. I was just trying to be funny, you know. About your face . . . I like you, but you're, like, in eighth grade—we can't get too serious or anything. . . .*No, that was another insult masquerading as an apology. *Sorry about that, what I said. I like you a lot, you know that, but whatever, you're just way younger than me and. . . .*But then he was thinking about kissing her again and there was no way into it. He had to remember to steal some of her lip balm next time anyway, check the ingredients for trace amounts of C. . . .

"I *hate* the stupid Chinooks," she announced.

"Yes. You've said that." The few other times, since they'd known each other, when the rain shadow had done its trick and the weird hot snow-eater winds blew down from the Rockies, she'd said it: The Chinooks were a fraud and a tease. Made a wind-burned mess of everything and drew you outside, thinking winter might be over, when it certainly was not. *Be real; stay cold*, she'd say in another second. *Don't tease me.* But he didn't entirely believe her. The hungry way she walked, her jacket draped over one arm, the extra movement in her arms—she was enjoying it.

"Don't you?"

"No. I mean, I don't care. It's all the same. Tomorrow will be winter again, soon enough, so whatever."

"What if it's like this all week?"

"It won't be."

"There wouldn't be any snow left."

"Hardly any now." He shrugged. "Global warming."

"You believe in that?"

"Duh."

"Al Gore–aphobia. That's what my dad calls it. Like the tooth fairy."

"Your dad's an even bigger idiot than mine."

"Probably. I say, stay real; stay cold."

The movie, that was it. She always liked hearing his ideas about that, the history, and his imitations of the sailors' voices. She even somewhat seemed to believe him about being related to Franklin. *Our ancestors, maybe they camped out in one of Franklin's pastures,* his father would say. *Shoveled his horses' shit and squatted in one of his stables. The name, that's about all we have in common. You need to divest yourself of this delusion, Thomas. This mythologizing. Do you figure we're related to Benjamin Franklin now, as well? Why stop there— how about . . . Aretha Franklin?* But it was more than the name, he was sure—too many other coincidences and little overlaps in interest. Anyway, it didn't matter. Related or not, if he wanted to believe himself a part of John Franklin's lineage and legacy (the explorer, not the high school teacher), then he'd believe it. Once, he'd even told her about the dead sailors visiting him in his sleep, stumbling around his bedroom comically with their dead feet, bleeding gums, and frostbitten faces, looking for food and a way out of their misery, asking him about the lamppost at the end of their walkway and the lights downtown. *Flying lights with machines attached! Did you see 'em? Blimey! Where'd they come from?* She'd bought that as well, or seemed to, or at least found it funny and engaging enough to keep listening.

His house was in sight. There was the lamppost and the bank of mailboxes under the tree at the corner.

"Yeah, like the summer right before Franklin hit Peel Sound and froze in for good. It was the warmest weather on record for hundreds of years. Totally false. Everything melting. No wonder they thought they'd just steam right down and through the passage in two weeks."

She nodded.

"So I had this new idea for the opening sequence today."

She nodded again. Made some noise in her throat that might have meant *Go on*, or might have meant she couldn't care less.

"There should be, like, a fight scene to set up Braine's death. He thinks it's because of a fight—like cracked ribs and stuff, so he can't breathe right, but it turns out to be pneumonia, so he's down there in sick bay, all cheesed off at everyone all the time, especially the guy that hit him. Loses his appetite and wastes away. But really, it's the lead poisoning. Makes you paranoid, so he's, like, going crazy and stuff, blaming everyone, and no one can figure out what's wrong with him. Him and the other guy, Hartnell—both of the guys who died out of nowhere the first winter on Beechey." Already, he was picturing some of the shots involved. Braine with Hartnell in sick bay. Someone hatcheting open a new tin of canned beef for them and heating it. Braine spooning it up from a nice china plate. Lying back. Pinwheel eyes. Yelling. Throwing the plate. Collapsing. Close-up of food splattered on the sick bay's wall and floor. Fancy tinned beef and split peas. No—no, wrong, because they'd only ever get rice in sick bay: *Sick bay rations limited to rice.* But here maybe a little poetic license was in order, to show the real culprit—the Victorian decadence and desire for a proper English meal wherever you were, which meant tons and tons of deadly tinned and contaminated provisions.

"Duh. They knew about lead poisoning."

"No. They didn't, in fact. I told you. That's why they soldered all the tinned provisions with lead. They put lead in, like, everything then—kids' toys, paint, dishes, glass, wine. You name it. Even some medicine. They even made guys take *mercury* back then. They had no idea. They thought it was good for you. But the amount of lead in those cans and in their water-purification systems. . . ." He croaked and did a little spastic death pantomime. "Lethal."

Two V-shaped dents like check marks appeared in her forehead, one above each eyebrow, and he wondered if he'd lost her, said too much, or been a little too enthusiastic in his death act. "I thought it was that other dude"—she snapped her fingers—"what's his name, that died first."

"Torrington?"

"Him."

"He came on board with TB. They knew that. They figured it was, like, therapeutic to send him on discovery service to the Arctic?

Good for the lungs? Then they had the bright idea to set him up as chief stoker down there in the engine room shoveling coal all day. Doh! Killed him right off. But Braine and Hartnell . . . totally mysterious. It *looked* like TB, but TB would never kill you so fast. Takes a while. Maybe botulism. Botulism is kind of like drowning. Your lungs quit and then you basically, you just . . . you suffocate. So says Devon."

"Why do you *know* so much of this stuff? It's, like, weird."

"I just read some books. That's all. There's nothing wrong with it."

"I didn't say there's anything *wrong*. Just there's other *things* in the world."

They'd reached the mailboxes and the walkway up to his house. Thomas stopped, but Jill kept going. She turned and walked backward, seeming to hurry from him now. He had the sense he'd scared her or hurt her feelings again. Maybe too much death talk.

"You need to wash with green soap. Your face. With a good green soap. And gargle salt water. No canoodling. It'll make the bleeding start again."

"Oh, so you . . ." She turned and kept walking. "Hey," he said. "So I guess . . ."

"See you later."

He raised a hand, half-waving, though he knew she didn't see.

"Later," he said, and turned to face the mailboxes.

Mom in the mailbox. Pop-up Mom in a square red or blue or bright green envelope bearing exotic canceled stamps, scentless and fat with paper. He'd seize it lightly in two fingers, as if not to touch any part of it too intimately, as if to keep his impulses in check, one of which veered toward an insane desire to rip the envelope open and pour all his attention greedily into her words, the other, with equal intensity, toward a desire to rip it *all* apart, tear print from paper if he could, and stomp the pieces into the grainy, icy snow without reading a word, because whatever she said, it would not be enough. The letters unfolded a larger window within the window of the envelope, all of it almost too electrifying to bear, none of it giving him anything like what he wanted. He didn't understand himself in the presence of such strong emotions—knew only that he wished, right now, there would be no letter at all. Or wished there would be many, many letters, better, more personal letters with pictures and kind words, and much more of her than that.

Deep breath. *Please*, he thought, and turned the key for their mailbox—familiar *tocking* sound—and peered in.

Empty.

Barren, gleaming little square Quonset hut, like where she might be staying right now—someone's makeshift sheet-metal hovel at the edge of a melting glacier maybe, watching and waiting. So the mail hadn't come yet. "*Yes*," he said. "Beat the mailman." He slapped the little door shut and pocketed his key. Safe another hour or two, until his father returned and came in the door braying orders and asking where he was, what was he doing, had he finished his homework, practiced his piano, remembered to take out the garbage, empty the cat's litter, start dinner. He was off the hook. He'd make some hot chocolate, or just eat some plain squares of it like the sailors, followed by canned tuna on Ritz crackers. Unwind a little with solitaire on the computer. Drop a note to Devon on his Facebook page. Dive into his storyboard notebooks awhile and see if he could draw some of the fight scene into frames—Braine versus Work. Hartnell in some of the background shots. It was too bad about Jill, yes—but probably a good thing, too. Skinny-legged Jill with her bare shins swallowed up in her black plastic snow boots and that blue-brown-red stain down her face. A kid, too young for him. Anyway, he'd survived plenty of afternoons without her already. He'd survive plenty more.

ONE THING HE'D LEARNED from his son's obsession with their namesakes, the Franklins of Arctic lore: Lady Jane, Sir John's wife, once traveled as far north as Muckle Flugga, in the Shetland Isles, then considered the northernmost point in the British Isles, in order to gaze longingly to sea after her husband's lost ships—to be as close to him as she might get without leaving British soil. A publicity stunt to gain attention and fund yet another search party, Thomas assured him—she'd even (according to rumor) invited her new friend Charles Dickens and her nephew Alfred, Lord Tennyson, along to write about it for the *Times*—but John Franklin the school-teacher imagined it differently. He'd been to Shetland once himself and knew you didn't make that sick crossing without a genuine incentive. His own had been a girl, of course, decades ago—a Dutch girl he'd traveled with for weeks through Spain and the UK, when without warning she'd given him the slip. Left him a note at the hostel's front desk, saying he should catch up with her when he was ready, and the address. Baltasound Unst. So he had his own picture of Lady Jane just north of Unst, prelighthouse, and staring out to sea from a deserted pile of wave-encircled rocks after Sir John. For him, it was not just more lore of the explorer: He'd seen those rocks and heard the gulls and looked straight north to nothing but more and more open sea (the Dutch girl, of course, long gone). Regardless, factual or mythic, because of his personal connection with it, the story of Jane and Muckle Flugga formed a kind of emotional touchstone for him, icon, whatever you wanted to call it, like his father's absurd dashboard Jesus figurines: something to look at and conjure as needed, to set on the horizon and steer yourself toward. Also a way of giving his own refusal to leave Alberta and move back to California a shape or explanation. (His mother's words to him just the previous week: *Honey, you're north of North Dakota! No, we're not visiting this year. You just come on home when you're ready.*) What kept him here? An oath, a personal resolution he mentioned rarely, if at all: He would not leave until Thomas had finished high school; he would wait at least that long so as to protect Thomas from having fully lost his mother, and to leave open for Jane the possibility of return. The chance for Thomas to visit her, too, though as yet that hadn't happened. If he pictured Lady Jane at Muckle Flugga, looking north after John, still hopeful after how many years, it almost made sense. So long as he and Thomas were here, they were that much closer to her. One day's travel instead of three. There was still the chance of patching it up.

Now he was in the parking lot at the end of the school day, done his classes, done the debate team, done grading, done with everything until tomorrow morning—familiar, happy release into the evening—hearing the wind bang and buffet the streetlight beside his car, the school-yard flagpole bare now but the halyard still chiming and chattering spastically against the pole, and thinking about Jane and Muckle Flugga and personal resolutions, because Moira had been text-messaging him every half hour or so since just after the end of classes. Three times, to be exact. Once just to pass him her number—a new one. Then the messages. *Call here when u can. Not urgent. Maybe urgen now yes, pls call now. Not the home number. Dial this #.* Picturing himself there at the point of his internal Muckle Flugga, gazing north, he wondered how much of it was dedication and adhering to an oath after all; how much was just stubbornness and being hooked on the romance of separation—the poignancy, stalled longing, frozen miles away from Jane—and how easily might Moira spring him from all of that? He'd sworn, too, when Jane left, that he'd never follow after her, even to visit, and had already broken that vow, months after she'd gone, though he hadn't actually managed to see her—his own fault for having flown up spontaneously, unannounced, while Thomas was back east visiting relatives. Three days he'd passed standing on the balcony of his rented room and getting drunk on ten-dollar well drinks in the hotel bar with some of the locals he'd run into, asking after her. He'd watched the sun circle endlessly, and once, on a one A.M. jog to the outskirts of town, thought he might be on the verge of appreciating something like the enchantment of the place, the bitten-down, inhospitable whatever it was that had lured Jane there and kept her. He'd stood at the top of a rise, alone and swarmed by mosquitoes, until some inchoate realization connected with the wind-tipped dwarf pines and the light so endless it seemed to come from the earth, felt as if it had worked its way through him, then turned and jogged back. Flying out, he'd been amazed, again, at the foreshortened strangeness of the perspective—the trees too stumpy to calculate height or distance, the land and water continually interrupting each other, so the higher you went, the more it looked like a swampy, cratered patchwork of endless puddles and waterways in which it would be impossible to ever know your way. And he'd felt relieved beyond all expectation to be home again and returned to hours of darkness and night (and somehow, consequently, *color*)—had known, too, he would not go back. It was enough, having seen where she was. If she'd heard from any of the locals that he'd been up there looking for her, she'd never let on.

"Moira, Moira," he said. Checked the callback number and hit *Dial*. Backed his car in a reverse arc from under the streetlight and headed out of the lot as digital ring pulses fluttered in his ear, connecting them.

She answered just as he was turning and accelerating onto the access road. All sand and bare pavement now, no snow. Just an incredible amount of sand. He couldn't remember—November? October?—when he'd last seen it this snowless.

"John! Hang on a sec," she said, and then moments later: "Back again. I'm so glad you called."

"Of course. You know I—"

They'd spoken at the same time.

"You first."

"No."

"OK," he drew a breath. "I was just going to say it was so good seeing you today. I'd forgotten how . . . how much I always enjoy your company. Whatever. It's just good, and I'm glad we're back in touch. Let's keep it like that."

"Let's do."

"So what's up?"

"Oh, you'll just think it's dumb."

"Never. What's wrong?"

"You haven't seen Jeremy at all since my visit there, have you?"

"No, I had class straight through. Talked to Legere, though, just a while back and everything seemed fine from his end. The boys will make a formal apology to Thomas, blah blah, and there'll be some work detail for them. Nothing goes on anyone's record. All sounded pretty reasonable, I thought. A little too reasonable, maybe, but he's got his theory about barometric pressure and *eccentric behaviors due to zee vinds,"* he said, trying to mimic Legere's accent. "Did he mention that? We were possessed by *the devil winds.*"

Her breath ruffled into the phone. A laugh? Not a laugh. "Jeremy never came home."

"Oh." Now he was maneuvering into traffic on the main road, Tim Hortons flashing by. Blockbuster, its formerly towering snowbanks shrunken to a meager misshapen few humps. The ridiculous new condo warrens. "Is that . . . that's unusual for him, I guess? Of course it is."

"It wouldn't be if I could track him down anywhere, but I haven't been able to. His girlfriend doesn't know. She never saw him after school. Alas, no one seems to have . . . a clue where he went. Ordinarily, he'd be in touch, call or text. Late after school, going to the Okotoks mall, busy with Belinda, whatever. I suspect he's gone to Davis . . . his dad, but I haven't been able to raise anyone there, either. Unsurprisingly."

"He'll turn up."

"Yes. Of course. Dead or alive is the question."

"I'm not touching that one."

"No, I'm sure he's fine." She sighed wearily. "It's just weird. He hasn't done this before, ever. . . . now it's going on six o'clock, and tomorrow he's got practice."

Franklin checked his watch. 5:27. Drove a ways in silence. There were certain things he could (and probably should) ask now—where was Rick, why was he getting drawn into this drama instead of Rick, how had this sudden collusion between them sprung up again—but to ask such questions would be to incite an impeding logic, when all he really wanted right now was for her to keep breathing (distraught, worried, whatever) close, in his ear, as he made his way home. He didn't want to ask her why it was so, why she was inviting him to share her concern.

"So . . . OK. Was he OK with Legere's disciplining? Did he mention anything to you about it after?"

"We weren't talking."

"Not at all?"

"I'd say he was a little disappointed, if I had to guess. But . . . I don't know. No, we didn't talk. I don't fight his battles for him. I told you."

"Yes. You said that."

"I can't anymore. Not for him or anyone. It's a road that goes nowhere."

"Yes."

She made a growling, exasperated noise. Laughed. "Fucking kid."

"He's all right."

"Probably having a hamburger somewhere or shooting pixels at imaginary aliens at some friend's house or at his dad's, according to a preapproved plan which I seem to have completely and inconveniently forgotten about."

"For sure."

"Anyway, I thought you might have seen him around. . . ."

"Sorry, no."

"I had this crazy thought maybe he would have sought you out to make good and patch things up, but . . ."

"Sorry, no . . . like I said." *Sorry.* He'd inflected the word Canadian-style almost before he could notice it to stop himself; some form of subconscious, unconscious mockery? Sabotage? Desire for inclusion? Hard *o* sound. Doubted she'd even notice. "Jeremy's not . . . not a kid I've ever had anything much to do with, actually, until today. If he was on the debate team, now, maybe. Otherwise"—he tried to lighten his voice a bit, speed it up—"I might've put it together long ago, you and him, you know. Turner Valley. Actually, though, aside from that, I don't really know how I would've figured it out. But I might have. Anyway, I had no idea. You have to realize that. No idea at all. Definitely, I wouldn't have grabbed him had I known."

"He'll show up."

"Yes, of course he will."

"I should go now."

"Call as soon as you know anything?"

Silence on the other end of the line.

"I didn't say that. Call if you want. Whenever you have a moment."

"I'll try, John. I will try to remember. I appreciate that you care."

"Well, of course I do. And I'm afraid I'm also at least somewhat culpable here."

"I wouldn't say that."

"Mmm . . . but I would."

His phone went dead suddenly, bleated and flashed on and off—*Dropped Call*—before connecting again to his service. The dead spot at the turnoff—he'd forgotten. "Damn," he said, snapping the phone shut as he rolled into the driveway. In the silenced car interior, he sat a moment, turning the phone over and over in his hand and staring idly at the thing as if willing it to ring. Should he call her back? To say . . . what? They'd been signing off anyway. You didn't redial someone to finish a call that was already ending. Did you? But this car—the Volvo—his pride and folly (and not many drives didn't end without a moment or two of appreciative reflection on this: the sweet blue-lit contoured dashboard and controls, all-automatic heated leather seats, heated mirrors), bought with money from the cash-out of their property in Calgary—it'd suit Moira. Rich girl. She'd like it. Had he chosen it (and Houndstitch over Cochrane, for that matter, where there'd been a similar position open) because of some semi-conscious impulse, despite all resolutions to the contrary, to be nearer to her . . . to be more *like* her? Possibly, all for Moira, yes. No, Cochrane was at least as overrun with new oil people as Calgary, and growing faster than Okotoks; moving there would never have satisfied his desire just to get *away* and clear of it all, back out to where your thoughts could stand in sharpest relief against the flat prairie light, the grass, the tall sky, the cold, the mountains—everything that had drawn him here in the first place. Never would have left him with the savings to establish such generous college funds for both boys, either.

No sound. Only the noise of the engine cooling. And then it dawned on him: no sound, no wind. The Chinook was done, or soon ending. If there'd been light enough still, he might have looked up through the windshield to see the sky clearly split in pieces, two or three bands of clouds like stair steps exactly demarcating the shifts in air pressure and temperature where one front ended and the next began—that dramatic. In hours, temperatures would plummet. Minutes maybe. Instafreeze. Welcome back, February. He swung open his door and gripped his knees a moment, trying to remember those lost lines of almost word sounds—the melting snowbanks, the reflections in the vanishing puddles, and the light high clouds whipping by. Nothing. All of it so illusory. "Another day," he said, and pushed himself upright to go inside, see about getting dinner ready for the lonely sailor-obsessed boy who was his son.

dude, did i just like roll a twenty on bardic seafaring knowledge while you rolled like a one?!? their antiscorbutics would totally have been so useless by the end of winter number two. the lemon juice would be like bad water, currants and raisins all full of worms, pickled cabbages and pickled pickles and whatever else if they had any left forget it, and everyone knows goldner's canned vegetable soups were like lethal. they probably figured that out. they had nothing antiscorbutic left except the rats rats rats and plenty of them to go around, if they would have thought to kill em and eat em raw. but who would do that?!? they were still holystoning the decks every day following royal navy protocol sticking to their rations. of course there was scurvy. the occasional random death from botulism and lead induced dementia too of course. they were . . .

He tipped back in his father's computer chair to read this through a second and third time, trying to find the right ending to it, the right way of making Devon see why it was important, what the sailors faced, and how the only realistic way of ever fully fathoming it was to experience some part of it yourself. No, he didn't have to kill himself from botulism or eat a bunch of lead filings until he went nuts; that would be pointless, irreversible. But scurvy . . . *call it a lack of imagination,* he tapped out on the keyboard, and then struck it, too. *call it a failure.* Backspaced over that, as well. *call it my deal with the dead sailors. my way of giving them a little honour and respect so I can put them in the movie. anyway i've got it so totally under control you don't*

have to worry. anything major bad goes down i can reverse it all in like
ten days tops with vitamin supplements. i'm on target. all's well. recur-
rent bloody nose (yes!). corkscrew hairs: negative. dad mopes as ever.
  hit points this round . . . sorry bro big zero for you.
  down for a visit soon?

But something peripheral to what he was writing had him distracted, so he kept wiping off the sentences and starting again, biting
the ends of his fingers, never quite feeling as if he'd said the thing
he'd meant to say, never finding the exactly satisfying and final way
of putting it. Kept glancing up and out the window at the dying
light—orange and yellow in the seed heads of the prairie grass bordering their backyard—and picturing that red-blue mark down Jill's
face. The freckles. Her mouth. Was that it? The thing bumming him
out? Her . . . her face? Could he ever get used to it?

Failure. That word he'd typed a few times and deleted. That was it.
Not just his own (though it stung some still, remembering the way
she'd dodged him there at the mailbox— . . . *wash with green soap . . .*
No canoodling. . . . See you later.) but her failure, too: how she must
have to survive some personal version of failure all day, every day,
never escaping it anytime she saw a reflection of herself or caught
someone staring and then quickly looking away, her so-pretty face
eternally disfigured by that blue stain and nothing in the world to
be done about it. It was too depressing to think about. Franklin, too.
Because, whatever else you wanted to say about him or his expedition, however horrible the ordeal, noble, stupid, doomed, surreal,
arrogant, absurd, colonial, whatever angle you wanted to take, there
was really only one thing at the bottom of it, from Franklin's perspective: failure. Failure as a commander to find the passage, failure to
break out of the ice, to follow orders and keep the men alive, failure
to get back home. Failure, period. And then death. No, first suffering, and then death. What good was a movie about that? Who would
want to see that?

To counter these thoughts, he shut his eyes a moment and pictured the grainy natural-light shots he so longed for. Meditated
them back into existence. Sleety, overcast, with dubbed-in howling

sounds so you almost feel the wind, just looking at the picture; sailors' figures like shadows lunging in and out of the frame, suddenly close, suddenly far away. No way of gauging distance, really, with all that wind and ice and blowing snow like static. Blinding snow light. Sound of one man's breathing, hard breathing, and then his face right in the camera. Black with frostbite around the nose and cheeks, eyes rimmed all around by ice, more white around his mouth and, hanging from his chin, a stalagmite of frozen breath and sweat in his beard hair so massively overgrown with frost, he'll eventually have to break it off with a hatchet if he wants to eat or talk—no, his face is wrapped in wool and wolf skin, which appears to have grown right over with ice from his breath like a giant frozen beard mask. Only the blackened frostbitten cheeks and nose show. Eyes bugged from hunger. *Sepulchral voices*—those were Franklin's own words for it, from the other expedition, the one where he ended up cooking his boots and eating them with lichen and someone's buffalo robe to survive. Sepulchral. Entombed. Hollow. "Eh!" the man says. "Hallo? Johnny? Thomas?"

The scene . . . he knew just the scene to look at in order to think this through a little further. Out of sequence, but it didn't matter. Movies were always shot out of sequence.

He pushed back from his father's desk, sending the chair spinning until one of its arms clobbered the edge of the desk. Turned to see if anything had been upset, but no, all good, and went out of the room, thinking, *Later—I'll finish that off, send it, not now.* . . . Down the hall and up the stairs to his room. Vol. III, the red notebook, on the shelf over his homework desk with his pencil jars and erasers, ancient busted Super 8, VCR camera, tapes and CDs, and all the other notebooks. He knew right where the scene started and where he'd left off: the officer in the boat—the two officers in the grounded, sledge-hauled longboat on King William Island, waiting to see who would die first. Leg bones and arm bones frozen and strewn around them. Strips of dried, frozen flesh on the bowsprits. In the prow of the boat, a musket under each arm, the cracked-up assistant sawbones from the *Erebus,* Harry Goodsir, talking, talking, though quietly enough that you can barely make out what he says over the ominous sound track; at the stern, Petty Officer Edmund Hoar, Franklin's steward, lips moving silently in prayer. All afternoon, they've wandered the area in search of anything at all to hunt or eat—rocks from which to scrape lichen, seabirds, seaweed, anything at all. The remaining food, the strips of sun-cured flesh and pounds of frozen chocolate in foil on the bottom of the grounded boat, will not sustain them much longer than another few days. So it's the insane waiting game, who will die first, which has to be shown really, primarily in the purplish intensity of the light. The glaring sun circling along the horizon and then dipping back up again in the sky, snow-blinding the men, but never warming them.

In his last drawing, he'd depicted Hoar with an arm over Good-sir's shoulder, something like what Commander Franklin used to do with Hoar—pulling him aside to enforce a pause in his duties, set aside the hot water, the polish, the razor strop, the tea service, the lint brush, be still and listen while Franklin clarified something about their purpose here in the Arctic, or explained a passage from the Bible as it applied to the icebound men. Until this expedition, Hoar had never been particularly religious; now it fills his head every waking minute (which is most of every single day from sunup to sunup), and is his only real source of solace. First, Goodsir babbling as usual (Thomas's note to himself here for later, for actual directing purposes, or for whoever else might eventually shoot the scene: *a little of this goes a loo-o-ong way*). New frame: Goodsir and Hoar, both men facing the camera, huddling for warmth.

Goodsir: " . . . At first they says *it's just the one man. We need him to stew, see, so's all the rest of us can survive. Of course! Just followin'* orders, sir! *Don't want to waste none of him, and none of his private bits in the mash, see—no fingers or toes or the like, nothing to discour-age the men from eating.* But of course, sir, Captain Crozier. *Goodsir's your man, handy with the saw and knives*, they says, *knows where to cut 'em to get the best meat*, says they. *The most nutritious.* So's it just the one then, says I? Just the one? *Aye. Aye*, says they, *just the one, to be sure.* 'Cause I'll only do it once. It's their heads and faces, is the problem, see, all scurvy and frostbit. Ever wonder what goes on in a man's head? I'll tell you what it looks like inside anyway. Tell you better how it cooks. To get the best bits ... listen, to unhinge a man's head for the cheeks and the brains, you make a cut *here* to break the jaw open first. You don't want to waste nothing. Listen! It's important. It could be me dies first and then will you ever wish you'd listened to old man Harry Goodsir. But you'll tell them for me won't you, if you make it home, their families that is, I never meant 'em any harm? Not a one of 'em. They was dead already anyway, most of 'em. If you make it home? *He's the man for the job,* they says. Wasn't my choice. *Handy with a knife and saw,* they says. Just the one then, is it? says I. 'Cause I won't do another. *Aye. Aye,* says they. . . ."

Two-shots and shoulder shots alternated down the page. Thomas lay on his stomach on the floor of his bedroom, face as close to the page as he could get without losing focus to become more deeply engrossed, feet lifted and swinging, spinning the notebook around and around for differing perspectives on the men: Hoar with his handsome, frostbitten blond face, a little like the evil Jeremy Malloy, really; Goodsir, the more he drew him, resembling Cody/Dakota, the proportions on his nose shifting from frame to frame, wider, shorter, longer, the frozen Welsh-wig hat thing on his head like Cody/Dakota's insane mess of tubular dread-locked hair.

Hoar: "Only pray with me. We've done 'em no harm. No one. They was *all* dead already. I for one, if it was me and I was dead, and the choice was life or death for my mates, I'd say make a stew of me! Come. Prayer. It's the only answer."

Goodsir: "That's Franklin talking."

Hoar: "No, it's me. Franklin's long gone. With *Erebus.* Died on board *Erebus.* Remember, sir?"

Goodsir: "Of course I remember. Who do you think'd remember better? And don't you be *sirring* me none, young man. I see right through your type. See right through your cunning, conniving skull. You're only waiting for your moment. Waiting till the time's ripe and then smack old Harry in the head with whatever's handy. Back, I tell you! Back!"

The next frames showed the snow increasing, each man at his respective end of the longboat again, Hoar muttering prayers, Goodsir just muttering. For a while, Hoar tries in vain to light a fire at the bottom of the boat using pages from a novel (from *Erebus's* one-thousand-volume library and hauled all these miles over the snow in hopes of being tradable to the Eskimos for food), scraps of wet rope, and the few remaining slats and wood shards from the deconstructed snow sledge formerly underlying the longboat. Close-ups of Hoar's hands working the flint. Flames catching and licking the pages, then flickering out; burned, blackened corners of pages. Again he works the flint; flames again, and here's Hoar's face in the sudden light of new warmth as he leans closer to blow gently, bringing the fire to life; then for two more frames, the blessed glow of flames strengthening against his frozen and now almost heat-blistering flesh, until—poof—a gust of wind snatches it all away: flaming paper extinguished, blown skyward, nothing but blackened bits of rope and wood left. Again and again he tries, more close-ups of his shaking, frozen fingers, and this time as the camera draws back, Hoar leaning in and curling himself around the failed fire at the stern of the longboat, finally giving up, face frozen in an expression of beatific rest and release; the camera pans backward fast, super-fast, Google-fast, up along the coast of King William Island thirty, forty, fifty miles north, in the path of the boat sledges—barely a trace anymore of the men in their misery, harnessed and hauling the longboats, two tons apiece, through ice, slush, rock snowdrifts—back all the way to Victory Point, the stone tent circle and the ships frozen in going on three years now, stuck dead in the polar ice pack; and back farther than that, up Peel Sound, past Beechey Island again and back out into the open bay until we're on board *Erebus* again, sailing. Again Hoar's hands work the flint, and this time there's the pleasing crackle of lit, smoldering coal as flames glow and jump to life. (Thomas's note to himself here in the margins: *Check this. Boiler? Coal grate in commander's cabin?*) The same happy expression on his face as he turns and rises, dusting his hands on his knees.

"There you are, sir. Fire's all fine now. Would you be wanting anything else, then, sir?"

Franklin, in the little ring of light thrown from his oil lamp, pauses from his writing, lays aside his pen, and calls Hoar closer. "Edmund Hoar," he says. "In your opinion, Master Hoar"—here he purses his lips and pauses to draw a breath—"would you say the punishment of twelve lashes and no rum in their rations the next fortnight was good and appropriate action considering the fisticuffs on board earlier today?"

"Begging your forgiveness, sir, and bein' a mere steward . . ."

"Yes, yes, but I *asked* your opinion, so you may give it. You are *free* to an opinion, Master Hoar. We are each of us free and fallen, every single one of us to a man, *and* made in God's image. Now then."

"Yes, sir. Bein' as it's only my opinion and all, still I'd say, sir, it was really Private Braine as instigated the whole thing. They're always after the sailors, them Royal Navy, always passing off their work if they can do, and sometimes stealing rations to sell back if no one's looking, especially their share of cook's prerogative, and . . . now as I see it, they made it so poor Thomas, there was nothin' he *could* do but fight back or suffer a beating, or else fight back *and* suffer a beating but at least save his dignity some. I'd say it was fair, sir, absolutely, the disciplining actions, only it mighta been more fair had it been Braine got all of it."

Pause and close-up of Franklin's face as he considers this. "*In your humble opinion,* that is, Master Hoar."

"In my opinion, sir. Yes. I said that, sir. In my own opinion."

"And *in your own opinion,* would you say the outcome of said disciplining will be of an overall positive and ameliorative effect? That is, are you more convinced of man's inherent decency and tendency toward goodness and godliness, as am I, or of his essential lack of empathy toward his fellow man and knack for finding trouble, always trouble, any sort of trouble, wherever it may lie, *regardless* the size of the rod and number of lashes awaiting? This is a *very serious question,* so please think a moment before answering."

"Beg pardon, sir?"

"On the question of discipline, Hoar. We're talking about discipline. Do you believe in a man's tendency toward goodness and godliness, or his eternal need for strictest disciplining?"

"With all respect, sir, I'd say, in my opinion, it's entirely depending on the man in question. Some's not as good as others, to be sure. And that Thomas Work, now there's a fellow'd never hurt a fly, but . . . you shoulda seen him in there with the Royal Navy one. Meaning no disrespect to the Royal Navy, but some of us was even bettin' on him to—"

"That's all right now, Mr. Hoar. That's enough. You may go. I thank you for your considered *opinion*."

"Would you be wanting your tea, then?"

"At teatime, thank you, and not a minute sooner. Now go."

Close-up as Hoar exits: Franklin's journal. *My Dearest Jane*, it begins—another letter: his spare, angular gentleman's scrawl, India ink, each word tilting exactly, artfully one to the next; the grooved and brown-black ink-stained calluses on his right thumb and middle finger—and farther down the page: . . . *mined from and later forged in the suffering endured during my previous Arctic experiences (excluding those with B—of which I may here make no mention, though, if you think on it, you will well remember) and further galvanized by our time at Van Diemen's Land (as, again, you know too well), I have in my soul now such an enduring and iron-clad faith in man's essential goodness as can never be shaken. Today's incident on board Erebus has again tested me to the core. Why must it be lashes, always more lashes?* . . .

Thomas spun the page again for refreshed perspective. Drew Franklin's fingers again, the ink-stained calluses, the nib of the pen flexing, the words, studying his own hand at work for a model, drawing, writing. If we're not related, he thought, how is it I can channel him like *that*—his voice. Coincidence? Words I've never even knew or heard of. *Ameliorative*. What's it mean? Who knows? He resisted the impulse, a common one when he was deeply enough into it, to pause and find the dictionary to look up the found words he kept stumbling into and for which he knew no true definition. Kept drawing, hands and more hands, lost enough in it that he must not have heard his father's entrance—the car pulling up, door opening.

"Hey, sailor. Time out for dinner?"

His neck hurt, his elbows, and there was a hollow numb spot in his rib cage from the way he'd been lying. All this he hadn't exactly registered until now—distant aggravations like the prickles in his fingertips. He spun the notebook a final few times to close the line connecting Franklin's thumb and forefinger, like a mapped bay or inlet, like the blank spot on the old maps Franklin had sailed straight into. Done, he glanced back up the page at his drawings: hands and hands and more hands like maps. Snapped the cover shut and sat up, folding one leg under the other.

"Whoa," he said. "I didn't even hear you. What time is it?"

"Just about six. Keeping busy?"

"No."

"Homework?"

His father was in his parka still and smelled faintly of cigarettes and cold outside air. Under this were the smells that always distinguished him to Thomas—burned toast, mothballed sweaters, citrus aftershave, and their shared soap and shampoo. Water stood in beads on the scuffed tan toes of his shoes and some had soaked into the cuffs of his khakis. If Thomas were drawing him, he'd want to add more angles to the way he stood now, because most people, he'd learned, came across better in a drawing that way—more active—if you included some kind of S-shaped curvature: a head tilt, hand on a hip, hip jutted and shoulder cocked at an opposing angle, something like that. But his father's natural stance, he realized, was pretty much in constant opposition to this bit of portraiture logic: He stood boringly straight up, hands at his sides, fingers tapping and swatting at something in his pockets. Twenty-five years between them. But, interestingly, in the decade or so during which Thomas had shot up from child to young man and became conscious enough to begin observing his father in anything like a neutral or semidetached manner, his father seemed to him not to have changed or aged outwardly at all. He had not gained weight, gone soft, lost hair, suddenly grayed.

He was pretty much as he'd always been: khakis and striped or plaid oxford shirts and flannel shirts, shoes and jackets rotated according to the season. Maybe he was a little more faded at the temples, duller-eyed, but not noticeably—and he was still the physically superior of the two of them. No question there. Occasionally, Thomas had had the shock of discovering ancient photos of his father in the hall desk or buried in some drawer, black-haired and regal, but the moment of surprise and discovery, seeing how, yes, he was not immortal, he'd in fact been changing and aging all along, however imperceptibly, somehow never stuck with him. Devon and his father had had their tennis and racquetball feuds, one of which had resulted in a dislocated shoulder for his brother, but to Thomas's knowledge there had never been a definitive knockdown game. Devon never satisfactorily wasted or surpassed their father; he just got better at giving him a pretty good game. Thomas and his father had no corollary physical rivalry, so there was not even that as a way of marking the distance between them.

"I figured I'd draw till you were home," he said. "How'd it get so late?"

"The debate in Cranbrook's coming up—we went a little overtime." His father's chin tilted upward slightly. "Anything good there?"

He shrugged. "Storyboard notebook stuff."

"For the movie?"

"Not exactly. More like research."

"Do I get to see?"

Thomas groaned. "Come on, Pop. I told you. When it's done. If you're lucky." He held out a hand, let his father pull him up, and they embraced lightly, each patting the other's shoulder blades, his father's parka making a faint hissing noise against Thomas's shirt as they separated.

"So." Here his father took a step back and squared his shoulders, hands on his hips, belt buckle showing, and moved to block Thomas's exit. He smiled and relaxed his shoulders. "Today, there at school . . . care to let me in on exactly what transpired?" But it was all wrong: The body language had the same fatherly, authoritative vibe as ever but not the vocal inflection. Thomas couldn't put a finger on it, but something had changed: He seemed overly judicious, too obviously concerned about something he wasn't mentioning yet—maybe like he was laying traps, getting ready to spring the big one on him later? "The fight?"

"It wasn't a fight, Dad. Just some really stupid grade-school antics from some of the school's lower life-forms."

His father nodded. "I understand, but it looked fairly serious, as well. You were bleeding."

"That wasn't related."

"How's that?"

"Probably."

"What do you mean?"

"Never mind."

"Answer my question."

He sighed, touched a hand lightly to his nose. "I've been having this thing lately. Like from the dryness or the wind or whatever. Nosebleeds."

"Really? It wasn't . . ."

Thomas shook his head.

His father drew a breath, annoyed now and apparently trying to calculate the phrasing of what he said next in order not to show it. "But would you say . . . was it Jeremy Malloy, primarily, instigating things?"

"He's . . . I couldn't tell you, to be honest. They were like all going at it at once and I couldn't see. They were mostly trying to get behind me anyway to . . . you know."

"Understood. But you wouldn't say . . ."

"Knowing Jeremy Malloy? Sure. I'm sure it was him. The rest of them are just like his minions. His little followers. Anyway, the whole nature-boy wedgie thing—that's totally jock behavior. Total jock homosadism, or whatever you want to call it. No one else gets up to that kind of crap."

"OK, but . . ."

"That's really about all I know, Dad. Sorry. No one to rat out here."

"That's not what I'm after. Because the other thing—other question, of course. The bigger thing . . ." His father sighed. "You kind of abandoned ship on us there, kiddo. Remember? Gave us the old slip? On the way to Vice Principal Legere's?"

Thomas thought about this a moment, scratching his head. He remembered the burning in his face and nostrils, the ridiculous feeling of his pants falling down at school while his underwear chafed and rode around, making him feel as if his whole back end were on display; his father's herding them to the building's double doors and then through and inside, and the sudden crash as the inner doors hit the wall, and his father yelling, *Any of you others want a piece of me?* His own father, that easily provoked and stooping to their level. But he hadn't seen this part of it because he'd already been making his way hurriedly from them along the north corridor to class. First, though, another hard left and a duck into the stall of the nearest boys' washroom for an adjustment to his destroyed underwear. What to do: fold them over the top of his pants? Tuck them down? Rip the elastic off all the way around and pray the things stayed up? Go commando? For a horrible few moments alone in the dented sheet-metal toilet stall, he could not tell what to do, his vision doubled up and speckling from sinus trauma and now tears, someone's enormous turd like a headless sea monster left in the bowl of the seatless toilet, and his blood dripping, huge splattering drops onto the bathroom tiling, all of it so incredibly awful and degrading. And then gradually he figured it out, rolled the elastic down, straightened things and cinched his belt another notch or two tighter. Went to class.

"What do you mean, 'abandoned ship'? I had class. I thought—"

"We were on our way to Legere's office."

"*You* were. But I thought—"

"No, we *all* were. You as well, ostensibly . . ."

"Why?"

"Look! I'm not angry, all right? I'm just saying—just asking."

Thomas nodded; scratched at his bare arm a moment and watched as his father's eyes followed the movement with something beyond mere curiosity. He looked closer at his own arm to guess what that might be about, but nothing suggested itself. Just his arm, vaguely red, with faint scratch marks; his usual bitten fingernails.

"I thought I should just go to class, Dad. Maybe the nurse's office."

"Yes, the nurse, that would have been a good idea."

"But I have biology fourth, so I don't know. I went to class. What, am I, like, in trouble?"

"No, no. I said . . ." His father trailed off, exasperated, and raked a hand back through his hair, pausing a moment, forehead in his palm. "It would have been a help, had you been there. That's all. Representing your side of things. A huge help, actually. But never mind. You're probably right—the more appropriate thing was a visit to the nurse. It just looked kinda . . . dumb. Your giving us all the slip."

"I didn't *give* you the slip. I told you. I went to class. I thought you were, like, making sure I was OK getting inside and that nothing else happened, and then once I was inside and everything, I could just . . . you know. It was so not a big *deal*."

"Right. Of course. Let's just . . ." He trailed off again. "Did you see the nurse?"

"No. I already said. I went to class."

Even more than usual, his father seemed unable to pursue any line of thought to a logical finish or full stop. "Well, let's forget it for now. There may be consequences. Let's . . . I could use some help with dinner."

"Sure. In a sec."

At the doorway, his father stopped and leaned in again toward Thomas, grinning, not meeting his eyes: "Avast, ye scurvy dogs. There's work awaitin' in the galley."

"Aye-aye, Cap'n. Down in a second."

He wanted a last peek at those drawings, a brief revisitation with Franklin and Hoar in Franklin's quarters, but he found, once his father had left, he didn't have the heart for it: That world, so contained and confined, destination coordinates set, a place for everything and everything in its place, each day known and accounted for, each scene and interaction in its frame—once he was inside it, the temptation was to stay there. Never leave, if he could help it. But getting back in sometimes, often, like now, when whatever was happening in his actual day-to-day life kicked him out this suddenly, could seem impossible. He'd find himself standing outside the imagined world of the movie and almost angry enough at himself and the whole stupid, fraudulent enterprise that he wanted to tear up the pages and walk away for good. He gritted his teeth, ground them together, and drove his fingernails into the palms of his hands to keep himself from doing anything stupid. Glimpsed himself in the window reflection: skewed black hair the same as his father's, skinny, pale arms sticking out of a misshapen bowl-necked brown-yellow T-shirt he'd been wearing since about grade six, pants still lopsided at the waistline. Had he ever even changed out of his destroyed briefs? No. But no time for that now. He went jogging after the clatter of his father's footsteps downstairs, realizing as he went how pressingly, urgently hungry he'd become—the thing making him woozy and sleepy with somewhat nauseated desire as he approached its cause and cure in the kitchen: food! Hunger. Rations and provisions. Salt pork and a lump of hardtack? Was today a flour day? He pinched his arm where he'd been scratching previously to see if it'd draw blood—*hemorrhagic sores*—see if he felt anything at all, and remembered then the other thing he'd been forgetting since coming in the front door.

"Dad," he said, and waited for his father, still wearing his parka, to stand back from the fridge, face him. "Any mail for me?"

As usual, they stood at opposite sides of the kitchen counter in the murky light and ate facing each other without looking up much or talking. For the umpteenth time, Franklin reminded himself, between bites, that more lightbulbs from the Superstore would be a really good idea; and sometime soon, this weekend maybe, he should try to remember to take down the kitchen light fixture for a scrub. Empty it of dead bugs, moths, and dust and replace the burned-out bulbs so he and Thomas would have more than this shadowy orange-tinged burnt umber light in the kitchen by which to eat and cook. The meat loaf was not quite hot, the salad limp and slippery with pickled green beans and olives—maybe it was for the best that they didn't see anything too clearly. If Moira were here . . . He glanced around briefly, wondering. What else? Many of the items they'd moved here from the house in Calgary a year and a half ago still had not found permanent places: the dingy, knife-marked cutting board always out on the range top; the mixing bowls shoved under the mug cupboard's overhang, unused for an eternity; the coffeemaker stranded at the wrong end of the counter, nowhere near the toaster or microwave, and splattered with old coffee. *If*, he thought . . . and almost killed the thought before it could swing broadside to its conclusion: *If* she were here for dinner one night, breakfast the next morning, he'd have a lot of housekeeping to do beforehand. Sort through the junk mail by the telephone, too. Figure out where the phone books belonged. Throw out those expired coupons piled on the windowsill and the Allen wrench orphaned from some repair job of a month or more ago. Was that all it took to start seeing things fresh and consider putting your house in order? The projected imaginary presence of a woman?

"Anything else new and exciting?" he asked. He knew it sounded as if he were trying hard to check back in and show an interest, and cleared his throat to mask that. Blinked and fixed his face into what he hoped was an attentive expression. But Thomas was already shaking his head no and helping himself to thirds on the cold meat loaf. "How about the big research project for Cullen? How's that coming?"

Thomas shrugged. "Mostly that's a rehash of the Franklin history project from last quarter. I think I'll throw in some more about Tennyson and Dickens to meet some of the assignment objectives, change some wording a little, but basically, it's totally done."

"Franklin—your all-in-one topic."

"Yeah, I could probably even get my biology term paper out of it, too, if I wanted, if I can find enough facts on botulism and lead poisoning and ice-core sampling."

"Devon's your go-to man there."

Thomas grunted in agreement.

"So, what's the Dickens connection?"

"Friends. No real personal connection. He wrote that insanely racist thing against John Rae, about the cannibalism, all because Jane Franklin asked. Or maybe Sophia Cracoft asked. Her niece or whatever. Everyone was in love with Sophia, right? But Tennyson—he was her nephew. He wrote the poem on the Franklin monument."

"Yes, I know. . . ." He closed his eyes, remembering. ". . . *the white north has thy bones; and thou/Heroic sailor-soul/Art passing. . . .*" He opened his eyes again and paused long enough to allow Thomas to jump in with the rest of it. In the beginning of Thomas's Arctic obsession, this had been more often Franklin's approach—share facts and information, stay attuned, involved, keep it from becoming a "thing" for Thomas to escape into ever more deeply and obsessively in order to distance himself. Maybe that's all he needed now was to pick up more of that former attitude. Neutralize the obsession with coolness.

"Just think," Thomas forked up a mouthful of meat loaf. "Our distant long-lost cousin, Alfred, Lord Tennyson."

"They are *not* our relatives, Thomas."

Thomas continued chewing and did not meet eyes.

"Thomas, seriously."

"OK, give it a rest. You think what *you* want, I'll think what I—"

"I think you're deluding yourself." So much for coolness.

"Fine then, I'm deluding myself." Thomas sniffed and wiped a hand under his nose. "So what?"

"Do you need a napkin?"

"I'm fine."

"Anyway, it's what, like twenty years ago now since I was there, but I wish . . . I mean, if anyone had told me one day I'd be sharing quarters with a young man so obsessed by the Arctic and convinced of a personal connection with the legend of his tragic namesake . . . well, for one thing I doubt I would have believed it. But if I *had* believed, I'm sure I would have taken better notes. Fact is, though . . ." He trailed off, distracted by the recollected singsong rhythm of Tennyson's lines, and thinking, not for the first time, how much harder it was anymore to strike the rhetorical stance of the versifier, tinkerer with lines, the one with anything relevant to say in poetic form for the masses. Who cared about poets? Just beneath this was the ghost of the

girl he'd followed north to Shetland and their day together in Westminster Abbey, home of the Franklin monument—a day when the
potency of poets and poetry had seemed to him anything *but* remote
or obsolete; had seemed, in fact, palpably, terrifyingly real. Odd to
be recollecting her a second time in so few hours when typically he
did not think of her at all. Or, no, he thought of her constantly, often
anyway, but never so directly—never the concrete image of her that
now presented itself: the gauzy Indian skirts and loops of springy,
dirty red-brown hair; the always intense and patchouli-covered,
unwashed-hair smell of her, of both of them together, and their endless shared hand-rolled cigarettes. The whole Sule Skerry project had
come to life there in that trip with her, or had its roots anyway in
that much younger version of himself blown north of Unst to find
her, and reading about changelings, selkies, betrayal, murder, sunlight hot on every stone. Yes, though surely he'd had no intention at
the time of staking the next twenty-odd years of his so-called poetic
ambitions teasing it out piece by piece, line by line, between jobs,
marriage, children. Interruption upon interruption.

Now it was time to get this meal done and cleaned up so he could
hit it for a while before bed. See what he might be good for tonight.

"Fact is?"

"Sorry. Mind wandered off there."

"You were talking about the Franklin monument?"

"Right. The fact is, there's so much history, so much old stuff to
see in Europe—busts and monuments and churches and battle-
grounds—you get saturated. I didn't pay enough attention."

"You've said that before, yes."

"Good of you to remember. Done?" He moved to the sink, running his catsup-smeared plate under the tap and throwing open the
dishwasher door to stack the plate inside with his fork and knife.
"Run this when you're done there, OK? We'll have clean dishes for
the morning."

Only a few good hours of awake time left. He knew this. Lowered
his lids halfway to conserve mental wattage and maybe induce the
trance state a little more readily as he exited the room and headed

down the unlit hallway. Padded into his study, instinctively sidestep-
ping the boxes of his unfiled papers, tax paperwork, magazines and
books, the rowing machine gathering dust in the middle of the floor,
the towel beside it from some workout a month or more ago. The
furnace kicked on as he rolled back his desk chair and seated himself,
jiggling the mouse to bring the screen up from suspend and simultaneously extracting his folder of hard-copy poem printouts from the
lower left-hand desk drawer. Impatient with meddlesome, exhausting Thomas, he hastily x-ed out any and all open Internet windows
of his, rubbing his hands together and listening to the computer click
and buzz. For a moment, he wavered between the file to open his
e-mail (Would she have written instead of calling? Would Jane have
written? No, Jane's Internet time was scarce enough that she could
never spend it on anything social or family-related) and the other
one, the yellow one with simply two words on it, "Sule Skerry." He
clicked open "Sule Skerry" and tipped back in his chair, marked and
revised poem printout in one hand, mouse in the other, the glow of
the computer screen shining through it and making the words and
his markings glow blurringly. He had not read more than a few lines
and begun inputting changes, thinking, *Good, good, yes,* before the
phone rang. Next, the thump of Thomas's feet on the floorboards as
he went up the stairs and then just as quickly back down. Again the
phone rang. *Sun oil water,* he remembered suddenly: the sound of
the wind, the reflections in the water, and the feeling that the earth
was about to open to him some secret, magical, alternate reality
wherein—

"Dad," Thomas called. "Dad! Phone! Where's the phone?"

"I've got it," he said, and stood back from his desk chair.

DRAWING THE FROZEN-IN SAILORS at mess had always presented
him with an array of perspective and lighting problems, none of
which he'd happily remedied. Midwinter, lightlessness around the
clock and then, gradually, the dim twilight of midday stretching up
a few minutes, then an hour, a little more, and lingering along the

horizon blue-brown for an hour or so longer. The ABs and petty officers all at their one end of the ship, cramped by the cook's galleys and eating salt pork, pemmican, hardtack, and the occasional peas or pickles or rotten currants, standing around their stow-away rope-suspended tables; later their sleeping hammocks, shoulder-to-shoulder, would be lowered from the same rafters, blackened and dripping, coated in an ooze of frozen coal smoke and condensation. The single biggest problem in all of this: no good available light source. Shadowy orange light. At the other end of the ship, the officers' mess, four or five courses on good china and served with silver by a handful of stewards, better lit with oil lamps, but still—not easily drawn. Yellow light and shadows. And probably much colder. A little above freezing, if they were lucky. But it was critical to do it right, exactly right, and clearly, because however mundane and daily the activity, it was absolutely central. It was, really, the whole story: food. Food had killed them. First contaminated food and then the lack of any food, which drove them from the ships to King William Island on the death march south for Back's Fish River, seeking an overland passage to North America. It drove them finally to eat one another. In some ways, the whole movie was just about that: sustenance.

He'd watched *Barry Lyndon* at least a dozen times for clues—particularly the long interior sequences lit solely by candles and shot on superslow film. Long single takes with few or no edits. He'd read what Kubrick had to say about this in interviews, and though a lot of critics had hated *Barry Lyndon* precisely because of those long murky candlelit interior segments, Thomas was pretty sure it was the right model for him. Those seasick granulated images exposed almost to the point of distortion, flickering shadows elongated intrusively to the background, they would convey exactly the right mood of claustrophobia, frustration, and exhaustion. Of cold. Then again, considering the length of time his sailors had to spend belowdecks, he wondered if it wasn't maybe asking way too much of viewers. Might be better to go pure Hollywood, like the night scenes in *Jaws,* or *Titanic,* or *Pirates*: flood the interiors with light and shoot through colored lenses; pretend there would really be anything approaching that level of luminosity for his sailors. Give the viewer a break.

His teachers from the SAIT after-school kids program would probably have reminded him that he was thinking too much like a cinematographer anyway. *Camera work is camera work,* they'd say. *Your job as a director is to* direct. *Actors act; cameramen run the camera. Directors articulate the vision and move the actors to reveal the scene. They call the shots, but they don't shoot them.* He knew this. Yet left to his own devices, as he'd been this past going-on-two years, he couldn't stop himself. Couldn't help drifting to this all-encompassing, all-pervasive stance in the material, always trying to solve every imaginable problem. So, he was viewer, writer, director, cinematographer, soundman, editor, makeup artist, and all the characters. Completely unrealistic and almost completely unuseful. Wasn't his fault, though. It was his father's fault for moving them here to Houndstitch, taking him away from everyone decent who knew anything about movies. *Check out Denys Arcand,* they'd probably tell him right now. *Our friend. Get away from the Americans. Why always the Americans? Try Patricia Rozema. Try some French or Italians. Truffaut. See some of the Indians. What's wrong with Fellini? That's where to go. Forget Disneyland! Hollywood's good for two things: pretty girls and loud explosions! Next year when you start with our friends at the Arts High School, we'll . . .* But the rest of that thought was too painful to finish without wanting to stab someone.

The sections in his notebooks dedicated to winter mess were gouged with lines and grooves, easy to flip to because of the extra ink and pencil coating the paper, wrinkling each page at its edge. Back he went, every day at least for a little while, usually when he was at his lowest or least hopeful about everything in general, or just had a few minutes (as now) to kill; still, he hadn't solved the problems of lighting and perspective. The sailors together at their hanging tables, faces inches apart, some, many, or all showing the first signs of scurvy—there was no good way of positioning himself to reveal them distinctly without falsely alleviating the viewer's sense of how jammed together they were. There was, literally, nowhere for a viewer to stand or have perspective. And no good light. For a few pages in the middle of one section, he'd solved the light problem by having the cook throw open his oven: Like a sun, it lit the sailors' oily faces—their teeth at odd angles, gums swollen and bleeding, suppurating hemorrhagic sores on their cheeks and arms. Into this section now he dropped himself, looking for clues on how to solve other related lighting problems later on. Hoar and Work together at the far end of one table.

Work: "Cooked the fat right out of it again, he did! Bleedin' idiot. Tell us again some of what they has, Commander Franklin and Fitzjames and them. Come on, tell!"

Hoar: "It'll only make you more miserable."

Work: "Scones for their tea and raspberry jam. Pearl onions and real stewed beef and soup and flour biscuits. Cream and butter. Bacon and eggs."

Hoar, shaking his head: "No more of that. That's all gone now since Greenland, since the tender sailed for home with our livestock. I should've never told you anyway. Only makes it worse. Lord knows, it's all I can do sometimes to keep from pinching a little of this or that, some real pepper and none of this gunpowder, while I'm heatin' up his bit of bouillon or mulligatawny or what have you on the steward's cookstove. If I can catch him just right, like yesterday, he'll give me a bit of a lecture, and then if I swear on me mum's grave the *twelve ways I'm walking with Jesus,* he'll give me a little something extra to go with." Hoar turns a pocket inside out to show Work a mauled half of a currant scone. "Even if me mum's alive and well, a little white lie . . . worth the extra rations."

Work: "Give us a piece then, eh?"

Hoar looks balefully around, shakes his head, but in the end he breaks off half of the scone for Work.

Work (whispered): "Much obliged!" (Full voice): "But why'd he cook the fat right out like that? Till it's all dry and stringy. Salt pork, salt beef, I'm sick of bleedin' salt pork and salt beef, pemmican and hardtack."

Hoar: "Sell you back the fat for a price or give it to them." He indicates the Royal Marines and petty officers across the way.

Work: "Sick of this bleedin' dark as well, I say. . . ."

Here, Thomas had run out of steam, and the next pages showed the same two young men on deck and then beside the ship, outside, against a backdrop of towering light spires and pillars of glowing, pulsating celestial smoke, looking skyward, wordlessly, and hearing the wind crack and howl around them. The masts of the *Erebus* have been taken down and her decks draped in canvas covered over in snow and then sand atop the snow for footing; still, the riggings left exposed to the wind rattle riotously—rattle and yowl like a broken harp beset by maniacal forces. The occasional groan or explosive BANG or RRRFFTTT caused by a shift in the ice pack under their feet and slowly squeezing the *Erebus* asunder.

Work: "God's way of reminding a sailor there's sunlight still in distant lands."

Hoar: "Have I told you? The dreams I'm havin' lately?"

Work: "Visions, like?"

Hoar nods.

"That's the dark and the cold and the rats bitin' all night, so's when you finally do manage to drop off for a couple hours, there's so much light in your head, you think it's somethin' else. You think it's a vision. My first winter in the Arctic, I—"

"I heard that one before, yes. But this is different. I *see* things, real things I never seen before, so close up, I could almost put my hands on them. Sounds and smells. Lights with flyin' machines and people livin' in houses so warm inside, you can strip down to the skin."

"Do that here all right, too. Might kill you, but . . ."

"And lights in the trees and hangin' from buildings, everywhere— bright lights, no whale oil or tallow. So many lights, it's like them Northern Lights only . . . more. Brighter."

"That's like I said. The rats and the cold and dark and the scurvy setting your brain afire. Happens to us all."

Hoar nods. "I'm not myself, I'll grant you."

"None of us is."

"Won't miss this place none."

"That's for sure."

"Come May, you figure, then?"

"May, June. The channel should open again and then it's heave and warp our way out of here till mid-August. Should be plenty of time."

"Figure Crozier's really in charge, then?"

"Nothing of the kind. Commander Franklin's is the first and last word, always was, always will be. Them ice masters says it's all Franklin's idea we sailed north around Cornwallis when the orders was plenty clear. Go south. Straight south into the channel and off the maps and through. No further exploration, but Franklin had it in his head to see was it an island or no, take his magnetic readings, so around we went. And then south again. If we hadn't've done that, where'd you think we'd be now?"

Hoar shrugs.

"Clear through the passage and homeward bound, they says."

"Never."

"Aye, they says."

"Ice masters don't know everything."

"They don't, but I'll tell you, when we get off this ship, if we do . . . there's talk of going overland if the ice don't break up. But if we do go overland, Crozier's your man. Stick with him, mate. You heard what happened in '19 with Franklin's bunch."

"Ate their shoes."

"Their shoes and plenty more besides. He's good as a commander and all, don't no one say otherwise, but I wouldn't stand by him in the ice and snow once we're off these ships. If we do get off. Don't know his way near as good in the ice as Crozier."

"The Irishman, then?"

"He's your man."

"Heard he was in love with Franklin's daughter."

"Daughter?" Work laughs. "Niece, you mean. The daughter would be a bit young for him, eh? You like 'em that young, Edmund? Nice hairless little twadge?"

Hoar shakes his head forcefully, coloring. "She wouldn't have him, though, the niece. And why's that?"

"Sophia Cracroft? Expect it's because of him being Irish. No other reason."

"Poor sod."

"I say, a murian on all things Irish."

"Why's that?"

Something peripheral had Thomas's attention now. He glanced up from the page at his bedroom wall and the hanging corkboard stuck full of pictures of Franklin, Crozier, McClintock, Jane, Rae, and maps of the northern, polar fringe of the territories, with Franklin's likely path emblazoned through it in purple Sharpie ink—the entry from Greenland through Baffin Bay and around Cornwallis and then south down Peel Strait; two x's showing the presumed spot where the ships froze in just off Victory Point; then overland down King William Island, more x's for known burial sites and boneyards, and across the last inlet (and the key to the passage), ending at the head of Back's River in Starvation Cove. Would Crozier really have wandered off with the Chippewa if he'd made it that far? Wouldn't he have? Why not? Why go back to England, having already been passed over for commander, turned down by Sophia Cracoft, and then having ordered his own crew to eat one another? There was probably a whole line of mixed-blood Crozier Chippewa somewhere still. Might look something like the stoner bus driver, Cody/Dakota.

And then it hit him—the thing that had been working its slow way through his brain circuitry ever since Devon's call came in and he'd been waiting for his father to get off the line so he could have a few words before Devon's minutes ran out: the Facebook message he'd left open and unsent on his father's computer. Thinking back to the precise moments in which he'd stood away from his father's desk chair, flung the chair around, that word *failure* eating at him, clotting the edges of his vision like something that would erase him altogether if he didn't act, and quickly, get a pencil and paper and just DRAW already, he was pretty sure he'd never closed his screen or hit send. No, he was positive. He even remembered the

stair-stepped last few lines he had not been able to knit satisfactorily to any logical, grammatical finish, and the promise he'd made
himself exiting the room: *Finish that later*. Later. Right. He furled
upward from his bed and went stealthily to the head of the stairs
and down, along the hall to his father's study. Stood a second in the
doorway, letting his eyes adjust, then went in, careful to sidestep
the boxes of his mother's old photos and letters, puzzles, books, and
other childhood junk, unsure at first if the hunched shadow aggregate at his father's desk was father and chair or just chair. Then the
shadow was moving, turning toward him and leaning to one side,
light from the hallway illuminating his face.

"Yeah, he's right here, in fact. Just a sec. Good talking to you,
kiddo. Right. Love you, too." He held out the phone.

Quick test: If Devon spoke first, all was well. Probably. If he
waited, if he let Thomas wade into it before saying anything, there
was trouble. That would be Devon's style: wait and lynch. Hang back,
let Thomas chatter away, and then snare him. The phone was still
warm from his father's hand and smelled faintly of his shampoo and
aftershave. His breath. Thomas held it to his ear and breathed once
into the mouthpiece and again, quickly retracing his steps back out
of the office and up the stairs.

"Ahoy, matie. T! You there?"

"Present."

"Scurvy dog. What's up?"

Safe. His father, true to form, had probably never read a word,
never noticed Thomas's open screen or thought to pry. It would not
even have occurred to him to do so.

"Same old."

"True not. Dad says you were treated to a little of Houndstitch's
finest today. Dude. Tell!"

Thomas threw his door shut behind him and sprang onto his bed,
plucking up pencils, erasers, and notebook and clearing aside his
knapsack of unopened school textbooks before dropping down, back
to the wall and pillow across his lap. "What are you talking about?"

"The school-yard fun and fisticuffs?"

"Oh—that. Yeah."

"*That. Yeah.* Dude, what planet are you on anyway?"

Together they gave the reply—a joke of long-standing family tradition: *Planet T, where the boys have big brains and the girls won't talk to you.*

"It was no big thing. Just some really immature homosadistic jock ritual. Who gives a rip."

"And what about the girl—what was her name?"

"Jill. From next door."

"We're still hanging out?"

"Sure. Whenever I'm in the mood or whatever. Yeah."

"This is the one with the harelip?"

"Not a harelip! Jeez. I told you! It's a birthmark, and it's not that big a deal."

"OK, OK. Sorry. Lighten up. No big score yet?"

"Fuck off. You'll be first to know if it happens. Promise. When it happens. I'll tell you."

"That's good. Because I might have some technical advice for you. Pointers, you know, from a procedural standpoint, like how to make sure she gets off, and be sure to put your dick in the right hole to pop her cherry."

"You're such a jerk."

Laughter. "Come on. It's my role in your life, giving you shit, just like it's your role in my life, to keep the malicious juvenile side of my brain active."

"Glad I can be of service. So when's the visit?"

"Actually, I was talking to Dad about that. I've got labs and exams right through the last day of the quarter, so I was thinking, on my spring break, I might actually just go up and visit Mom for a few days."

Ice in his belly and sudden numbness, the clotted dark spreading up at the edges of his vision again. He kicked his legs out straight and clenched his thigh muscles, then knotted a fist around his pant leg and pulled hard, making the material constrict cuttingly around his leg. What? Visit Mom? "You what?"

"Yeah. I don't know. I figure why the hell not? Right? Catch a ride with one of the mining planes and get someone with a snow machine to haul my ass the rest of the way. Haven't seen her in an age."

"Sure. But did you . . . have you, like, talked to her about it?"

"Oh yeah, sure. Of course."

"When?"

"Couple times. I don't know. Last week, I guess it was. Week before that."

"You're talking to her now?"

"Not all the time. Every week or so since the start of the quarter, something like that."

He unballed his hand and turned it over on his leg, palm up, stretching open the fingers until they bent backward and the white of bones and tendons stood in speckled relief against the surrounding tissue and blood. Squeezed the hand shut and open and shut again and drove it into his leg as hard as he could.

"Sorry, man. I guess I just assumed. I figured, you know, if she was calling me . . ."

"No."

"That wasn't too swift of me, was it?"

"Letters."

"Pardon?"

"She sends letters."

"I see."

Again he drove his fist into his leg. Not hard enough. You could never hit yourself hard enough to do damage or make it hurt anything like enough to drive out the other pain. His fingers stung now and his joints felt etched with nerve endings; in his leg, a dumb nothing of an ache.

"She probably just doesn't know when to call you. You know, like when to be sure Dad isn't around or whatever . . ."

"They could talk. Wouldn't be the end of the world."

"Sure. But I don't think that's exactly what she has in mind right now. It isn't really in the cards, as they say."

"Too bad!"

Devon sighed audibly. "Anyway . . ." He'd said it like their East Coast grandfather, *ann-a-way*—another family joke of long standing.

"Gotta go already?"

"Yeah, actually, I should. Tons of studying here. And I've already been on like an hour with Pop."

"Twenty minutes!"

"How about you?"

"How about me what?"

"Studying?"

"Please. These classes here are so undergeared, you would not believe, dude. If I have to open a book before the end of the term, I'll be really surprised. *Honors* math we're still talking about parallelograms and polyhedrons. Last week in history class, some dufus actually asked how Julius Caesar got his name from a salad. I kid you not."

"Smoking a little too much of the salad himself."

"No doubt."

"So get Dad to pass you up to grade eleven."

"Uh . . . think I'll just stick with the stupids, thanks."

"Well, I gotta study here. You go on back to your movie or your Facebook or whatever it is you waste your time on these days."

"I'm not wasting time, Devon."

"Well, that's good. Better than I could say at your age. Do me a favor, though?"

"What's that."

"Eat some LEMONS. Eat some good juicy lemons and ORANGES. And then suck on some of those ester C lozenge things. Ain't worth killing yourself over a little art project. Believe me . . ."

"It's not a little art project."

"Have it your way."

"But wait. You didn't—did Dad say anything to you about, you know?"

"What?"

"You know, did you talk to Dad at all about the whole . . ."

"Relax, bro. Your little *secret's* safe with me. I didn't say a word."

"OK. Same goes for here, then. I guess."

"I don't follow. Same what?"

"*Your* secret."

"You mean the new tats and—wait. Are you *blackmailing* me, Thomas?"

"I'm just saying . . ."

"Because for a second I thought that's what I was hearing."

Silence.

"*Ciao, fratello.*"

"OK, Devon. Bye."

Sunlight hot on every stone . . . sometimes he could see his way right into it and remember all his original inspiration: man-faced seals, two of them, riding the inner trough of a wave, the older one chin-to-chest, back-swimming, younger one following, tail weaving in and out of water. Father and son. Flash of light in the lifting water between them, brilliant, hot as the sun-hot stones ashore—and at the crest of the next wave, the white longboat, gunner at the prow, gun raised. The older seal knows what's next even before the puff of gun smoke and delayed report of the gun. He doesn't dive to safety through the wave or look away from the gunner's eyes. *Oh but you will be sorry,* he wants to tell the gunner. *You would kill your own wife's only son.* But he has no language for it, no man speech anymore. Only knowledge.

Franklin had been aiming for this moment, the final death scene, final wave, for as long as he'd been compiling the poems leading up to it: birth of the selkie changeling in blood and seawater; man eyes peering from a seal-whiskered face; and later, the poems of his shape-shifting to come ashore—rounded black seal eyes in a man-whiskered face, drunk as only a human can be and air-swimming, bar to bar, touch of sweet nighttime on him everywhere; seduction of the land mother in a firelit laundry room; firelight on the stone hearth and sheets; more blood; departure, and then the return to land seven years later, again man-formed, fur hidden in a heap under a rock, to purchase his son with a bag of gold and foretell for her their deaths (his own and his son's) at the hand of her future husband. When he could, when he believed, he flew straight in: his own transmutations of icy Albertan prairie, white prairie light, oil fields, distant Rocky Mountains and cottonwoods, into poetry—into seals and men and seal-men in the waters off the northernmost coast of England, and the imagined underwater selkie kingdom of Sule Skerry—all of it cohering in lines and words he understood about as well as he did his own blood circulation. Other times, it was drudgery. Swimming against a tide of ill-matched words and worlds. Lines that didn't breathe or scan right, iambs and spondees sticking through line breaks isolated and treacherous as shoals. Almost like he didn't know the first thing about putting two words side by side—almost like he didn't speak the language. Always it was a game, seeing his way back into it. Always, he was losing. And then getting it right again. He trusted neither instinct, not the one that said *Quit now*, nor the one that said *Go on*.

The call from Devon had thrown him out, of course. Happily. He was always glad for a call from his son, never considering it a bona fide "interruption." If Thomas had inherited all of Jane's mysterious gloom, coupled with his own tendency to prefer, above anything else, hours alone lost in worlds of his own imagining, Devon had gotten both the more socially functional, calculating, outgoing, and observant self Franklin brought to his own teaching job *and* most of Jane's analytical, technical smarts. All Devon didn't have of their sunnier attributes was her music. She was gloom illuminated by and interpenetrated with string sound. Thomas was gloom, period. Fascinating gloom. Devon was . . . something else. He was almost like a kid from a TV show; sometimes, he was that perfectly, surprisingly apt in every social setting. A stranger. An (at times) overly energized, athletic stranger.

Parts of what Devon had said to him now remained stuck in his head, forming a subcurrent of argumentation just beneath the poetry as he sat trying to hear his way back in. One thing in particular, which had to do with Jane and a catchphrase of hers he'd been

almost surprised to hear coming from Devon: *Time to face facts,*
Dad. Shit or get off the pot, don't you think? What it meant was, he
and Jane had been talking about him. Of course. But what it also
meant was that he had to examine, again, in response, his own ratio-
nales for not serving her with divorce papers until Thomas was out
of the house. She, of course, was free at any time to file. He wasn't
sure how he'd respond if she did, but he was pretty sure she wouldn't.
It just didn't make enough difference to her, one way or the other,
no loss or gain, no contested custody, and she wasn't one to waste
time and money on inessential legal paperwork. Aside from needing
to protect Thomas, stay in Canada, and keep the door open for her
return, and aside from the fact that making their separation final
and legal might involve more officially sharing with her his cash-out
on their house in Calgary, he also knew that as long as he was still
attached to the idea of a reconciliation (and he was), if he served her
with divorce papers, it would be (a) only because he felt forced into
doing so by her, or, worse, (b) because he was playing for a reaction
from her (i.e., reconciliation). Once Thomas was grown and out of
the house, if nothing had changed in the interim, then would be the
time to serve. But Devon saw things otherwise. *You're stuck, Dad.*
File first; get over it later. Thomas can deal. He hadn't said it in those
words exactly, but Franklin knew him well enough to know it was
how he saw things, what he meant. *You need to move on already. As*
long as you hang on to a dead marriage, how can you go forward in
your life? But I am going forward. I'm in a new house, new job. I'm
working, writing. I've got prospects. Having hope is not the same
thing as hanging on. *But, Dad, in this case it kind of is. Time to face*
facts. Time to shit or get off the pot, I say. . . .

He glanced at his watch—9:40. Bedtime anyway. Saved his files,
shut down. Pushed back from the desk chair and stood stretching
a moment before heading out of the room and up the darkened
hallway.

One foot on the staircase, he froze. Heard the exhaust fan running in the downstairs washroom and saw the bar of light shining
beneath its closed door; again, the thing that had stopped him—the

unmistakable sound you didn't ever want to identify but always had to, instantly: puking. Throat clearing. Curses. Private, repercussive coughs bursting against toilet porcelain, and more retching. Instinctively, until you were a parent and learned the care associated with it, learned the other response of needing immediately to go in and find out what was wrong, help if you could, you wanted to run. Still, there were the warring impulses in him: one, to swallow back his own bile and head upstairs fast, pretending not to have noticed; the other, to go in, see what he could do. And even as he was registering all of this, he was already halfway to the washroom door.

Deep breath. Hand on the doorknob, testing, twisting to see if it was locked. "Thomas?" He rapped once, hard, and again. "Thomas?" He pulled the door open. "Hey, T—everything all right in here? I thought . . ."

The boy was on the floor, legs around the toilet and arms outflung as if he were embracing it, head back. Sink water still ran and there was a guttering noise as the toilet drained, so he was spared that much anyway. No stink, no puke to look at or clean up.

"Kiddo?" In spite of himself, he sniffed after the smell.

"Yes, Dad."

"I asked if everything was all right in here." From this angle, he could see that the boy had never changed out of his mauled underwear. The elastic waistband had entirely separated from the shredded rest of the briefs and rode, solo, midway up his back. "Are you OK?"

"Fine. Yes, I'm fine. Think I must have eaten something. I wasn't feeling so hot. But"—and like that, he was pulling himself upright, stooping to unwind a massive wad of toilet paper from the roll (Franklin almost didn't stop himself in time—*Hey, hey, easy there!*) and wiping down the rim of the toilet, the underside of the seat, slapping down the seat and lid, flushing again—"it seems to be passing." Fist touching his upper lip a moment, he faced Franklin. "Yeah, I'm fine now, I think." Shrugged. "I don't know what it was."

"Well, I do."

"What?"

"It's that crazy diet you're on, whatever it is."

"What diet?"

"How should I know? You tell me *what diet*. No fruit, no yogurt, no trail mix, no lettuce, no orange juice, raisin bran . . ." Some of these items he counted on his fingers, as if that would make his case more convincing; held the fingers in the open palm of his opposing hand, and then abruptly found he'd run out. Sushi, he remembered. One of Thomas's old-time favorites. "No sushi," he added, but didn't use a finger for it. "I mean, you've *never* been particular about food. Ever. Why all of a sudden? What are you trying to accomplish here? Is it like some special grade-ten form of self-torture through dietary self-abnegation? *What*?"

Again the irritating shrug. "Tastes change."

"*Tastes change!* Jesus." He sighed. Scrubbed an open hand over his forehead and then pressed the heels of both hands to his eyes. Released them, sighed again, more explosively, and leaned to the doorjamb. "Are you turning bulimic on me?"

"Do I look bulimic?"

"No. Christ."

"If you don't mind . . . I'd like to go upstairs now. Brush my teeth. If you don't have anything more to say, that is. It's not the most pleasant aftertaste, you know."

"Of course. But Thomas. Look. If there's something, if there's ever anything we need to talk about, you know—right?—you know we can just talk about it. No fuss, no trouble."

"Sure."

And as they moved around each other, Franklin raised his arms to draw the boy in for an embrace. "Come on," he said. Felt Thomas's arms go limply around his own back, the light reciprocative pressure of his forearms, and at precisely the same moment his own arms dropped, the pressure vanishing. Stood back a step to see him and to observe, not for the first time, that Thomas was actually an inch or two taller than he was now, and had precisely his mother's eyes.

"It's been a hard couple years, OK? I know that. Hard times for all of us, Mom leaving, moving here, Devon starting at university, all of it. It's normal enough to stress about stuff and have a few bad days here and there, but the worst thing, the last thing you ever want to do about any of that is pretend it isn't real. Pretending it isn't happening or isn't a . . . problem, that's psychotic. That's where you get into actual, real trouble."

Thomas nodded. He was entering his other mode now, a new one Franklin was coming to recognize more and more lately but for which he had not yet devised strategies to cope—his disengaged but attentively listening-son mode. The eyes were open and trained on Franklin, the mouth relaxed, no smirk, no smart back talk. In every outward respect, he gave the appearance of *earnest young man hearing and accepting words of wisdom from parent*. Seemed, actually, to have become suddenly years younger in the process. Meanwhile, Franklin was pretty sure nothing, or at least very little, of what he was saying was actually getting through. He wondered if Thomas even heard him.

"But we've been over all this already, right?"

Thomas nodded.

"Talk. Talk is good."

Again the nod.

"To bed with you, then. Tomorrow's a new day."

"Must've been like some bad jerky from the Jerky Shack or something. I don't know. Maybe something I ate at school."

"Sure. Could be."

Inexplicably, the boy seemed stuck in place now. Something was holding him; Franklin had no idea what, but it forced him to reconsider everything. Maybe he really *was* listening.

"OK?"

Thomas nodded some more and cleared his throat. "But . . ." he began. "So did Devon tell you?"

"Tell me. . . . You mean his grand scheme to drive the ice roads north for a tête-à-tête with your *mère* in, where was it, Norman Wells? Someplace like that?"

Thomas nodded.

"Well, yes, he did. And it's probably about time. You should, as well. Go with him if you want."

"As if."

"As if what?"

"Never mind."

Thomas pushed past him and went wordlessly up the stairs.

"What?"

"Night, Dad."

Occasionally, as now, it hit him, what the kid must be up against. He'd grown three sizes or more since Jane had left, and had recently begun shaving every couple of weeks; there was a new slouch in his shoulders, a digressive sideways tilt in the way he climbed the stairs, like a boy so dead set on avoiding all notice, you couldn't help but stare, noting, too, how angry and hurt . . . how separate from the world he seemed to hold himself. Most of the time, Franklin could stay focused enough on his own concerns not to realize; when he did, it was almost too much to bear. Truth was, if Jane were here now, she would not be able to give Thomas what he must need from her emotionally—too much had been lost already, too much time passed, and Jane was . . . well, Jane. Thomas was better off not understanding that and not knowing Jane's limitations, though he was decidedly *not* better off without her. And to counter all of this, there wasn't a whole lot Franklin could do, other than to keep things going. Keep things normal—as normal-seeming as possible.

"Good night," he called after Thomas. "Love you."

NEXT SHOULD COME THE RELIEF. It always followed. Scraped gut, sore throat, horrible taste in his mouth, burning nose and sinuses and then . . . a little light-headedness and temporarily all the twisted fucked-up badness of everything going wrong all the time just *gone*. Purged, cauterized in physical sensation, physical tension, whatever, but *gone*. It was a trade-off, one thing for the other, and always pretty much worked . . . only, this time it hadn't. Because again, looking at himself in the mirror over the upstairs washroom sink, scrubbing and scrubbing with the toothbrush, all he could see was how wrong it all was and how everything ought to be different. Kill the clean black swoop of hair over his forehead, the cornflower blue eyes from his mother, the straight, clean chin and jawline from her as well, fresh bloom of young pink blood under the surface. Kill it, rupture it, make it go away. Break open the gums with suppurating sores. Grow the teeth down and crooked, distorted as fangs. Swell shut the eyes with sores and blacken the cheeks with broken capillaries. Crack the lips. Why? For the first time, it hit him, the real truth of the matter: *Because I fucking hate myself to death is why.* But why? This, he wasn't so sure of. Did it matter? He'd caved and eaten half a fruit leather after all—that was one thing. Stupid. So, he had no resolve: He was a failure where anything relating to self-discipline or self-control was concerned. A failure, period. But that wasn't it, wasn't the real bottom-line thing causing the self-hatred, because . . . he wasn't sure. He just knew it wasn't. And anyway, it hadn't worked this time, purging. Still, he was stuck in the same old outlines, same old routines. Still himself. No relief. Maybe because his father had stopped him before he was really done.

He spat and swirled the pink-green-white glob of foamed toothpaste and blood down the lavatory drain with water. Drank and spat again and let the water run a moment longer. Grimaced a last time at his reflection and held up a fist as if he'd shatter the glass, then turned and went abruptly back out of the room.

Edmund Hoar was all wrong, too, in the boat drawings. Of course. Too pretty, too much like Jeremy Malloy, too clean and healthy. No blackened cheeks and sores. No rotten fanglike teeth. Maybe the other drawings, the new ones, Hoar with Franklin, were salvageable. But the boat drawings? He flipped to them to be sure and leaned closer to make out his own garbled writing, the hand marks and fingerprints smudging lines between frames, the crooked and misspelled words. Felt around in his bedsheets for a pencil and started fixing things, rubbing out lines, changing words, grinding the pencil into the page to broaden away prettiness, pressing harder, harder until he felt the paper almost give once or twice. Stood back a second to see if it was better, and abruptly stabbed the pencil down straight through Hoar's eyes and forehead, ripping a zigzag rent through the page and snapping the pencil in half in his hand. The blunted half still in his hand, he stabbed again a few more times into the pages, without much effect, and then threw it pinging across the room, followed immediately by the notebook, whose pages riffled and caught air before spinning and plummeting, sliding out of sight under his desk.

"Fuck you all," he said. Dug notebooks, knapsack, papers, pencils, everything in a pile off his bed onto the floor, then stripped and slid between the sheets. Lights out. Lay faceup and cold, eyes open until they stung, staring through the dark and waiting for the men to come. He could still halfway make out his map of Peel Sound, Victoria Strait—the open inlet gleaming bare and white as a breast and the Sharpie-drawn line, two x's for the frozen-in ships, draping down it like a broken necklace.

THE EVENING DRIFT: check doors were locked, lower thermostat, turn lights out, freshen food and water for the cat. Line up shoes in mated pairs by the front door. Hang Thomas's coat, fallen or just dumped there on the floor. Now he wasn't tired. Jarred into full wakefulness by the business with Thomas. He was even vaguely hungry.

Back in the kitchen, he noted with some annoyance that Thomas had not started the dishwasher as asked. Of course not. Reflected, filling the soap cup and shoving the door closed, dialing the cycle to START, that Jane or no Jane, the whole bathroom episode—the puking and evasive talk afterward—all of it was so familiar: Always there was *something* in Thomas's personal life, some variant of psychic stress or trauma, some illness or other debilitation, physical or emotional, or both, overriding what you might ordinarily expect from a kid his age. Excusing him. Was it *real*? Yes. Always real and often medically documented. Every era of the boy's life, in some ways, was marked and made discrete from the previous ones by what had compromised (complicated?) him and what no longer did. Now it was the diet and the Franklin obsession. Before that, it was Thomas's refusing to put down his camera. Everything, from morning to night, seen from behind the buffer of his DVR, VCR, or the Super 8. Easy enough to understand: He'd needed some way to protect himself— Jane's withdrawing, Devon's getting ready to leave home, Franklin's own retreats into poetry, work, preoccupation with Moira. Before the cameraman phase . . . sleepwalking, bed wetting, milk allergies, hives, fevers that came and went. The list went on.

He peered idly into the refrigerator, not hungry really, or not hungry enough anyway to select any one item he craved. Mentally, he blotted out the foods he knew Thomas would never touch—actually, he wasn't altogether clear, but he could make a pretty good guess: juice, lettuce, yogurt, tomatoes, canned peaches, milk, carrots. Whatever. He slapped the door shut and stood back.

His phone was vibrating on the kitchen counter. Odd how attuned you could become to such a meaningless, unlikely cue—the mooing buzz of electronic circuitry encased in plastic, rattling in a half spin there on the Formica. Enslaved by it. And the anticipation, uniquely, sharply hopeful, as he lifted and flipped open the top; glint of blue light on his fingers and the message there on the screen. *New Text Message! View Now?* Well, of course. He clicked it open. From Moira: *All well son home!!! death sentence administered. drinks stime soon? xoX M.*

He hit *Reply* and realized, as soon as he had, that he'd never actually texted another person in his life. He'd often enough witnessed students, palms aglow with their private feuds and correspondences, thumbs twitching over keys, eyes lowered. Called them out for it, seized phones in class and made a pile of them on his desk; delivered his little set-piece lectures on the indolence of texting culture, mocking the butchered English it engendered, worse even than emails, and the spirit of codependent instant gratification it fed. Well, the joke was on him now, wasn't it? His entire existence seemed concentrated into his thumbs, eyes straining through darkness to make out the letter combinations on the too-small phone keypad, which one to press, how many times to get the desired letter and symbol, phone slippery in his palm. *Of course! When & where? Glad boy is well. Consider amnesty?* Hit SEND and snapped shut the phone and

stood back, noting as he did that he had entirely forgotten his surroundings. Had not heard the cat crackling food at its bowl or the
dishwasher cycling into wash with a gushing, vibrating hum.

———

ALL DAY AND NIGHT NOW, light stabbed him to the roots of the eyes,
severing some essential aspect of reason and stranding him in a
walking nightmare. His makeshift attempts to deadlight his cabin's
skylight and block the sun—rags and scraps from sail mending
tacked to the surrounding boards with finishing nails—and to blot
the noise and smell rolling in from beneath the India-rubber curtain
partition with more of the same, none of it worked. The light didn't
stay out; the sound and smell seeped in continually. Every night, he
lay exhausted and enervated, eyes torn-feeling from sleep loss, mind
reeling between dreams and random details relating to the day's
tasks, the service and cleanup, endless preparation and polishing,
or veering suddenly to pictures of home, or of ice and sun, snow,
glowing spires and clouds of Northern Lights, and the rest of the
crew. Hideous-faced bearded men with frostbitten cheeks and noses,
eyelids, lips drawn back from bleeding gums. Snippets of Franklin's
Bible-jargon interpenetrating it all with no apparent pattern or sense.

Are you awake? Edmund Hoar!

Stupid is all.

Wake! Now!

On the double. Crozier's asking for you. Come on, then!

Crozier?

His curtain partition was, in fact, open wide now and he saw that
these were actual men addressing him, not phantoms: Fitzjames and
the bosun's mate, Hardy. Trouble? Almost certainly, if it was these
two. Lashes and half rations, whatever it was. But what had he done?
Nothing he remembered. Sneaked once weeks ago with some other
men into the storeroom on orlop deck for rum but . . . hadn't they
paid him off already? They had, he was sure of it—more rum than all
of them took together given to Fitzjames to keep him quiet.

He rolled over and felt boards pressing through his horsehair mattress to the small of his back. Sat up.

They were still there, the two of them, Fitzjames with an arm extended through the doorway now—fat, spoiled drunk . . . well, not so fat anymore—Hardy a step behind.

What's it about, then? Hoar asked. *Something afoot?* And as the words came, he realized that all night there had been some form of commotion outside his cabin, footsteps, men speaking in low voices, mixed together with the usual din from the front end of the ship and the ceaseless howling, moaning racket of the ice pack beneath them.

Fitzjames seized him by the shoulder, pulled him through.

On the double, sailor, he said. *There's no time.*

Seconds later, they were in Franklin's quarters: iced floorboards, frosted windows half obscuring the endless, heatless sun beyond. Only that afternoon, he'd stood in this very spot with the luncheon tea service, cold early-June sun streaming thinly under a low layer of advancing snow clouds, and carried on a halfhearted, mostly one-sided conversation with Franklin about easier days ahead. *Seal and whale abound in these waters, I'm told,* Franklin had said. His breathing wasn't right, or the timing between his words. Almost like he couldn't focus or ever get quite enough air in his lungs. *And if one of our hunters is an especially good shot, a little south of here, bears big enough to feed the entire crew for a fortnight. Can you imagine? The Eskimo hunter, when he's killed a bear . . . will drink his blood and eat his still-beating heart. Considered a sign of honor and respect. . . . Our men are as good a shot as any, but I do expect we can refrain from these more barbaric aboriginal demonstrations . . . of ultimate* respect, *would you not agree? Plenty of game, though, once we're sailing. Never abandon ship, I say. Never. There will be plenty for all. This channel in particular, I expect . . . rife with opportunity for better marksmen, perhaps even a . . . pelican or two. Some beaver and quail, dovekies . . . a musk ox.* So persuasive were his descriptions (though Hoar knew that in most respects they were pure poetry: There would be no beaver, quail, pelican, musk ox, probably no whales, and few bears or seals), he almost felt the ship tilt and roll under his feet, drawn on the current southward—any day now, they'd been hearing; any day, temperatures should rise, ice break up—half-expected the horizon outside Franklin's windows to swing and veer around suddenly; clang of the bell on deck and men calling to one another from above and below. But no. Of course not. They were solidly frozen in. Coldest June on record, so far as they knew. Cold without a break, continuous snow and blinding white sun all day and night. The mercury in the thermometer approaching freezing but never going much above, never the first glint of real meltwater.

In his seat by the coal grate, legs outstretched, quilt on his lap and another around his shoulders, Franklin had continued a half-intelligible line of inquiry: *Any regrets, lad?*

Regrets, sir.

Misdeeds, failures, things you might not have done or wished you'd done better, women left with child, objectives never met and carried through . . .

None worth a mention, sir. No.

That's a blessing, then. My one real regret, and my other real regret . . . both females, one alive, the other dead . . . one I'll see again ere long, I fear, the other . . . perhaps never, or not for a long while to come. And then, pointing at the tea service, grimacing: *Take it. I've no appetite, and you look hungry enough for twelve men.*

Now, well past midnight, same room, same commander, same endless light, but nothing else the same. Crozier, Fitzjames, the surgeon, Lieutenant Gore, all men he'd served day after day going on two years now, others from *Terror* he'd never served, all of them standing idle but attentive, waiting, speaking in low voices. On his side, on the floor where he'd apparently fallen, lay Franklin, covered in blankets, bits of foam flecking the corners of his mouth and chin, breathing shallowly, with convulsive effort.

Here's the lad.

Who's that?

Hoar, sir. Captain's steward—the one he was asking after.

Crozier faced him. *Well, you're just a little late, then. Apologies. Can't say nothing anymore, our fearless leader, but he was asking for you.*

Asking for me?

Like them others, I expect. The exact same progression. Like they was poisoned.

But what . . . Hoar began. *Why . . .*

Wanted to see you. Wanted you to have this. For your services. And this. We'll hold them until your honorable muster-out—navy protocol—but you may look briefly now.

One was Franklin's Bible—familiar worn green calfskin cover with gold embossing and felted overleaf. The other a shallow reflective surface of silver, octagonally shaped: a serving plate engraved with the Franklin crest. He'd used ones like it dozens of times serving Franklin. Same weight and heft, same fluted edges, cold beveled undersurface against his palms and fingertips, all of it the same as ever. Breakfasts, lunches, teas—all those mornings and afternoons serving the commander, bringing his hot water and towels, fresh linens, barely believing his own good fortune to have been so well positioned and on such a great ship, first in service to the commander, the greatest Arctic explorer of all time! He'd been so sure of it, sailing out of London and later departing Discko Bay—everything, every aspect of this trip to be savored and memorized for future retelling: *Voyage of a lifetime,* he'd told himself. *And a career-builder, too!* He'd even, in some perverse way, been anxious then for his first winter of endless night and cold, coal stink, bad food, bound up eternally in darkness belowdecks. Anxious for hardships of every kind to test himself and know his limits, what he might endure. *Our nation's heroes,* Franklin had called them once, Hoar, and all the crew. *There will be poetry for us, and ballads. Statues, I expect. And, of course, my book . . .*

May I? he asked, and before permission was granted, he knelt by Franklin. From his pocket he drew the handkerchief he used to conceal bread and hoarded bits of fat or meat. Shook it clean and pressed an edge to Franklin's mouth. The lips twitched apart—thin, sad, always downward-turning, serious, even when he was at his most jovial—and the eyelids moved, eyes seemingly fixed on some remote middle distance beyond Hoar, maybe inclusive of him, maybe not.

Hard to tell. He wiped the cheeks and mouth and smoothed a hand along the slope of Franklin's cool forehead. Tried to ease shut the eyes. *There,* he said. *Give us a hand, then. Let's get him in his bed at least.* But no one came to his aid. And then suddenly, it seemed Franklin was seeing him—really looking straight at him, those deep-set gray-blue eyes—as if some awful thing were bearing down on them, his face going redder by the second. *What, sir?* Hoar asked. *What is it?*

He can't breathe. Come, lad. It's no use. He won't stay abed anyway. We've tried. Believe me.

They were pulling him upright and back.

Won't be long now.

It's an unusual form of consumption or tuberculosis, to be sure. Exceedingly fast, observed Goodsir. *May be related to the prolonged cold. We've not seen it before and can't say for sure the cause, though once it sets in, it does seem there's little to be done, save morphine to ease his passage. . . .*

Back into the freezing light and down the ghost walkway Hoar went, past the empty officers' cabins, all with curtain partitions gaping open, all officers in with Franklin now, waiting for the end. How had he missed this? How had he been the last notified? He couldn't bear the thought of confining himself back to his quarters for another few hours of tortured sleeplessness before reveille.

Through the thickening darkness to middeck, where the smell was worst—human, fungal, rotten. A rank cheese of shit, coal fire, sweat, rotten and burned food. Beyond cook's stove, the humped shadowy mass of men strung up in hammocks shoulder-to-shoulder, groaning, snoring, one swinging upright now to shout and wave at phantoms, all of them too cold, too hungry, too often rat-bitten to ever fully sleep—a constant, senseless shifting like the pack ice alive beneath them and slowly devouring the ship. Dark. At least they had the darkness here. *Here come I with a sharp blade and a clean conscience!* Oh, that would get them all up in a hurry. But this was no night for pranks.

He had to get out, even if it killed him. Even if it meant wandering around pointlessly on the ice until reveille, walking the trail back and forth, back and forth between *Erebus* and *Terror,* or Fitzjames's "exercise" loop, and being more than half-asleep on his feet the following day. Didn't matter.

The Bible and plate. He'd forgotten both in Franklin's cabin.

No they weren't his yet. *Navy protocol. Honorable muster-out.* Probably never would be. Up the ladder he went; pushed open the door and out.

Burn of colder air, ice mist and bright ice-rimed riggings. Stinging first intake of breath. Twenty-four degrees, he guessed. Maybe colder; not much. Warmer than it had been for months, but not warm enough. Anywhere men had walked on deck, the silver slickened outline of boots in compressed ice dust and melted and refrozen snow. Outgrowths of ice on all railings. Dead, everything dead and still. If they abandoned ship, how long would it stand alone, looking exactly like this, icebound, no men aboard, light creeping end to end all summer above decks and then the winter-long dark? Years maybe . . . or months, before the ice claimed it. Over the side he went, and down—into the eastern zigzag gulley of footprints through old ice toward *Terror,* crunch of ice underfoot, and then he was scrambling up, up the embankment and out to pure open space. Pure open ice. Horizonless. Sun glaring inches above the eastern rim of the world, white, steadily upward-bound; one or two in the morning, he guessed. Out of habit, though it was no longer cold enough for it, he held his eyes open as long as he could between breaths to prevent their freezing shut, narrowed against the snow glare, but open; felt tears burning along his cheeks and neck. Blew out straight to keep the breath from icing his beard. Dressed as he was—sleeping clothes and jacket, scarves, mittens—he could survive hours, days even, if he were careful and kept moving. Or he could die. Walk into a whiteout, fall through a crevasse, or just stumble along, ice-blinded, disoriented, and compass-less, until he fell down in a last peaceful ice coma. Never have to face what was coming: the burial of Franklin and the ensuing despondency and fear; Royal Navy protocol and formality overcovering it all, and the growing certainty among all men that they were on the verge of a most colossal failure and collapse, and closer than ever to the end: sail now or, if the ice didn't break up, open a lead, abandon ship. Begin the march out. Never have to ask, *And what next for me? What service for captain's steward on* Erebus *or off it, now the commander is gone?*

As he often did, in moments of worst disappointment and doubt, he tried to conjure his last few nights ashore. Jenny. The abandoned crofter's shack on her father's land where they'd lain those nights and the feel of her lips on his, her fingers. Gray-rose sunrise illuminating the window at dawn; maple and elm trees just outside, thick with steaming new leaves, and a sound of rain cascading through them as the wind gusted. Jenny dozing against him—cheeks flushed from sleeplessness and kissing all night, and those perfect pursed red lips. Smells of old straw, rain, wet earth. When she awoke, he'd ask her. Say, *So, can you wait for me, or no? I got to know. You won't be sorry if you did. On my honor.* And the silver locket from his grandmother with a cutting of his own hair for her, to seal it, if *Yes* was her answer. Meanwhile, these moments alone soaking her in, the sight of her asleep, and trying to memorize every last detail, as if that would stop or slow the passage of time: the little bump on the bridge of her nose, the color and sheen of her skin, the exact placement of her freckles, the shape of her eyebrows, even the number of eyelashes against her cheeks.

But it wasn't working. Instead, interrupting his picture of Jenny, another, grimmer image: his last sight of his mother, before sailing. He'd forgotten his Saint Christopher's medal, and returning for it at a dead run (full day's travel to London ahead), he'd heard her singing from the back of the house, an air or popular song he felt sure he knew but somehow couldn't place. *Sailed a falling sky . . . chartered hazard's path—I have seen the storm arise, like a giant in his wrath. . . .* He ducked the neighbor's hedge and came up the walkway, expecting to find her there at work already, singing to pass the time, but no. She just sat, eyes lowered, singing. No work. Like hearing your own eulogy or standing at your own graveside. Too much bad luck acknowledging or intruding onto a scene like this; besides, it was plainly private and he didn't have the heart or courage to start all over again with the tears and good-byes. . . . *My last boy*. So, he'd waited a few moments longer, watching. Whispered *Good-bye,* and *Bye, Mum*, and *See you again soon* under his breath before turning back around. He didn't need his Saint Christopher's. If he really wanted, he could get one new before muster-in or somewhere else along the way—the Hebrides, Greenland.

Some crewmen and officers, he knew, would be glad for Crozier's ascendance to commander. They'd never say so publicly. Most of them had been hoping for some time now that Crozier would win his campaign to get them off the ships and at least partially entrenched onshore, stone tent circles built, supplies cached, cook-stoves in place, so on, just in case the ice never broke up, in case the ships went down or, at the very least, so they'd have another place to overwinter and a change of scenery. Some relief from the constant drear of being entrapped belowdecks—the terrifying noise of the ice pack. According to some of the more experienced sailors, the ships couldn't last another winter, frozen in. They had to go down. They'd mourn Franklin's loss, of course; all of them would, but they might, some of them, feel relief. And hadn't he, Edmund Hoar, had his own little part in spreading some of that word, fomenting the talk among crewmen, sharing with them details from exchanges he'd overheard between officers at mealtimes? Of course. They all had, all the stewards. Trouble was, none of it was half as neat or black and white as what he always heard later coming back from the men: *Franklin says he'd sooner die than abandon ship . . . says we got food for twelve more years in a pinch. . . . Fitzjames's with Crozier and the ice masters and them; word is, he wants to double our rum rations for winter. . . . Gore is a Franklinite, says the ships won't ever sink.* Half-truths at best. And the questions. *Says the whole Anglican liturgy at every mealtime?* The reason for the confusion . . . partly it was the men themselves and their tendency, retelling a story, to embellish and distort. Draw wrong conclusions. Spin yarns. But there had always been something of Franklin you just couldn't impart—some aspect of his manner and comportment. What might appear as carelessness or feckless privilege was something else . . . was really a way he cared more deeply, more personally for the crew as individuals than did any other of the officers—more than any high-ranking officer Hoar had ever encountered. It set him apart, always, gave him a glow that could seem dandyish or silly. Removed. Could too easily be misread anyway. But Franklin never missed a thing. He knew every detail of every one of the crewmen's lives and had cared for them. . . .

The ice would break up soon. It had to. Then they'd sail. Maybe Crozier would shift quarters to *Erebus,* take Franklin's quarters, and there he'd be, Edmund Hoar, first in service still to the commander of the greatest Arctic expedition of all time, current tugging them out finally, free and homeward-bound. Yes, things were all about to take a turn for the better. The greater the sacrifice, the greater the good. Wasn't that how it always worked? Better to believe than not. *Believe on Him and His will be done.* . . . Franklin's words.

He slid from his perch back onto the track, walking to keep warm and pumping his arms. No way to guess the time. Maybe hours left before reveille, maybe minutes—anyway, what was the point of going back belowdecks and trying to sleep when so much was about to change? The sun had pitched farther above the horizon, bloated white disk of light and no heat, glaring eye, medallion, locket, a summons to all his young blood: no sleep, no sleep, no sleep. *Wake up,* he wanted to shout. *Come on everyone! Up! There's no time left! Franklin's gone.* His feet crunched over the ice and cold magnified the sibilance of his breaths in and out. A shiver ran from his gut to the sweating, cold top of his head. Maybe he was the one asleep and all of it, the endless sun and cold, himself in it, Franklin belowdecks dying, all of it, just one long bad dream.

———

LATE THAT NIGHT, THE COLD RETURNED. He could tell from the ache in the joint of his left big toe (bone spur, ingrown nail, or callus, precursor to arthritis—he didn't know, and didn't necessarily want to know)—a small discomfort he'd happily and instantly forgotten with the Chinook. He rolled onto his side and drew up his left knee to reach the offending joint, rubbing through the ache with both hands and occupying several planes of awareness simultaneously. One involved the cold, which he felt now not just in his foot but beyond the walls and through the hot air blown over him from the furnace. Yes, it was back. Winter. He could almost make out trees swaying and backlit against the dim Calgary-lit predawn glow on the horizon. Shadow of something vaguely human-shaped there as well beside them, erect and flickering in and out sight against the wind. Fence post? No, there was no fence post there. The notion of one materializing suddenly, magically, or of his own sleep-muddled disorientation causing him to misidentify whatever was really there (trick of shadow and light projected onto the plastic-covered glass?), pleasingly beguiled him. He almost didn't want to know any better what he was seeing. Just beneath this was another layer of thought, this one having to do with Moira, and again her imaginary presence beside him—because once, near the end of their days together, Jane had awakened in the middle of the night with leg cramps, and he'd been amazed at how fast the years of their intimacy trumped all the tension between them and her unshakable resolve to leave. Without a word, he'd gone to work holding her legs, pushing back the cramped toes, soothing and massaging until, still half-wrapped around each other, they'd both fallen back to sleep, as if nothing were wrong. He'd known then as certainly as he also knew she would be gone in less than a week that this would be the thing he missed most in her absence—this silent companionability and the assumed kindness between them; the automatic, unquestioning *doing* for each other. Nothing needed to be said about it. If Moira were here? It would be like that again, yes . . . but different. Better? So maybe, sure, it was time after all—as Devon had put it: *Get off the pot.* Just beneath this thought stream were the dreams that had absorbed him until the sudden pain: a fake oceanic surf sound, female figure morphing from Jane to Moira and back again, sound of someone singing. And with those recollected sounds and images, the sudden revelation that, no, it was not a voice that had awakened him, nor was it the dull, sticky pain in his foot; it was an actual sound. A door. The downstairs back door opening and then blowing shut hard. He'd known this without really knowing it even as he'd heard it in his sleep. And that . . . that was no fence post below his window, but a human figure. His own son. His son was standing outside in the backyard, doing something weird.

Upright, fingers on the plastic seal overlying cold glass, he tried for a better view, simultaneously pulling on pants and then slipping into a sweater. Yes, the kid was outside, naked, it looked like, a blanket around his shoulders, and ducking and weaving his head and shoulders as if he were in a slow-motion boxing match against someone. Sleepwalking? But he hadn't done that in years. Again, Franklin held a hand flat to the plastic-covered window. Cold. Very cold. Imprint of condensation surrounding where the fingers had been. Closed the hand and rapped futilely at the windowpane, through the plastic, to get Thomas's attention. "Thomas!" He leaned into it, considered the work of resealing the window in plastic, and stopped just short of clawing through to pull up the sash. "Goddamn kid," he said, and went down the hall for his coat and shoes. Out the back door.

Cold, but not terrible, and instantly his eyes were tearing. Underfoot, the ice-encrusted grass broke oddly, collapsing under his weight and dampening his bare ankles, causing him to widen his gait and walk stiff-legged over the yard. "Hey," he said. "Thomas!" From previous experience with Thomas's sleepwalking episodes, he knew better than to expect the boy to rouse instantly. They might carry on a full-fledged, if completely illogical, conversation about aliens or swimming pools under the house before the boy was really himself again—usually not until they'd gotten him laid out in his bed again, back to where the sleep-induced physical transmigration had begun. Only then his eyes might snap open suddenly and he'd ask what they were doing here in his room, what was going on? Sometimes not even that. Sometimes he never wakened out of it at all. How many years now since the last occurrence? Several anyway. Since the house on Beverly. One of Jane's theories: She'd likened it to a form of faulty reception—like an old TV getting too strong a signal on the wrong channel. Another: He'd been dosed incorrectly with general anesthetic while having two cavities filled at age three.

A kind of latent autism triggered by the anesthetic. Franklin wasn't sure what to believe, what was true or false, and he was pretty sure neither he nor Jane had ever had a similar problem growing up, but he'd been thankful when it all appeared to have resolved itself and gone away. The sight of Thomas at five and six years old stumbling trance-footed down a stairway, bumping into banisters and walls, pj bottoms soaked to the cuffs with urine, it had more than once sent him almost over the edge of panic. With this was another recollection: Jane walking the mostly asleep Thomas to the toilet on Beverly Street and instructing him, as loud-voiced as possible, *Wake up, T! Are you awake now? Good. Lift the seat now, honey. No, not yet! Pj's first! Are you awake? Point it down, honey. No! Down.* And watching as she suddenly, tenderly but with exasperation, took hold of Thomas's penis at the last second, cradling him back against her waist and pointing the stream of his urine into the toilet bowl. Watching and sharing with her amused looks of frustration, and not for the first time registering his gratitude that this woman, his wife, the one with whom he'd chosen to bear and raise children, did not have any of the weird moral scrupulousness or twisted foibles regarding sexuality that had, in his opinion, more or less ruined his parents and so many other people from his parents' generation. A penis was a penis. No big deal, nothing to be ashamed of.

Meanwhile, here was Thomas, almost man-aged and standing in their backyard, evidently asleep, and covered in nothing but a thin blanket. Barefoot.

"Honey?"

He wasn't up to this. This was never supposed to have been his job.

"Thomas."

"Yes, Dad."

"Hi. Thomas. Are you aware that you're standing in our backyard in your Skivvies on a winter night?"

"Yes, Dad."

"Good. You are. That's good. Then you're probably also aware that it's not such a good idea?"

Face-to-face now, he saw Thomas had done something to his hair; he couldn't tell what in the half-light—maybe just the way he'd been lying on it, asleep, but it appeared as if he'd been fully shorn on one side. His nose ran freely over his lips and mucus dripped from his chin. His neck, too, appeared wet. Crying? Had he been out here crying?

"OK, Dad. But I liked it."

"Pretty cold, though, wouldn't you say?"

"Cold, yeah."

"OK, then. Let's go back inside. Get a little hot milk in you?"

"No milk. See—bad for my health."

"OK. But you agree we should go back inside?"

"They were going to bury him, I think. Right here."

"Who's that?"

"You know."

"I do?"

"Sure."

"OK. I—"

"And they needed our help."

"Help. With . . ."

"Well, I don't know yet. They'll tell us when they need it."

"Who's 'they'?"

He turned Thomas to face the house and, hands on his shoulders, pushed him along step by step back across the yard.

"Just some guys."

"'Some guys,'" he repeated. "And when do you figure they'll tell us if they needed our help?"

"I don't know. Soon as they're ready."

"But how do you know they needed our help at all?"

"Because. It's obvious. And they said so."

"Right. Here come the steps. Easy, tiger. One up, next one." When it was happening more often, he'd read some of the articles and books on somnambulation. He'd heard of people breaking bones in their sleep. The mind could anesthetize itself well enough, apparently, you could walk right off a curb or stair, twist an ankle, and keep going. Crash a car and never wake up. He didn't think any of this would happen to Thomas, but all the same, he worried. Now, as when he'd been younger, Thomas was remarkably compliant and agreeable—easy to direct—but not really in control of his body. "No. You've got to lift first, here, and then step up." Thomas had stopped moving forward. Both feet on the second stair going up to the back doorway, he seemed intent on shuffling forward without raising his feet. Franklin tried again. "Up. Honey? Are you listening?" And when Thomas still didn't move, he drew him back, tilted, caught him in his arms and lifted, staggering up and sideways through the open doorway, and inside.

"Jesus," he said. "Thomas. Are you awake yet?" The boy was surprisingly heavy, dense and awkward to carry, and it didn't help that once they were inside, heading for the couch, where Franklin intended to dump him, only then did Thomas start fully coming to his senses. He stiffened in Franklin's arms and tried to bolt, crashing back with his head and nearly clipping Franklin's chin. "Stop! Can you just wait—"

"What's going on here?"

"You tell me."

"PUT ME DOWN NOW THIS INSTANT."

He angled Thomas floorward.

"What were you *doing*, man?"

Briefly, they faced each other in the darkened living room. Thomas's hands were in fists and he looked poised to strike—a reflexive, meaningless stance, Franklin was pretty sure. Thomas had never hit anyone in his life. Probably. Maybe Devon once or twice, and then in self-defense.

"Easy there. You were sleepwalking, kiddo. Outside. OK? I had to get you in."

"What the . . ."

"Yes, exactly."

Thomas straightened and breathed once in and out. Combed fingers through his hair and flopped it side to side until, to Franklin's relief, it all appeared more or less proportional. Good. So he hadn't done something ridiculous to himself with scissors or a knife. "Sleepwalking," he said. "But I don't *remember* . . ."

"No, you never do."

"Did I say anything, though, like what I was dreaming?"

"They were going to bury him, I think you said, and they needed our help. Something like that."

He nodded. He seemed vaguely pleased by this, or amused—at pains to conceal an embarrassed pride, and attempting to overcover that with puzzlement. Like he had an unfair advantage over Franklin, a secret, but didn't want to have to say so. "Yes," he said, still nodding. "It's coming back now. Only, they didn't bury him. It was a concrete cairn. I'm pretty sure of that."

"Let me guess. Franklin?"

Thomas nodded.

This was getting ridiculous. So many things he could say now and so many different tones in which to say them—dismissive, chiding, jokily concerned, mad—he couldn't choose. Could not chart a course or deduce ahead of time what might give him any leverage. "Thomas," he said. Just as likely none of his words would ever make a difference. He turned and started out of the room. "That back door is still unlocked. Would you mind, please, locking before you head to bed?" Turned again. "You're sure you're all right?"

Thomas shrugged. "Fine, Dad. All's well."

"To bed, then. And stay there."

2
KABLUNA

ALWAYS, IN THE LAST TEN MINUTES of second period, it happened, as if some hitch in the day's passage hung him up and kept him from engaging until he'd bumped past it—some internal thermostat cued to the school clock's minute hand ticking infinitesimally ahead, 10:05 . . . 10:06—Thomas's blood suddenly, unreasonably released, moved faster, his bladder filled, and his head swam with good feelings. He couldn't help it. Always the accompanying thoughts and emotions were more or less the same: He'd survive. The day had passed its hump. He was safe. He'd even occasionally tried not looking, keeping his eyes down on his open math book and the sheet of graph paper on which he was supposedly working out the evening's homework problems, straying only as far as quick sideways glances at the desk to his left or right. It made no difference. Clock or no clock, he knew.

Tick. A new lead opening into the rest of the day.

He'd be all right.

This day, waking up over what should have been a set of inequalities and was instead turning into yet another sketch of Franklin's hand, this time holding a spoon, a series of sketches, actually, morphing from the outer edges of the page ever inward, two things occurred to him almost simultaneously. One was that his feet hurt. He'd been registering this all morning—a new tenderness in the balls and sides of his feet—without giving it his full attention or really identifying what it was or how it had come to exist. Something related to the sudden change in temperature and his depleted vitamin C levels, he'd figured. But now, as he came awake, he knew what had caused the pain and what it signified: It was from walking barefoot outside the night before, sleepwalking, over their backyard of frozen grass and rocky soil. Maybe, if he thought hard enough about it, he could even read backward from the sore spots and abrasions on his feet to retrace his exact movement across the yard—remember where he'd

gone, what he'd been dreaming. Picturing it—the seldom-used picnic table by their property line, the old apple trees, bumpy ground
and frozen grass—the second revelation came, the thing he'd never
considered before: He could walk. Like the men. To suffer as they'd
suffered and know their miserable end without having to endure it
himself, he didn't need just to starve himself of vitamin C until his
gums swelled and bled and his skin turned black; he could *walk*.
Walk north from here, say to Edmonton, or west to Banff. Somewhere tragically, heroically far. A few hundred kilometers, sleeping
outside and hauling a heavy weight of some kind, eating nothing but
tinned meat, jerky, and chocolate.

Idea. He printed this on the page, below his drawing of Franklin's
hand. *WALK NORTH.*

He spun the page around to start over—more drawings of hands
and wrists, ink-stained calluses, a miniature of a man's face and then
another, ice-blinded eyes and blackened cheeks—and to let the new
idea settle more deeply. View it from another perspective, inverted,
sideways—*WALK NORTH*—make it more questionlike. Determine
whether or not he might really mean it. Walk? North? Could he
do that? How far? What preparations would be involved? Sledge of
canned foods; tent, pad, sleeping bag; cookstove and mess kit; spare
boots and runners; all of his warmest clothes. . . . Anyway, how had
it been when he first decided to quit foods containing vitamin C—
how definitively had he made that choice? He didn't remember. It
had been summer, that much he was sure, because it had been so
very hard at the start, with a lot of backsliding. No fruit, no milk
shakes, no frozen fruit Popsicles, no lemonade, cherries, melon,
berries. All the good summer foods—all the foods that were best
all summer. It had been almost impossible, really. Pleasantly impossible, and infuriating to his father, which, he supposed, was a sweet
natural side effect of the experiment, if not the whole point itself:
mystifying the old man and leaving him baffled. Unconcerned as
ever, of course, and positively wrapped up in himself and his *book,*
but still aware that *something was going wrong,* even if he had no
clue what it was or how he might control or stop it. Fool. *Let him*

come after me, he thought. He would, too. If Thomas walked, his father would follow. He'd be desperate . . . insane, even, reading his son's disappearance as a measure of his own epic failedness. Might not find him, but he'd try.

Again, Thomas spun the page, and this time he wrote out the inequality from his math book. Stared at it a moment and could not focus. Something his father had said that morning on their way into school was echoing in his memory now—not the exact words at first, but the feelings the words had woken in him, which, he supposed, had been resonating all morning without his having realized it.

Of course your mother wants to be an activist. She'd love nothing more than a life of total activism. Protest. What do you think she's doing up there? Counting snowflakes? But you've got to understand that just . . . how stubborn she can be. I could tell you stories. . . .

Please, Dad. No stories.

She wants to change the world, but not according to anyone else's agenda. That's all. She won't be part of any organization or its political talking points, smear tactics, manipulative press, what have you. Which is to say, no Greenpeace for her, no Earth First! None of that "save the polar bear" crap . . . "save the baby seals." Essentially, she's all on her own out there, a one-woman nonprofit taking on the world with her "quantifiable observations." And sad to say, but the historical record is full enough already of examples for how that particular equation works itself out, right?

His only comeback: *You don't know everything, Dad. When's the last time you talked to her?*

Not the point. She's my wife. I know her and I can tell you exactly where her deal is headed.

The conversation had ended there not just because they were arriving at school, his father lovingly gearing the transmission to PARK and leaning up sideways in his seat with a rumble of seat leather to face Thomas, keep him there talking. But Thomas, vaguely alarmed and panicked, wishing simultaneously to run and to hear much more of whatever his father would say (they never discussed his mother openly, let alone clashing over interpretations of her plans and intentions or what she was doing up in the north), found himself suddenly in the grips of an uncontrollable physical corollary to his panic, unkinking days of his bad diet and causing him to cramp sharply and go limp through the core, stricken. All other concerns vanished.

Dad. Kind of an embarrassing question. Can you let me into the teacher's lounge—the toilet there? It's early enough; no one will care. . . .

Now Thomas tipped his head to the side, wondering what the relationship here was.

I can tell you exactly where her deal is headed.

WALK NORTH.

What did one have to do with the other? Anything? Or did it matter? Did he always have to be reacting to his father?

As often happened at about this point in second period, Dalia Harvey, seated two rows back on his left, done with her homework, was reclined in her desk chair, feet lifted to the lower rung of her desk and wool skirt taut across her lap, paperback novel propped open on the edge of her desk, and all her attention sucked into its pages. If Thomas (or any number of boys seated in the rows ahead of her) leaned forward and tipped his head at just the right angle, he could see straight up to her floral-print underwear. It was astonishing and irresistible—a miracle of sorts: a more than halfway pretty girl regularly displaying herself to the world. What was wrong with her? Didn't she know? As soon as one boy sensed it from another's body language, they were exchanging smirks, tipping casually from desks, peeking from under forearms, pretending to have dropped things. He tapped his pencil eraser on the page but wrote nothing further, drew nothing, the sticky pressure mounting in his groin as he looked and looked again, waiting for the end of class. Today after school, maybe it would happen finally . . . him and Jill on the floor of the basement rec room, *canoodling*. Worth a try anyway. As long as he touched her over the clothes, she was fine with most anything—receptive even, cooperative, grinding back against him—but the moment she sensed him fumbling with a button or strap or snap, she stopped. Went rigid. Picked away fingers. Closed her mouth. Said,

"No. Don't. Thomas, stop." Once, he'd been delicate or fortunate enough to open the top button of her corduroys without her noticing and had slid in a hand for a glorious full few seconds before she realized what was happening, at which time her hand closed viciously over the back of his wrist and a noise began in the back of her throat. The trick was . . . obviously the thing he needed to do. . . .

Bell. End of class.

He stood, slapped shut his books, lowered them to waist level, and strode out and down the hall with the rest.

It was still true. He could walk. Maybe all the way to Inuvik. Offer his help. *I'm here, Ma,* he'd say. *I'm going to film you being the world's greatest one-woman activist team. I'm going to make you famous. Together, we'll save the world.*

Coming out of the boys' washroom and heading east again up the orange corridor, he became aware of a force mounting in the crowd behind him, some nameless chaos or commotion, but did not connect it with himself in time to brace sufficiently, so the shock of someone's body hurled against his and slamming and pinning him to the lockers on his right was almost total. Black hair, jeans, turtleneck sweater. One of a pack of wild younger kids he'd seen around sometimes. "Hip check!" the kid yelled. And immediately following that, another body—blond hair, plaid shirt—flew against him, shoulders ramming against Thomas's rib cage and causing his arm to whip out spastically, the back of his hand striking locker metal. His books spilled to the floor and were kicked out, skittering from under him across the corridor. "Shoulder check!" the kid yelled. "See you on the ice, pussy!" And both of them, whoever they were, were gone, ducking and weaving out of sight through the crowd of students so fast, Thomas could determine where they'd been only from the disturbance left in their wake. Not Malloy. Neither kid had been Malloy. He was pretty sure of that. But he was just as sure they would have been acting on Malloy's instruction.

"Hockey morons!" he yelled after them. "Douche bags!"

He bent, and bent again to begin picking up his books. "Sorry. Scuse me. Do you mind?" Stinging heat of embarrassment in his face, thinking, *Stupid, stupid, I'm such an idiot*. His math book was on the other side of the hall, splayed facedown in a puddle, notes and homework sheets scattered everywhere. His notebook binder and history text were back closer to where he'd been standing. The drawings of Franklin's hand would have blown upstream with the rest of his loose math papers, all of them being kicked along, caught against feet and legs and then kicked to the wet, sand-tracked linoleum, stepped on or stepped over. Thomas went after them, one by one, retrieving bent, scuffed, and footmarked pages, old tests and homework assignments. "Thanks. Sorry. Hey—yeah, that's mine, too. Thanks."

And out of nowhere, here was his father, stooping to retrieve the last few pages of notes from in front of his own classroom door, jovially flushed and energetic in his *Hey, I'm Mr. Franklin, the new teacher* persona, the blue of his eyes infuriatingly snappy and accentuated by his blue oxford shirt, causing Thomas to speculate, incongruously, *What's up with him? Something's up. He's in love again? Holy smokes. Who's he in love with?* He didn't realize he'd drifted this far afield of his normal route. He'd never make it to his next class on time. And now here was his father, holding the last of his papers, shaking them in his face, causing him to reconsider all of his perceptions. Mad, not jovial; vengeful, furious, not in love.

"Who did this?"

"Some kids. I don't know. Didn't see."

"I need to know. Was it Jeremy Malloy? What—"

"Negative."

Their eyes slid together briefly. Thomas did not want to witness or apprehend his father's emotions; did not want to give away anything like his own emotional condition, either. He wished they'd come to a tacit agreement about this immediately, keep it cool for school, wait, talk later, if at all, but from the way his father kept staring, clench-mouthed, eyes flicking from Thomas's right eye to his left and back again, he knew there would be no such agreement. His father smelled of teacher's lounge coffee and that unique singed garlic smell Thomas only ever noticed on him at school—something to do with his metabolism maybe, his failing antiperspirant and the work of teaching. Or maybe it wasn't him at all. Maybe it was from the school—some combination of elements he absorbed out of the air here and converted through a personalized reverse osmosis process into his own soap-and-garlic-tinged funk.

"Dad. It wasn't Jeremy Malloy. Just some kids in a rush to class or something."

"'Or something?'"

"I don't know."

"You listen to me, Thomas. . . ."

"No." He shifted his books to his other hand. "Not now. OK? I've got class. It was an accident."

"This is unacceptable."

"It's pretty normal. Actually." He flipped a backward wave and went back the way he'd been heading.

"Thomas!"

Only later, sliding into his seat seconds after the final bell and patting down his pockets for a pen, zipping open his notebook binder and settling lower in his seat so as not to be registered as tardy, did he notice his hand: the middle knuckles of his left hand split, red and skinned where he'd struck the lockers, fingers already swelling. This was no ordinary wound. He pressed between the tendons, made a fist, and flexed his hand open again. The fingers were tight where they'd begun swelling, but otherwise he felt no pain. He placed his hand flat on the table. Maybe a slight ache spreading up from the palm through the knuckles. But that wound—it was like something from the movie! Ghoulish. Like the pictures of hemorrhagic sores Devon had sent. *Easy bruising*: one of the top ten symptoms. It was happening!

"Dude." It was Griffin, the stoner-huffer kid who often shared Thomas's table and who, in exchange for being allowed to copy answers off multiple-choice exams, had always been mostly kind and friendly with Thomas. Griffin leaned closer, moist mint-over-smoke breath covering the side of Thomas's face. "What happened, man? Girlfriend bite you again? I'm so sorry."

Thomas laughed. Shrugged. "It's nothing."

Again, Griffin leaned in. "Check it out. I got just the thing for you." He pressed his knee to Thomas's and directed his gaze downward, under the table, open palm flashing an amber pharmaceutical vial. "Hyrdros and methadone or some shit. Stole them off my old lady after her operation. Only a few left. No shit, hey? Take them."

"Thanks. No . . ."

"For reals! Shit like that has to hurt."

"It doesn't, actually. But . . ." To make him happy or at least prevent his getting them both busted with all the whispering and nudging, Thomas accepted. Squeezed the bottle's cylindrical warmth in his busted hand and tucked it into the front pocket of his jeans, nodding, all the while fixing his gaze on the front of the room: Ms. Johannesen—poor misled, iron-haired Ms. Johannesen, thinking anyone was listening to her or wishing to learn anything about the current state of world affairs or the history of Western civilization. "Thanks."

Griffin was nudging him again. He was a handsome kid with dark blond hair to his shoulders and reddish beard stubble, a few millimeters of it always covering his chin and cheeks. Pink chapped lips like a little kid, and perfect skin. To look at him, you wouldn't guess he was high more than half the time. In fact, Thomas had not believed at first, but had learned gradually, that Griffin was not lying—he'd seen enough folded paper packets of pills, stolen pill bottles, flattened green buds in Baggies, and had too often witnessed Griffin snorting hits of something from a brown vial, after which his eyes would roll back and his eyelids twitch shut for minutes at a time while class droned on. "Oh man. What day is it?" he'd ask afterward. "Did she even notice? Did she say anything? Of course not. Fuck yeah, dude . . . you gotta try."

"Go on. Take them."

Thomas waved him off. Almost giggled from all the attention.

"Can't dry-swallow?"

Thomas shook his head.

"Dude, this is serious. You have to keep ahead of the pain. That's what my mom says. She's a nurse. She should know."

"Doesn't hurt."

Again, he nudged Thomas. Again, Thomas shook his head. Pretended to write something in his notebook. Watched his pen moving—circles, squares, dashes—and wondered, *Why not?* And then he remembered. His feet. Still aching. Had to keep his head on straight. Figure out a few things. Plan.

"Later," he whispered. "For sure."

"Dude, whatever. Live life. That's all I got to say."

ALONE IN HIS CLASSROOM after hours with the debate kids, no sound of other classes in session or corridor traffic, only the solitary click of the custodian's mop on the hallway floor scrubbing from side to side, his AM talk radio coming a little nearer, a little louder with each mop swipe, Franklin often felt a peculiar kind of loneliness (really an awareness of the general isolation of a single life and the ridiculousness of most social conventions) so keenly, it made him want to laugh aloud. That or blurt weird, inappropriate things to shock the kids and get them riled. The pointlessness of these hours spent after school, pooling information, testing logical semantic tricks on one another, rhetorical positions, and surfing the Web for every possible statement of truth or half-truth to learn their given debate topic, could seem to him so terribly, comically obvious. And, of course, that the whole essence and raison d'être of the debate team itself (the thing he was always harping at them to bear in mind: *People, people, please lose your sentimental attachment to truth; believe what you want outside the club, but here truth is immaterial; here linguistic and reasoning skills reign supreme; truth is whatever you make it!*) so neatly intersected his existential gloom only made for a perplexing overlay of irony. *Bunch of goofballs alone after school arguing and practicing verbal gymnastics. What for?* Well, to keep his job, for one thing. Score big in the upcoming tournament in Cranbrook, for another, and thereby maybe assure his reassignment to this extracurricular post instead of being assigned, say, assistant coach of basketball.

Meanwhile, outside, the bronze tones of afternoon turning to

early evening and the hammocky tree shadows lengthening across
the school yard cued some half-pacified animal part of his brain in a
way that contributed to the melancholy (Wright: . . . *I lean back, as
the evening darkens and comes on. / A chicken hawk floats over, looking for home. / I have wasted my life.*), making him long for an action
he couldn't name or specify, but which might look a lot like throwing on sweats and runners and going for a jog, if he could, feeling
the blood surge to the surface of his skin, the sweat freeze, breath
race—if he weren't committed to the rest of the afternoon here with
these lonely, misfit teens. Twelve of them, total. None handsome
yet (though more than a few, he suspected, would one day mature
into surprising attractiveness), many with crooked, metal-encaged
teeth, bitten, bloody nails, most of them a little overweight, two
severely underweight. Bumpy, greasy skin. Dandruff flakes on col-
lars. Eight of the twelve wearing glasses. Nine of the twelve, boys.
Not a one of them sporting a pocket protector or carrying a slide
rule or oversized calculator—none of the classic nerd indicators of
his own bygone era.

So far, they'd done admirably in one debate, marginally in
another, and had been shut out in the others. Not too impressive.
They needed to knock heads in Cranbrook next week if they wanted
a shot at the spring invitational in Ottawa. The topics were good for
their particular mix of talents and intelligence, especially the number one Lincoln-Douglas proposition: *Quebec should be allowed to
secede from the union.* This they could nail. He was pretty sure. He
just needed to keep his focus, keep all of his attention in the room.
Help them. They liked and trusted him, even if he was new; he was
pretty sure of that. And he'd earned their trust, he supposed, by lik-
ing them back in his way—by letting them more or less run the show,
giving them that respect, and by breaking up the session unpredict-
ably with dramatic free-association exercises (also new to them),
which they claimed to love, though he suspected mainly they loved
it because of his own occasional hilariously overplayed bumbling
participation, freely making an ass of himself. *Cued extemporizing.*
"Get used to it, people. Being comfortable speaking in public is a little

like controlled barfing, puking on command . . . a skill like anything else, and especially valuable in this context. That's what we're here to improve, right? Out of ideas? No problem. Just keep talking and stay on point." The club had such a feeling of isolation, he sometimes wondered if a person coming in or overhearing them from the hallway would have the first idea what they were up to. Some cultish, argumentative variation on Toastmasters.

Right now, they were working independently in teams of two and three, some clustered around computers at the far side of the room, others with their desks repositioned to face together, quizzing each other from note cards and books, all of them busy. In earlier years, as a young teacher straight out of college, nothing had pleased him more than this, witnessing his students' self-directed industriousness and enthusiasm. Used to make his face flood with warm feelings and eyes burn at the corners. Those days, he'd sometimes wander out of the room and back again just for the joyous rush of sentiment he experienced returning, seeing them all there, still at work, so engaged and earnest—*Oh people, my people, my favorite chosen few.* Debate team, he'd tell anyone who might listen then, *"Is not just an interesting and fun way to develop your public-speaking skills, practice forms of consensus-style governance; it's maybe the only remaining formal piece of your education that will actually train you in the fundamental civic responsibility of every person in a democracy, which is knowing how to take a stand in the world about anything—how to formulate an argument and articulate it forcefully, in public. Where else are you going to learn that? Tell me anything in the world more important to know how to do!"* Now what? He still believed in it, but he couldn't keep his thoughts from meandering, floating in and out. He no longer ran the convoluted free-form congressional-style practice sessions. Too involved, too much time and effort. He sat on the edge of his desk, letting them work on their own, eyes drifting from the stack of Sinclair Ross mock-essay pop quizzes on his leg to the clock . . . the window . . . the students . . . back to the essays. No rush of good feelings. Exhaustion. What had happened?

As ever, another part of his mind stood aside, occupied with the poem and working it out. In particular, one of the three girl debaters, Carol, he thought might possibly embody the most accurate physical model available to him for the seal-man's human lover. He needed to pay attention. She'd be about the same age, sixteen or seventeen, with that greasy northern skin and tied-back scarf of dirty black hair, those seemingly unyielding hips, and not quite innocent eyes. Was she pretty enough—sexy? He supposed not. Something odd about her mouth, its shape or proportions—down-turned, vaguely Muppet-like. Not that it mattered. What drew his attention was the stiffness or detachment about her generally—not yet in possession enough of her own sexual potential to control or participate in any of its effects, but not unaware, either. That's what the seal-man would respond to and desire in her. She yanked her hair over her shoulder. Twirled the strands together and picked at the split ends with bitten fingertips. Wrote something on a note card, slid it across the desk, and wiped a hand under her nose. Caught Franklin's eye and shifted abruptly in her seat, looking away; said a few words to the girl she was working with. Again, her eyes met Franklin's. Cheeks flared.

He'd been caught staring.

At the same time, he realized they were short one boy. Misha. Where was Misha and how had he not noticed until now? Silver-tongued Misha, the only one with a three-year history in the club and a real gift for argument and oral presentation. Diligent, sweet-natured, reliable, Misha had come to represent to Franklin both an ideal and an aggravating paradox: Here was the high-water mark, where every member of the club should be by now—tangible proof it could be done, and easily, so why? Why weren't they all as good? Why only Misha? Again, Carol looked his way, and this time, without his own prurient-by-proxy examination of her, all strangeness went out of it.

"Where's Misha?" he asked.

She shrugged.

"Hey, kids," he said, louder. "Anyone know where Misha is today?"

More shrugs and blank eyes.

"Anyone?"

One boy, perennially twirling and flipping a pen around his

thumb, said, "I saw him before. . . . I think he, like, signed himself
out early sick? Pretty sure . . ."

"Never mind, then. Change-up time. Benjamin!"

"Mr. Franklin!"

"Everyone! Listen up. Eyes here. Are you ready, Benjamin?"

"Yes!"

"Approach the desk and grab a topic."

Benjamin's sneaker laces were two different colors, and not for the
first time Franklin noted the hairs growing from the butterfly-shaped
mole on his right wrist, sleek and long as whiskers. Seal hairs. Part
Métis or Inuit, he guessed—dark skin and hair, owlish gold-green
eyes. The boy twisted his chin to one side, squinting as he fished a
slip of paper from the "topics bag" on Franklin's desk.

"Shopkeepers," Benjamin said, glancing around the room, nodding. He handed the paper to Franklin.

"Indeed. Shopkeepers it is. Two minutes." Franklin looked at his
watch. "Go!"

"In today's economy, I think there should be more shopkeepers
because of the whole idea of your corner market, you know, where
you used to go and pick up your daily paper and a quart of milk, you
know, and talk to your neighbors, pick up some bread. I'm talking
about community here, and that's the important thing—that's what
I'm saying we need a lot more of these days. That's my number-one
criterion. Because, you know, there just isn't a lot . . . with all those
malls going up, there just aren't so many corner markets and. . . .
OK, strike that. To define community. Community is where you get
a lot of like-minded citizens together? Civil-minded anyway"—here
he glanced nervously at Franklin, and Franklin understood these
must be something like his own words or concepts coming up now,
albeit scrambled and reconstituted—"according to . . . Rousseau?
. . . which is to say people acting together for the greater good and
always caring for his fellow man. One man can change the world.
That value right there is the founding cornerstone of civilizations,
that civil-mindedness, like the corner store, you know, as you can
see in the Old Testament and Gandhi as well as Rousseau, so you can

see why shopkeepers today are so crucial and why we should have
more of them. . . ."

He tried to keep his attention on the boy. Stared and nodded and
stared harder, until his eyes stung, as if by following his every singsong phrase he might cause what Benjamin was saying to add up or
make better sense. Might cause the argument to gel, the sentences
to untangle. But the longer he spoke, the more difficult it was for
Franklin to follow. He narrowed his eyes to fuzz the room. Heard the
boy's voice droning on—his typical up-and-down local inflection
not connected with any particular stress or emphasis. Leaned back
on the heels of his hands and drew in a breath, which he held for as
long as he could, still staring, still trying to hear, and like that, he
was face-to-face with the central fundamental puzzle of his teaching
life: ignore the stuttering and incoherence of his students, try to see
through it to some implied meaning and authority, and then supply
that meaning to them in an attempt to lead them through their own
confusion to a better statement of truth, or say, *No, stop right there.
Please. What did you just say? You're making no sense. Get command
of your language before you try to say one more thing.* Well, of course,
and of course. Some of both and never either one, exactly. Always a
balance and an approximation.

Benjamin seemed to be winding up to a premature conclusion
now, having drifted from Gandhi and Rousseau to a consideration
of architecture, fountains, Frank Lloyd Wright's Taliesin, and the
function of the cornerstone. He was positively free-associating. Better to study the girl through this fuzzed field of vision and imagine
the scene of her deflowerment by the seal-man. Firelight. Mounds of
wet, dirty laundry. Her clothes in a heap on the floor. Those stiff hips
and plump little hands. And then it wasn't her at all anymore. It was
Moira or Jane, the curve of some unknown other woman's hip.

" . . . Which by the commutative property, you'll have to agree,
applies equally to the shopkeepers, because what's a corner store
without shopkeepers? A shop without commerce, which is to say
without community . . . commerce equals community? I rest my
case."

Franklin glanced at his watch. "Twenty more seconds! Keep going
. . . redefine the topic. Take the opposition. Doesn't matter. Just keep
it going!"

"When I was a kid, my grandfather and I used to go to this store
where we'd get sour balls. . . ."

Hands waved at them. "Personal narrative!" someone blurted.
"This isn't story time!" One mouthed words but didn't say them,
another tapped his pen restively, and several rolled their eyes. Carol,
the girl he'd been studying too long, for inauspicious reasons, added,
"Plus, I heard a lot of *be* verbs there."

"Yes, you're right, you're right. You're all right. That was very
strong up to the point where you broke off, Benjamin. But I have
to agree that after that you were waxing a little personal. Folksy. Go
back and find the argument. Keep on topic."

Benjamin's eyes went ceilingward and he began squeezing his
pencil at either end, pushing out against it with both hands like he
meant to snap the pencil in half. Franklin had seen him trapped
in this kind of funk before. Thrown off track, he could become
weirdly, tragically withdrawn in a way that made everyone anxious.
Franklin was never sure how much to apply the brakes—when or
where.

"Hey. Benjamin. What are you doing to that writing pole?"

Benjamin shoved the pencil in his pocket. Grinned. Went back to
studying the ceiling, his blinking accelerated.

"OK. Now, think. Ten more seconds and we'll restart you. You
were on a tear with Gandhi and Rousseau—remember?—just shredding it up."

He nodded, brushed aside hair.

There were points Franklin was going to have to mention later,
aside from the general praise and confidence bolstering, but deli-
cately: *Eyes forward; don't look up or to the side; avoid fidgeting; stay
focused; seem confident even through the fluff; avoid the question form,
which includes* you know, *you know? And yes, avoid the* be *verbs. Ms.
Alison, our be-verb buster, got you on that, and it's true. Stronger
verbs a stronger argument make.* The point of this exercise was to be

free—extemporize and get validated. Get comfortable. Gain confidence. But also practice doing a few things right.

Franklin's phone was buzzing in his pocket. At first, he misidentified it—thought someone had pranked him or thrown something at him to hit his breast pocket. He swatted at it, hit himself in the chin, and, realizing the cause, blushed, waving at the students who'd noticed. "You keep it going. Paul, start him when he's ready. Make it thirty more seconds for good measure. And you can get into some good comments without me. I'll be right back."

He slid from the side of his desk, flipping open his phone and clicking the door shut behind him almost fast enough not to hear the chorus of mock love-struck oohing and aahing from his students. They knew. How did they know?

"Moira," he said into the phone. "Just a second." He looked up and down the hall and crossed to the empty, unlit classroom facing his, pushing the door half-shut behind him. Crouched into one of the desks there and folded his legs one over the other, phone to his ear. She'd begun saying something else to him already, most of which he'd missed. "Sorry. Didn't catch that. Hello? Moira?"

"Right here, John. I was just asking. Is this a bad time?"

He peered into a corner of the darkened ceiling, reflexively imagining it pierced by arrows. Shot full of arrows. This was a habit of perception he'd developed during his last few months with Jane, all those nights lying awake beside her, or talking with her in the living room, bedroom, or not talking, but still silently trying to work out solutions. He hadn't been able to control it. As his mind chased after ways to balance their mismatched lives, some final formulation to make sense of the impossible situation, his eye created this visual analogue: a flight of arrows, each seeking the exact point where wall and wall met ceiling.

"Bad ... not really. Debate team. I've got a few minutes here. They're critiquing. . . ."

"Do you teach them to become master debaters, or merely cunning linguists?"

He laughed in spite of himself. "That is such a *bad* joke, Moira.

You know, I can't believe . . . it's about the first thing I hear from *any-one* when I say I run the debate club."

"Proves how depraved we all are, I guess, John. And unoriginal. Always sex on the brain."

Heat prickled his face. Such directness, he knew, could as easily be a bluff as a genuine provocation—a form of indirection, and a way to conceal vulnerabilities. Like all flirtation, he supposed. How to respond? In her poems, too—one in particular, a striptease from the perspective of an onion—there was often this disjunction between form and content, appearance and essence, the one merging with the other, drawing you in deeper, deeper, until at the heart of it all . . . nothing. Mortality or some grim, empty joke. A gimmick and a farce, he supposed, but also always smart enough, true enough, and relevant anyway to keep him going.

"Well. If I *had* a brain, I'm sure I . . ."

"Poor you! I hear it's a man's one true erogenous zone."

He laughed. "Uh, I'm going to have to ask for a source check on your information there, as we say in debate."

"You'd question my authority on the matter?"

"Maybe not. Just saying. Need some supporting evidence and documentation. What have you got?"

Her breath fluttered into his ear. "Hard evidence? Let me think. . . ."

He was still anxiously peering into that darkened corner, envisioning it shot full of arrows, none finding its mark. "Please! Only the evidence. No personal narrative."

"Is that how you coach them?"

"More or less. Though the subject matter is, shall we say, a good deal drier, but . . ."

"I'm sure. Listen, though, I wasn't . . . I was calling because I had a little break here and wanted to share with you this bit of just incredible, incredibly wonderful weirdness."

"And I thought you were calling to arrange the drink you texted me about last night."

"That's a possibility as well, for sure."

"Impossibility?"

"*A* possibility"

"As in *a*moral?"

"You *are* a cunning linguist." She laughed. Something in her laugh he'd forgotten—a brashness or quality of emotional extroversion that sometimes caught him off guard. He pictured her alone, leaning over a table at her house and doodling pen and ink designs on a sheet of paper or writing notes to herself as she laughed. Some static on the line suggested it—an intermittent noise like a fountain pen scratching over paper. No, she'd be at work in her office or a conference room in downtown Calgary, or telecommuting from her desk at home. He tried to remember what she'd ever told him about her work—part-time at the Securities Commission and some pro bono work for the Alberta Arts Foundation—but it'd never seemed to interest her enough to talk about beyond a passing detail. *I shuffle papers. Sometimes a lot of money.*

"Well," she said, "bad jokes aside, here it is: Jeremy has taken it into his head to convert your son."

"He *what*?"

"He says it came to him all of a sudden yesterday that he needs to quit being such a bully. Anyone can be a bully. It's nothing. Proves nothing. So he says he wants to get your Thomas on the ice. Build him up and give him a chance. Try to like him a little. If he's to take it out on him in the end for being such a wuss and a weirdo, it should at least be a fair fight."

"He obviously doesn't know Thomas."

"Well . . . but apparently Thomas's older brother . . ."

"Devon."

"Yes, Devon. He was quite the athlete? Quite the star, right?"

"Somewhat, yes." Franklin winced. She seemed to be waiting for more. "Never hockey, though. Wrestling, track . . ." He'd learned to say this as if it were nothing, in a tone of voice that might even be misread as pride.

"Well, he has a reputation anyway. Different schools, but a reputation will travel . . . so Jeremy feels it's got to be an innate thing for Thomas. He must have it in him, as well. So now he just needs to man him up and get him in the rink. Kick his ass fair and square, if that's how it's going to go. I suspect Davis's hand in this. More than suspect, actually. Did I tell you that's where Jeremy finally turned up last night? At his father's? In fact—fair warning and full disclosure— I'd guess you'll be hearing from Davis yourself in person before all's said and done, if I know Davis. And sadly, I do. Nothing to worry about there. Just treat him like a wild animal. Avoid sudden movements and direct eye contact, you know? Show no vulnerability. It'll be fine."

"No kidding."

"But isn't that something? I'm not saying it's Jeremy's moment of amazing grace or what have you, but . . . maybe, just maybe, there's some hope for him. Revelation, growth into new insight and sudden maturity—it can strike the best and worst of us when we least expect."

"I don't doubt it for a second."

Pause. "But you do doubt everything else."

He sighed. Again his eyes probed the ceiling. He imagined his arrows—the corner of the ceiling stuck full of them. "I guess I'm still thinking about the whole wild animal thing."

"Oh, don't worry. He won't bother you. Much. If he does, you just say a few things about the Flames and you're home free."

"Noted."

"So why don't you call me here when you're ready. This number. We'll figure out where to meet."

"Give me thirty-forty minutes. But . . . Moira. You told Jeremy— that is, you *didn't* tell Jeremy or Davis about us, I hope? Our, whatever . . . history. That we knew each other already?"

"God no. They have no idea. They *have* come to their own conclusion that you're an abomination and a menace to the school."

"Me!"

"Part of why Jeremy wants to save your poor son, I suspect."

"From me."

"Good-bye, John."

"I'll call."

He flipped his phone shut. Breathed once in and out. Gathered himself and pushed up from the too-small desk chair, thinking, *Moira, Moira—what am I doing?* And realized too late as he stood, the back pocket of his chinos refusing momentarily to detach from the seat plastic, that he'd done it again. Sat in some kid's bubble gum. Not pranked this time, just blind and dumb enough with infatuation to sit right in it.

HE WAS EXHAUSTED, but not in the ordinary way—more like someone had taken out his central power source. Downed all major power lines, leaving only trickles of energy where random portions of the grid remained intact or an emergency generator had kicked to life. Residual strength here and there in places it had lain untapped. What an excruciating process to bend and raise legs, lift feet, repeat, repeat, repeat, press on against the wind, bits of blown ice and snow burning his cheeks like glass. Exhaustion in the corners of his eyes making the lids scratch, as if he'd rubbed them with dirty fingers. Poked them. *So tired,* he thought. *Why so tired?* And his hand—not that it hurt really, but he couldn't put it out of mind, either—numb and prickling with weird edges of feelings that didn't belong in a hand. Once, years ago, he'd been afflicted with something like this, accompanying a high fever: hallucinations that had caused his senses to invert, especially hearing and touch, so certain sounds became unearthly harsh and magnified, while others faded in a wash of static, and his fingertips, numb on the outside, had felt bloated with the prickly weight of his circulation and the narrow pressure of bones inside skin.

They'd been harassing him all day, running up from behind and blurting cryptic hockey slang—*face wash; deke the pylon; butt-ended ya, ha-ha; catch you in the rink, mo-fo*—alternately poking him, waving things in his face, knocking books from his hands. Nothing as forceful as the first attack following math class, so either they'd decided, en masse, to lighten up, be more polite, or he'd gotten better at anticipating them, bracing himself and continually checking over a shoulder to see what was coming. Consequently, her light taps to his head and shoulder as she ran by, jumped a snowbank, and swung around in his path, facing him, didn't startle him half as much as her presence there in front of him, so incongruous and with that incongruous blue-purple stain creeping out to her cheek and vanishing into the fringe of her hood. Almost before he could stop himself, he was winding up to swing at her.

"Thomas!"

"Oh. Hey. It's you."

"What?"

"I didn't say anything."

"You looked like . . . Never mind, weirdo." She turned and they started walking. "Fun at school today? Any more fights?"

He attempted a sputtering noise of dismissive contempt and scorn, but the breath caught in his throat more like a sob, surprising him and requiring more. "Not exactly. Today was the day of random hip checks and other surprise moronic hockey moves. Someone's going to have to pay."

"Scuse me?"

"There's this scene I'm thinking of, like probably one of the first real cannibalism scenes, maybe close to the end of act one—somewhere around there anyway—hacking up one of the frozen corpses for stew." He slid his eyes at her and noted how she walked like a kid still—shoulders hunched and swinging, hands deep in her coat pockets. Or maybe it was the way she flung her feet out. Reckless, kiddish. "Anyway, Hoar realizes it's this one sailor he's hated all along, this guy who's just bugged the snot out of him and pranked him on dog watches, stolen stuff, you know, so you think he'd be glad seeing him chopped up for dinner, right? But instead, he wishes he were alive still, because that would be better than watching everyone die. Better, too, because of Franklin's teachings . . . you know, he figures he's lost the opportunity for grace by forgiving his worst enemy? Anyway, sometimes . . ." He trailed off.

"Yeah?"

"Just trying to sort it all out. Sometimes it's not so bad having your worst enemies around. I mean, it beats a lot of other things, especially if your enemies are just a bunch of dumb jocks and morons."

They trudged on against the wind, neither of them saying anything further, Thomas realizing that in her company he'd almost quit feeling bad and had miraculously regained all or most of his energy. What was that about? All it took was a girl to make you feel better? Even if she was only, what, thirteen? She had tits, though, and from things she'd mentioned to him, he was pretty sure she'd started having her period. He was no cradle-robber. The mailboxes went by in his peripheral vision—the tree and the walkway up to his own house—almost before he could fully consider what he was doing or what it signified, as well as the danger averted (because surely there would be a letter from her today, and surely it would mention things he didn't wish to hear about from her—Devon's visit north, the inevitability of divorce). *Mom,* the voice in his head said—*I have no mom*—then it was gone. Easy as that. Single-file, they marched up the walk to her house, Thomas holding the door open for her as she fumbled with keys and then stood just inside the door, entering the alarm code. Stomped in, unzipping coats fast for the inside air, shivering and stripping away hats, gloves, kicking off boots. Unlike at his house, the thermostat here seemed permanently set to full blast, the air so warm and saturated with smells of plug-in potpourri freshener and cinnamon-raisin bread baking in the automatic bread machine, he wondered (as always) if he would be able to breathe at all—*alien life-form visiting inhospitable biosphere.* He drew a cottony lungful and then another. All well. Lifted and pulled out the bottom of his T-shirt for the warmer air, remembering as he did that he had not showered or changed most of his clothes since the previous day. New underwear and socks. "So . . ." he said, rubbing fingers into his hair to unmat it.

She stood over the heat vent beside the kitchen door, bent at the waist, with her head down, hair catching the current of warm air. "Want hot chocolate?" she asked, inverted still, wiggling her fingers at the heat. "OK, I admit it. Today I miss the Chinooks."

"Told you."

Abruptly, she swung upright, hair floating down around her but still lofted and blown-looking, so she appeared older and radiant, bigger anyway. She went to the enormous fish tank beside the front picture window and sprinkled in a pinch of flaked food. "Look at them go!"

"Indeed." He couldn't have cared less about fish and had never understood why people kept them as pets. Trapping creatures from the wrong parts of the world and putting them on display in a tank in your living room, for what? Pathetic. Maybe they were supposed to be sexy, with their exotic multicolored armor and trailing fins. Pacifying?

"Today's Mom's late day at work."

He almost missed her meaning. "Oh. And your dad?"

"Same, duh. They carpool. It's Thursday, right?"

He nodded. Didn't trust himself to come up with words that wouldn't give away a too-eager tone. "Last I checked, yes."

"So Thursday's the late carpool day. They won't be home until, like, six."

"Sweet."

Together, they went to the kitchen. He hopped onto a counter and watched her slide around the linoleum in her socks, humming to herself, pouring milk into mugs with Hershey's chocolate, stirring, then carrying the mugs to the microwave. "What do you think," she asked, "three minutes? Four? I can never remember. Let's go with . . ." She punched in numbers, hit START, and spun again. "Apple?" she asked, and almost too late he remembered: real milk. Raw, pasteurized, deaerated, didn't matter—it almost always contained some C. Well, no big deal. Low potency. He'd sip a little and leave the rest. Be polite.

"No. No apples, thanks. But hey, don't you guys have any of the powdered mix stuff that goes with water—like Swiss Miss or whatever?"

She made a face at him, chewing. Had another bite of her apple and wiped spray from her cheeks. "Disgusting. You'd rather have that?"

"Sure. Maybe. Just asking. It's actually better for you."

She chewed and swallowed. "You and I would so totally never be a good couple."

"Who said anything about *that*? You're way too young for me."

"And you're *way* too stupid. And weird. This is vile." She turned and stuffed her apple down the drain, ran water, and hit the switch for the disposal. Went back to the refrigerator and leaned in, searching. "OK, let's see. Turkey meat, salad, something icky that looks like I don't know—oh, that's Dad's *beets*—spaghetti leftovers, cottage cheese . . . more cottage cheese . . . What do you want?"

Though their houses were mostly alike, the sliding glass doors here led onto a spacious elevated back deck, icy with new snow, in the far corner of which a covered barbecue grill hunched like a short man standing watch. Thomas's eyes were drawn from that to her reflection in the glass and back out again, past the hunched sentinel to the late-afternoon light streaking up through the trees at the far edge of the yard. He was not supposed to be here now. He was supposed to be home, poking around in boxes of his father's junk for the old Mom movies. Earlier today, this had seemed to him like such a perfect idea and definitely the next step, the plan for the rest of the afternoon: locate and study his old Mom footage to see if any of it was worth a damn and maybe lay in a course for how to film her up north, or at least how to propose it to her to sell her on the idea. But here he was with Jill.

"Thomas? *What do you want?* Anything?"

"I'm good, thanks."

She slapped the refrigerator shut and spun toward him. "You . . ." she began.

"What do I have in my pocket?" he asked, because for a second he didn't actually remember what it was prodding the side of his wrist and pressing into his thigh.

"How should I know? Freak."

He wiggled his eyebrows. Hissed, "*Nasty hobbitses. Wants to know what he has in his pocketses? Prec-c-c-ciouss-s-s.*" A perfectly good series of books ruined by a movie that missed no opportunity to sensationalize and Disneyfy without irony. So said his teachers. Personally, he'd mostly felt cheated and sold out by Peter Jackson—as if his own personal fantasy world had suddenly been raided and made much too accessible to the rest of the world.

"Puh-lease." She was smiling in spite of herself.

"But seriously." He hopped down from the counter. "Check this out." With his good hand, he worked an edge of Griffin's pill bottle up from his pants pocket to where he could see it and grab hold, shaking it so it made a dim rattly noise like a miniature can of spray paint. "Buddy of mine gave this to me in history class. Some kind of magic painkiller pills. We should try them."

"Stupid, and weird, *and* now you're a druggie?"

"You gotta live a little. For reals. You grind them up, like with a whatchamacallit—the mortar and pestle thing—and then get a straw or something and snort it. For maximum effect."

"You *are* a druggie! Thomas, you have to leave now. My dad would so kill me."

"How's he going to find out?"

"Because I'll tell him, and then he'll call the cops!"

"Why would you do that?"

Her mouth opened, but no words came. Behind her, the microwave dinged, and Thomas observed, looking through the radiation-proof glass of the oven door, that both of their hot chocolates were silently boiling over, foam steadily streaming down the sides of the mugs, though the oven had switched itself off. "Jill . . ." he began. She was closer suddenly, eyes lowered, reaching for his hand. He shoved the pills into a back pocket and reached to draw her in, opening his arms, but she dodged him. Sidestepped and took hold of his hand.

"Thomas! What *happened* to your *hand*?"

"Practicing hockey moves, like I said. It's nothing. Sometimes you get a little carried away. People get hurt."

"*That's* not nothing."

"You should see the other guy."

"Shut *up*."

He nodded. "I tell myself that all the time. Half the time, my every other waking thought is that I should just shut up, or go jump off a bridge. Doesn't seem to work. I—"

"Would you please be quiet for one second? I've got to think what to do."

"Nothing at all. You don't have to do a thing."

"Give me those pills."

"No."

"*Give* them to me *now.*"

"No. Why?"

"Because I said! I need to see . . ."

This time she didn't resist or sidestep him, though for a moment she continued the pretext of trying to get at the pill bottle. There was the usual sweet smell of her shampoo and lip gloss, lotion or whatever else she wore, and the faint hot-cold pressure of her breath against his neck, then her arms going around his waist and the familiar insistent weight of her against him. He closed his eyes not to see it—not to notice up close the same light fuzz that covered the rest of her face, but stiffer-seeming, blanched and stranded against the alien purple skin. Felt her lips on his chin, teeth grazing the corner of his mouth and then right against his mouth, lips pursed, lightly sucking, tongue probing the fronts of his teeth. By habit, he turned so that if his eyes did happen to open, he'd be looking at the other cheek, the good one; spun with her once and again, but she wouldn't let him have the angle he wanted. She pushed back and kept pushing until he was against the kitchen counter again. OK, he thought, fine, and slid his hands in under the bottom of her shirt, inching from her hips to her rib cage, then higher, until he touched the lower straps of her bra, at which point, as always, her arms clamped down, blocking access. The pain bridging from the back of his bruised hand up his arm was a good thing, he told himself: a warranted rebuke and good contrasting physical sensation by which to distance himself and keep control. *Down beast! Tame the monster!* as Devon would say.

She tipped back, staring right at him. "Look at it," she said, nodding. "Touch it."

"Do what?"

"You know what I'm saying! Get your hands out of my shirt and quit pretending. Touch it."

"Your . . ."

"Yes."

"But . . ."

"No *buts*, Thomas."

He'd been about to point out that he'd touched her birthmark plenty of times before and that she'd always been the one to make him stop, when it dawned on him that without her explicit invitation or instructions to do so, it was almost like it had never actually happened. This was different. A lead opening onto a fresh inlet going who knew where.

He held his palm flat to her cheek and neck. "OK," he said. "Then the pills?" He noted as he had before that there was really nothing discernibly different to the touch. Just skin. A slight puffiness or serration at the edges of the birthmark. Nothing else.

"You and your pills."

"Pills for Jills." He kept his palm flat against her. "See? I'm not pretending." He smiled and said nothing further because he knew (he had no idea how) that any remark or observation or attempt to relate what he actually experienced touching her would offend her. If he said it was nothing, something, the same, different, special, made her beautiful, didn't make her beautiful, anything, he would be understood as insulting and his words turned against him.

She closed her eyes. "You have no idea how strange this feels."

"No," he said. "Maybe."

"It's like my head is buzzing."

"That sounds OK."

"And hot."

"Better."

She placed her hand over his and after a moment, searching his eyes, he understood that she meant to direct him further. "There's more," she said, and with that she pushed his hand into the front of her shirt. Reached around to release her bra strap. "But first . . . since you've been so insistent. Go ahead." He kept his eyes on hers. Didn't

look down or question her. He stared until he felt he might be seeing her face whole for once, not as if a corner of it had been bitten
or peeled to the side: a whole shape, though partially darkened. The
waxing moon on a clear night. "Have you ever . . ." she began.

He shook his head. Knew better than to lie. "First. And you?"

She nodded. "What do you think?"

Again, he knew he couldn't or shouldn't try to describe all of what
he actually thought: weird, pillowy-soft excess of flesh, not like anything he'd ever felt before, the skin on top so smooth and delicate,
it hardly seemed real or human, actually, more like the inside of a
balloon or the way he'd imagine a baby bird might feel, and yet for
whatever reason all of it so perfectly, exactly matched to what he
most craved about her and about girls generally. "Nice," he said. "It's
really, really nice." And then weirder still, the skin was changing,
poking up into the palm of his hand. "Should I stop?"

She shook her head. "If you want." Closed her eyes. "No."

"So, that's good?"

She nodded. Eyes still closed. "It must be. Sure."

He wasn't certain if there was more he was supposed to do. *Feeling
up* a girl had always seemed to him, by its name alone, to indicate
something more active on the boy's part, like squeezing or rubbing,
but he couldn't connect anything like that with a genuine desire on
his part. *Pinch her nipples till she pees herself*, Devon had said once,
but he was pretty sure he was only kidding, or else deliberately passing on bad intelligence. He didn't *feel* like squeezing and pinching;
Jill was so alien and fragile-seeming, his only real impulse was to be
sure he didn't hurt her—didn't do something inadvert to screw it
all up. Far easier, he thought, to lie on the basement floor with her,
knowing where he was and wasn't allowed to go, *canoodling,* and not
worrying about all this strangeness.

"Hey. Shall we?" he asked.

"Sure. You go ahead. I'll be down in a sec."

But they didn't go anywhere. At first, this surprised him, until he
connected it with other endings and leave-takings. She'd say, *Time to
go,* and then ten minutes later, fifteen minutes later, still canoodling,

OK, really now you need to leave. Mom'll be home any minute. In fact, some of their most advanced intimacy had occurred between the time when she'd told him he needed to go and his actual leaving. It was like a weird kind of procrastinating, which somehow opened a breach in time, changing the way time itself passed and allowing in new urgency, new permissiveness and feelings, until all boundaries might break. It almost made sense: If she said one thing, he should probably expect more or less the opposite. For now, she seemed positively rooted to him.

"Let's just stay like this forever," she said.

"Sure. Let's."

"Screw everything else."

"Absolutely."

And sure enough, as soon as he'd said that, she was leaning away from him, breaking her hold, separating and backing up a few steps. Then, hands on her cheeks: "Oh my fucking God! Our hot chocolate! You didn't say anything. Thomas! Look." Burned brown milk oozed from the front of the microwave down the counter and dripped in streaks from the cabinets to the floor. "I *hate* that stupid thing, I swear. I'm going to throw it in the garbage right now."

"Come on," he said, "it's not your fault—we'll clean up later . . . come on!" and led her by the hand back out and down the hall to the basement family room.

HE WAS ALONE IN HIS BOOTH at the Pearle's in Okotoks long enough to lose some steam and reconsider the wisdom of what he seemed embarked upon. Long enough to finish a cursory reading of all the Sinclair Ross quizzes and to revisit a familiar set of observations relating to the young person serving him (common verbiage, he knew from the boys, was no longer *waitress* as in his era but the more egalitarian *server*), and Canadian youth culture generally: a kind of 1950s mid-America attitude of small-town vanity or self-importance too easily confusing itself with *freshness,* but with all new pierced and semipunk costuming. That the cut of her top invited

in the eyes (glitter-sprinkled expanse of very muscular and suspiciously suntanned orangey bosom) and that she carried out her job
with seeming and ostentatious indifference to this, not as invitation
or provocation but as simple *display,* did not convince him, as he
suspected most of the props at the restaurant were designed to do,
that he was *part of* the place's over-the-top hipness and style, part
of some cutting-edge global culinary/social experiment featuring
fragrant seared meats, cinematic lighting, and twelve-dollar drinks.
Nor did it make him feel completely *excluded.* Invited to spectate.
Like a visitor from another planet. Time and again, he caught himself looking up from his stack of papers and staring idly, foot tapping to the scratchy sound track of the night—*I don't want to be your
ghost, I don't want to be your ghost*—and not just in hopes of seeing
Moira there (fifteen minutes late now, and counting) speaking to the
handsome young greeter at the door. This was still *Okotoks,* after all.
Not quite nowheresville, but awfully damn close. Who was anyone
here fooling?

"Appies while you're waiting?" she asked.

He shook his head and slid his empty beer mug toward her,
smiling. Noted the stud in her left nostril—glint of blue-green glass
or stone to echo the blue-green glitter in her cleavage—and thought
of Devon. All Devon's first requests for nose and lip and eyebrow
piercings. No, and no, and no again. But what was it Thomas had
hinted at recently regarding Devon? Something to do with a surprise concerning Devon's longtime girlfriend, Charmaine. That
they'd broken up? Hardly surprising. That they were engaged to
be married? Well, equally, not surprising. He had no idea how that
one would turn out. Only knew it made him cringe and feel as if
someone was standing on his chest when he heard her name, heard
anything about them as a couple, really, almost in the same way
Devon's prolonged, addictive dedication to wrestling and track had
at times made him wish with all his heart that he could just find the
cure—the way to break in, reorganize Devon's brain—anything to
make him set his priorities straight. But that had all worked its way
out in the end, hadn't it? So Franklin had learned and had, for the

most part, in fact, butted out and tried to quit caring so much what became of Charmaine, the scatterbrained high school girlfriend, or of Devon and Charmaine together. She was all right. So they'd get married and kill each other, or split up and kill themselves in grief. Either way, they'd get over it. Not really his problem anymore. He just hoped whatever it was went down well before kids and before any kind of alimony settlement that might permanently sap Devon's future prospects.

"Another Moose Drool?"

He nodded. "You from around here?"

She shook her head. "Yellowknife."

"Well, never mind, then. Thought you might know my kid."

"I did do a year at Douglas High, though. Grade twelve. Ran out of courses up there at Frankl—"

"Really! I know some Douglas teachers quite well." What was he trying to do? Flirt with a girl his son's age? "Excellent school! Buddy of mine I used to run with . . ."

Moira had slid around the server and seated herself across from him in the booth without his having seen her coming. Faint scent of cold emanating from her as she removed her coat and gloves and, with a rattling of jewelry, the Russian-style white fur hat perched on her head. She leaned toward him over the table, bracelets knocking together. "It's so cold. Warm me up, John! What are you drinking?" Raked aside hair, glancing sideways at the drink list and back at the server. She had applied lipstick for the occasion and looked generally more dolled up or polished than the day before. Eye shadow? He was not actually a good judge of these things, but he sensed more preparation than usual had gone into her appearance, and though it might not mean *sex* positively, he was at least pretty sure it indicated some kind of heightened festive mood into which sex might be incorporated. "Oh, I'll just have whatever he's having. No, I won't, either. Make mine an Irish coffee. No-no-no, what's that other, that wonderful, superlative drink you have here? I'm so sorry. I can never remember." She flew through pages of the drink menu while the server tipped her order form on a hip and named some favorite specialty martinis, until suddenly Moira stopped her, pointing. "Yes! That's the one."

"So," he said, leaning toward her over the table as soon as the server had gone.

"And so, and so," she replied.

MAYBE IT WAS THE PILLS—an ensuing numbness and dizziness mixed with heart-racing sleepiness—or maybe it was just as she said: It was his turn now. She'd shared something that terrified her, a secret of sorts, and also let him put his hand in her shirt. Now it was his turn. He needed to bare something too, share a secret. So he did. He told her everything. Spilled it all—about the diet and making himself throw up and eating antacids to block or neutralize stray traces of ascorbic acid, the whole deal; what he hoped for and why he kept failing, breaking down, eating fruit leathers and puking them up again—hemorrhagic sores, teeth falling out, blackened skin, old scars reopening, long-healed broken bones unmending. Didn't go as far as to share with her the thing he'd discovered only the night before, that it was purest self-hatred motivating him and making him wish he'd disintegrate from the inside out. That was too new, and anyway he was not entirely sure of it.

Afterward, she was silent for so long beside him in the thickening shadows, he wondered if the pills had kicked in, knocked her out or sent her off to a similar state somewhere between sleep and waking. He lay on his side, facing her, a hand on her rib cage moving up and down with her breaths, and trying to discern whether her eyes were open or shut. Beyond her, in the corner of the basement beside the exercise bike and NordicTrack machine, her father's upright golf bag had transformed into one of the sailors. He was sure of it. Maybe more than one. Their eyes blinking at him where the club handles would have been, bodies bent and bulky as overstuffed bags, blackened, bearded faces indistinguishable from the shadows. He heard them whispering back and forth, a sibilant, senseless stream of sound. *See-see-shoe-shoe . . .*

"See, sea, C," he said.

Jill raised herself on an elbow, pulling hair from one side of her face. "What? See what?"

"Nothing. I was just saying. I was thinking. They're all the same thing . . . sound the same. C, sea, see. See? Isn't that cool?"

"What in the world?"

"Never mind."

"You are very strange," she said, and again lay down. "And I am . . . very tired. Is it affecting you that way? Just *so* sleepy and maybe a little light-headed, and actually like . . . I feel pretty good, actually."

"Can I?" he asked, and again slid his hand back inside her shirt, where it had been most of the time since they'd come downstairs.

"OK, but the weird thing is . . ." she began.

He waited, but nothing more followed. He squeezed lightly. Her flesh felt warm and clammy under his, still weirdly pliant and unskinlike, nothing he was accustomed to, but now behaving more like actual skin in response to his own skin and getting hot and kind of annoying. "Yes," he prompted finally. Removed his hand. "The weird thing . . ." Still no answer.

He rolled onto his back, sat up, and looked around.

The men had detached from the shadows and come forward, not shimmering and holographic like cheesy Spielberg specters, nothing Disney or CGI about them at all. Completely real. He waved a hand at them. No reaction. *Guys,* he wanted to say. *Hey guys! You found me!* They were more like paintings of the old Flemish masters he remembered from his mother's art books—a onetime favorite of hers—grim and sorrowful, big-nosed and terribly detailed, with heavy greens showing through the underpainting. One younger, one older. Hoar and Work. Had to be, though mostly unlike his drawings of them. Both bearded and wearing clothes that seemed assembled from canvas or burlap sacking, maybe sailcloth, combined with wool and fur and felt. Boots torn and nobbed with brass nails, completely wet, and wrapped all around with more wool and canvas or burlap cloth, fur, mummified, so it looked as if they'd tried putting on motley shredded socks over the top of their boots in order to hold them together. No, it would be because of the swelling. Of course. Feet would swell from cold and frostbite and infection to the point where boots no longer fit except by brute force or by having seams relieved or cut away, so why not put the socks on top for additional insulation? How else could you do it? Just beside the enormous TV, they stopped and leaned against each other, breathing hard, and toppled together into a seated position. Again he waved at them. *Guys!* he mouthed. No response.

"The weirdest thing is . . ." Jill began again. He scooted halfway around to face her. "Well, what I was going to show you before, when I said *There's more,* you know—" Again she broke off.

"Yes?"

Work removed something from his pocket. Looked like a golf ball. So they *had* come out of Jill's father's golf bag! They passed the ball back and forth, holding it up, scrutinizing it, sniffing and licking it, rolling it between their blackened, broken-seeming fingers, and shaking their heads at each other until Work produced a pocket watch and something else—looked like the remains of a pipe bowl—and began juggling the three things together, to Hoar's apparent delight. Thomas's, too. He grabbed his knees and leaned toward them. So real! They couldn't be mere projections of his own imagination, bits of too-intense dreams left floating around the room when he awakened, as usual, though he was sure, too, they must still have *some* connection with his dreams and imagination. So he needed to be careful. Play dead and stay to the side; don't stare too long at them. He'd been wrong to hail them, but never mind that. They were here for now. Soon enough, they'd evaporate back to wherever they'd come from; no need to hasten it. Meanwhile, this fantastically fun show. Juggling! He'd had no idea.

"OK," she said. "Thomas?"

"Yes."

"Don't take this the wrong way, but . . ." She rolled upright, stood, and removed her pants. Stepped out of them and snapped the elastic of her underwear higher.

"Jill!"

"What. It's *not* an invitation, I said. All right?"

"But you just took off your pants!"

"Very observant." She nodded and again lay beside him, belly down, feet kicking. "OK, now look. On my butt," she said, gesturing with her chin. "Go ahead." Thomas didn't move. "Look!"

And finally, sliding closer and leaning right over her, he understood. At first, he wasn't sure, thought it must be a shadow or some other trick of the light, but no. From the outer fringe of her underwear's waistband to the top of her left thigh seeped another blue-purple patch of skin.

"See?" she asked, lifting and pulling aside her underwear, lowering them until the mutant shoreline shape of the stain was mostly in view.

He nodded. "Yes. But what . . ."

She snapped the underwear back. Rolled to a seated position, facing him. "Birthmark. Same as my face. Covers like the whole left side of my butt. Nothing anyone can do about it and nothing to feel bad about. Doesn't *hurt* or handicap me or whatever. It's just *there*. And it's not that uncommon, either—not an uncommon place for them, I mean, on your butt. Lots of Korean girls get them."

"Korean girls get . . . what? Where did you hear that?"

She shrugged. "But don't you think it's *weird*? Like, here you are trying to *give* yourself scurvy and I already *have* it."

"What are you talking about. *Scurvy*. You don't have scurvy. . . . It's nothing like—"

"Not *all* of it. Just the one thing. Look." She slid an arm from inside her shirt and bent, hugging herself to present a view of her bare shoulder and, as she snaked her arm back through the armhole of her sleeve to face him again, a half glimpse of bare breast, all so fast, he almost didn't catch what she'd evidently meant to show: another inlet of purple-blue, smaller and backward C-shaped, ending just below where her bra strap would have connected. "See?"

He nodded. Reached a hand toward her and let it drop. "Wow. So it's like . . . all over?"

She shook her head. "Not *all over*. Jerk. Just those places. So *what* if I never get to wear a bathing suit or an evening gown, or even most *tank tops,* for that matter . . . or get to sunbathe with my friends or sit on the beach or go on a real date. It's not like it anyone *cares,* right?"

"Jill, I . . . That's not necessarily . . ." Again he lifted a hand toward her.

"I'm *not* a freak show! Just get, *get*—" She slapped at his hand, and then, realizing what she'd done, covered her mouth. "Oh no," she said, and began to cry. "I'm so sorry. Oh my god, Thomas, I'm sorry."

That fast, when only moments earlier she'd seemed fine, ready to take off her clothes and say crazy things about scurvy. Crying. What was he supposed to do about this? He had no experience. Sometimes, when they were younger, Devon would erupt into terrifying fits of rage against him or one of their parents, and these had nearly always ended in tears. Not the kind you'd dare get close to (angry, face torn open, snot everywhere, teeth bared), though generally one or the other of their parents had eventually had to wade in, wrap arms around him, to put a stop to it. Aside from that, the only person in his family to cry openly was himself. Less violently than Devon, to be sure, and requiring much less in the way of provocation. There was also the one time, more recently, weeks after his mother had left for good, when he'd walked in on his father alone in the study, lights out, and found him sobbing and making a crazy, repetitive hiccupping *wa-wa-wa-wa* noise so much like a windup toy, that at first Thomas had thought it must be a joke. But it was not a joke—in fact, there was nothing funny about it—and he'd slipped back out of the room, unnoticed.

None of which prepared him. Jill didn't sob or gasp, or crumple her mouth and wave her fists around like Devon. No theatrics or hiccupping. She just stared and let the tears slide down her face with strings of mucus until the front of her shirt was soaked.

"It's OK," he said. Rubbed his hands together. "Didn't even hurt. See? Those pills . . . I'm totally numbed up now anyway. Didn't feel a thing." Flicked a finger at the back of his hand to prove it. "Really, didn't hurt. No worries."

She scrubbed knuckles into her eyes and smiled at him. Laughed once. Lifted the bottom of her shirt to wipe her nose and cheeks and said, "Relax, OK? It's no biggie. Girls *cry*, all right?"

"If you say."

She leaned her elbows on her knees and hunched toward him but made no move to put her clothes back on. Like she'd forgotten. "Are you really *stoned*, Thomas?"

"A little, yeah. I guess. Mostly numb. You?"

"My mouth feels all, like, rubbery. Does it look weird?" She stuck out her lower lip at him.

"Like that it does, sure."

"And I'm just super*tired*," she said. She yawned, stretched her arms over her head, and abruptly fell onto her back. Closed her eyes. Said, "I hope you don't mind. Nightie-night."

"Really?"

For a few moments, he watched her. Wondered if this was some kind of joke or test. Was he supposed to leave? Keep her awake? Go to sleep himself? He didn't get it.

"Jill. For real?"

Her eyes stayed shut, hands folded over her solar plexus, feet tucked one against the other. The picture of tranquillity. He started thinking maybe she truly was asleep, or even in a coma.

Devon: *Dude, she took her pants off for you and pretended to go to sleep and you did nothing about it? Let me get this straight. Are you on crack or are you just some fairy who lost his balls in his art project?*

Thomas: *It wasn't like that. She was crying. There was other stuff.*

Devon: *Other stuff! Dude, Thomas. I've got news. A girl takes her pants off for you, you can bet it means one thing: She wants you to jump her, harelip or not.*

Thomas: *It's not a harelip. Fuck off and leave me alone.*

Beyond her, the men were still crouched by the TV, Work attempting to skin or otherwise pick apart Jill's father's golf ball with what appeared to be a large bone-handled hunting knife. Having already nicked a thumb and twice caused the ball to become airborne, both men swatting desperately at it, catching it and returning to their study with renewed awe and intrigue, passing the ball back and forth,

Work seemed at last to have settled on a more aggressive course. He braced the ball between his feet and spun the blade of his knife point downward on it like a top, like how they'd taught Thomas to start fire with sticks in Scouts; and, having at last penetrated its surface, he set about methodically sawing it in half with the edge of his blade. Only, the ball wouldn't stay put. Kept rolling from under his numb and ruined feet. They were like twin Chaplins or two of the Three Stooges! Hilarious. It had never occurred to Thomas that the men should be funny. But of course they should be funny. Funny was the answer to everything!

"Jill! Hey, Jill!"

She rolled toward him finally. Blinked. "Oh."

"My turn again?"

"Turn?"

"Yeah. Come here." He scooted to the back of the couch with an arm out. "Just come sit here right next to me and tell me what you see. Try it. Come here."

Weirdo. She didn't say it, didn't have to say it (he knew her well enough to predict), and given how things had developed between them this afternoon, probably had lost the grounds for saying it anyway; still, he saw the word on her lips. He narrowed his eyes, looked back at her, and shook his head. Said, "Don't even think it."

"What?"

"I'm no weirder than you are."

"Says you, duh."

She walked on her knees to him and sat so her shoulder fit under his arm, the side of her head pressing his neck and shoulder. He tried hard not to think about the fact that she really had taken her pants off for him, still had no pants on, and was now sitting there with her bare knees halfway across his lap, the side of one thigh fully pressed against him. In the corner of his vision he could just make out (almost didn't dare seeing it) the white V shape of her underwear and the way it ended at the leg holes. Glanced once and again to be sure and felt her shifting beside him, tucking her legs up under her shirt and hugging both arms across before leaning firmly back beside him.

"Cold," she said. "There. So? What am I supposed to be seeing?"

"Look. Not at the TV screen. Right . . . there. Next to it. See? In that kind of shadowy area right there?"

Hoar had impaled the golf ball on Work's knife and was alternately stabbing it at the ground to fix it in place and then lifting it and nipping at it like an apple on a stick or some other kind of shish kebab. Again and again he tried. They must think it was some kind of spherical and extremely overcooked hard-boiled egg. Stabbed the knife at the ground. Bit down. Now he pressed a hand to his mouth. Gaped and held the knife and ball out for Work to see— *look, look*: Both of his front teeth had ripped out and were stuck in surface of the golf ball. Blood ran down his chin. Work pointed and laughed, tipped to the side and kept laughing, clapping and slapping his legs. Hoar shook a fist and got ready to throw the whole thing end over end, knife and ball, until Work stopped him, clamping a hand over his wrist.

"They're so funny! Oh my God!" Thomas said. "Can you see?"

And so, and so . . . As always the feelings of most intense confluence and ongoing interference talking to her, both at the same time, conversation drawn unexpectedly into currents he didn't anticipate, tearing wide, stopping, and just as suddenly moving ahead again. On the table between them, her open phone buzzing and blinking periodically, summoning her attention, but never fully—*Oh, that's Marguerite, my sister. You remember. I'll have to call her later. . . . Oh, look at this, from Paul. You remember him from the group? He's just sent a link on Eavan Boland's new book*—also their drinks and gloves, her hat, and the remains of the food he'd mistakenly ordered on her insistence—*I'm not hungry, but you order something. Really! I'd know that starved-bear look anywhere. . . . You MUST eat. I'll order for you if I have to!* He'd tried, and mostly failed, to eat discreetly. He knew this was against all dating protocol: Don't order if the girl doesn't order; don't eat more than the girl; don't share her food even if she invites you to. Don't talk about your ex. But he couldn't help himself, and anyway, maybe they were more familiar with each other than all that. Besides, he was buzzed from the beers and needed ballast if he was going to drive home; and given the prospect of another dimly lit meal of three-day old leftovers with gloomy Thomas when he was here already . . . why not? *Please*, he kept saying, motioning at his plate, fingers slick with steak juice, catsup, and chipotle mayonnaise, *help me out. Have some.* Bad signs, all of them, he was sure, and yet here she was still, across from him and nodding her head to another scratchy youth pop number of indecipherable lyrics, hanging in there. Maybe the signs didn't apply. Maybe in her case, all signs went contrary.

"I guess you could say Jane fell in love, but not in the usual sense," he said. He glanced at his beer mug and wondered, How buzzed? The glass was tall but had seemed to him thicker than it was deep— designed to look as if it held more than it actually did. A higher than normal alcohol content? His general tendency drunk was to say too much, too fast—never anything he didn't mean or overly regretted later, but more than better judgment would have allowed. It always surprised him, afterward, to realize he'd done it again. "She was pretty radical in college. Dedicated. We had this one teacher . . . never mind. He was always calling her on it. *Remember, the fascists were idealists, too*, you know. To get her going. *Stalin, now there's a real idealist for you. Take any ideal too far, it becomes hypocrisy. Dogma.* Anyway, where your ordinary person might have seen some articles about the impacts of climate change on those little native fishing-hunting communities up in the territories and said, *Well, that's just god-awful,* and then basically forgotten about it, she couldn't. For her, it was critical. It was right now, do or die. She had to get involved." He drank. "She had to actually *go* there. Be there." The explanation left a lot out, of course—namely, his own part, which was probably too close and too convoluted to describe. He still doubted he could have done much to change the outcome, but he knew, too, that his worry and grief about the open-ended uncertainty of it all had turned him in ways that would have helped anyone find reasons to go.

"Huh." She was smiling and tilting her head—a mixture of

provocation and finger wagging. He could guess what was coming. "Not unlike you with your selkies."

"Totally different!"

"How so?"

"Sule Skerry doesn't exist anywhere. It's a made-up underwater city. Shouldn't hurt anyone else if I get stuck there now and then for a few hours. I mean, I always come back. Truth is, if I was a little more single-minded, a little more selfish or dedicated, like Jane, I might have finished the damn thing already. And better." He popped another fry in his mouth. Drank. "But you know me. It's not just excuse making, either. I actually truly believe there are other things in the world at least as important as my *art*. I mean"—he poked a finger against the table-top in rhythm with his words—"kids, wife, work . . . these things *intrude* because they're *supposed* to intrude. They have as much right in the world, and most of the time a more legitimate claim on my attention than *poetry*. Come on. I can't see it any other way. So, whatever, maybe it's illusion or false hopes or what have you, but I always tell myself it's"—he gestured vainly—"part of the gestalt of the thing? All the going back and forth, coming in and out of the work, stopping, starting, being constantly, constantly interrupted. You know all this. And lately I've decided maybe it actually *helps* me to understand the shape-shifting parts of the narrative—selkie going from seal to man and back again—so he's like a process analogue for me and subject, both at same time. Leaving his fur hidden under a rock, finding his human lover to court and make love to, propagate the species. I mean, isn't all literature the story of transformations? Death, sex . . . just another transformation, so this is like a transformation within a transformation to achieve another transformation." Shut up, shut up. Why wasn't she stopping him?

She dipped a fry and ate it. "*Good* sex, maybe."

"All sex is good."

She laughed. "Coleridge. *No such thing as a bad poem.* Remember? Only good poems."

He shook his head. He'd forgotten that—her use of the word *remember*, common with one or two other members of the group. As

if there were some presumed pact between them that they were continually at study and had memorized every book under the sun and
needed only to remind one another of passages by saying *Remember?*
to call it up, bring it all back. Always something vaguely embarrassing and pretentious-seeming to him about it. But also genuine in her,
not chiding or show-offy. Sincere enough that he was willing to let
himself be swept along.

"No," he said. "*Remind* me."

"It's in his . . . oh, I forget where he says it actually. But for him,
for a poem to *be* a poem, it must be good. Therefore, if it's not good,
it's just not a poem. Doesn't achieve poem-ness and therefore doesn't
exist. Handy, no? A poem-like-object."

"Well, if you could remove subjectivity from the equation. Sure."
He snapped his fingers. "Poof. There goes—"

"All the language poets."

He nodded. "Makes a certain amount of sense."

"For poetry. Not sex, alas. Bad sex is, sadly, still sex, as I suspect
bad poems are mostly still poems, just badly. Believe me, I know
whereof I speak, on both accounts . . . and—"

"Maybe not. Maybe it's—"

"Now John, I'm afraid you'll hate me for it, but I really must go."

"So fast?"

"Fast! So must you, if I'm not mistaken."

"Right. Sure. Just . . ."

"I told you it'd be a short night. One drink. Somehow, you got me
to two. Now let's pay and you can walk me out. *Uno momento,*" she
said, and slid from the booth.

"Where're you—"

"Be right back."

He settled against the booth and eyed the beer left in his mug,
wondering again, How buzzed? Well, the important thing—they'd
met, they'd talked, spent time together . . . it could happen again.
It *would* happen again. A beginning of sorts. A rebeginning. And
probably for the best if nothing more happened tonight. Still, though
he didn't want to (as if it were another omen to circumnavigate), he

couldn't help but imagine the picture he must now make from the server's perspective—lonesome middle-aged guy, stranded with the detritus of drinks and his solitary dinner, flushed from beer and talk, and probably in the middle of trying to do something icky with the lady in the white fur hat. She'd probably been waiting for just this moment to circle in and get them out of here. Collect her tip and seat the next customers.

"Anything else tonight, or can I . . ."

He smiled. "Just the check."

And when she'd gone again, he flipped open his phone to see if there had been a call from Thomas, a voice message: *Dad, where the hell are you? Hello! It's a school night!* But no. Not surprisingly, there was nothing. Thomas would be in his room, drawing or goofing around on the computer and likely unconscious of the hour altogether. He'd have to call from the car. Say, *Sorry for the delay, kiddo. Busy day. You should go ahead and start something on your own to eat. Doubt I'll have time for it.*

There came a subtle modulation in the tone and lighting of Pearle's—more rose-tinted and darker; happy hour shifting over to dinner hour, he supposed—and someone had changed the music channel to jazz. This was taking too long. What was she doing anyway? *Uno momento.* He tilted his head back and closed his eyes, waiting, and was happily surprised (relieved?) when he knew to look up and refocus at exactly the right moment—that walk, those eyes on his as she approached.

"Sorry for the wait," she said, showing him her phone by way of explanation. "Shall we?"

He nodded, stood, remembering as he did the gum adhered to his khakis. "Hey, check this out," he said, turning and pointing at it for her to see. "Can you believe?"

"Is that from here?"

He shook his head. "School."

"Use white vinegar," she said. "Soak it."

He offered her his arm, which she slapped at once and didn't take. "Are you nuts? Do you think we're the only people in the world?"

And outside, sheltered from the wind between her Escalade and the SUV parked alongside it, the sudden rush of her mouth on his, her arms going around him, her hair blown in his face, the smell of perfume trapped in her coat collar distilled by the surrounding cold and isolated in his senses. He couldn't stop himself. Couldn't even be sure who was leading, who was following. "Oh my God, Moira, I have wanted this for so long. . . ." Her mouth on his, her breath in his throat. Sounds of their coats hissing together, snow compacting underfoot. Absurd to attempt intimacy this bundled up—he could barely feel her through all the layers of clothing between them. "Jesus God, you have no idea how much," he said.

"Yes, but I'm getting the picture, though," she said. And after another moment: "Oh, John. It's always so complicated, isn't it? Why so complicated?"

He shrugged. "Maybe. But then again . . ." Touched her nose. "You," he said, and touched his own nose, "me. What could be simpler?"

"You really *do* think we're the only people in the world."

"How else should I . . . I mean, how else *could* I think of it, and still be standing here with you? I mean, I'm assuming, with your marriage and whatever, you've got your reasons, your story, and I'm more than open to hearing about all of it, as much as you want to share anyway. Just . . . seems to me like that's up to you."

She didn't answer immediately. Sighed once and smiled. Pressed suddenly closer and turned her face so her cheek was against his. "Of course, John. And I promise. Another time, you can hear the whole sordid tale of woe."

He waited for more. Stared at the light on the snow-blown pavement, the dirty half-melted and refrozen snowbanks, tire tracks in ice and snow, everywhere the desolate glitter of orange-blue sodium lights on frozen asphalt. This was not a place in which to linger. Not a place in which anyone was trying to entice you to spend a single extra moment and definitely not a place to attempt romance. Things he could say now but didn't know how to choose from: *We can take our time. No rush, no pressure. I'm here for you, not going anywhere; whatever it takes to make you comfortable, just say. . . .*

She was laughing.

"What's so funny?"

"It just occurred to me. Please don't be offended." Again she broke off laughing.

"What?"

"The word in French for seal . . . you know it? *Phoque*."

"Fuck?"

"Sounds the same anyway. Perfect for you, isn't it?"

"What are you . . ."

She was still laughing.

"You're making fun of me!"

"Only in the best-possible way. Mr. Phoque."

As she tipped back in his arms, laughing, it dawned on him—the tapered line of her jaw contrasted with her cheekbones' prominence and the slenderness of her neck, the delicate skin there just beside and below her ear: like Joni Mitchell. All this time he'd been attracted to her because of a physical likeness to Joni Mitchell? Because of some hangover adherence to that younger version of himself, adrift following his trip to Unst, listening to too much Joni Mitchell alone in his dorm room and imagining a Canada populated with squarish-jawed blond beauties singing tragic folk songs? Impossible. Therefore probably at least partially true. She was his ideal of youth: a prettier, more approachable-seeming Joni Mitchell. He nuzzled aside her hair and fit his lips there at the juncture of neck and ear. Breathed the warm smell of her and opened his mouth to taste her; felt her surge against him and after a moment go liquid under all the winter layers.

"OK," she said. "Uncle. Tell me where you live."

Later, as she drove off and he made his way across the icy lot to his car, he realized—the thing that had looked *wrong* or different about her since they'd left the restaurant: her white fur hat. She'd forgotten and left her fur hat in the restaurant.

Clamping the finger of one glove in his teeth to remove it, he flipped open his phone. Punched up her number and stuck the glove in under his arm, changing course and marching *scrunch-scrunch* back toward the restaurant, through the double doors, and into the front foyer as she answered, overhead heaters blasting hot air at his head. Like entering an airlock chamber, Thomas had once pointed out, and he'd never been able to see it differently since.

"Dearest," she said. "So soon?"

"Forgot your hat."

Silence. "So I did!"

"I'm on my way inside now for it."

"Thank you *so* much."

"De rien."

She laughed. "Phoque."

Inside, there were other waiting guests to cut past like the pushy American he supposed he was still, and the confusion: No, he didn't want a table; yes, he'd just been in; nothing wrong, no. A hat, had they seen a hat? A very nice, probably very expensive white fur hat? Looking around for the young server from Yellowknife to help, it occurred to him how unlike the mythic taverns and inns of his imagination this Pearle's was—the seal-man swimming upright through air, seeking his fertile human female, and later his bonnie wee bairn—and yet how similar in purpose; how eternal the purposes of public drink and food.

"Haven't seen it," the greeter was saying. "A number where we could reach you, if it shows up?"

"Sure. But let me go have a look first, if you don't mind," he said, and pushed by, already knowing exactly where he'd find it: marooned under the table in a crust of sand and snowmelt and dropped fries, rice, the rim of it probably slightly damp. Otherwise, untouched. Knowing, too, how the fur would compress luxuriantly under his fingers—the ridiculous plushness of it; how he would not want to remove his hand from it all the way home.

HE MUST HAVE FALLEN ASLEEP. His arms were numb and prickling and his mouth felt as if it had been packed with wool. Then he remembered: the sailors coming out of the golf bag, the birthmarks, Jill with her pants off. His explanation for her as he tried to fill her in and make her see the men: *Like a reverse hallucination, I think, because apparently the ice on the shoreline, the pack ice and bergs and all the other formations everywhere would sometimes look so freakishly much like an exact replica of a city, with streets and houses and cathedrals, the whole deal, the sailors would think they were going bonkers. But they'd all see it together, too. These empty ice cities exactly like England. They'd be sailing along and one of them would say, "Look, it's Westminster Abbey, right there!" Probably only because they wanted so badly to believe. Or maybe it was real. Anyway, instead of that, I'm seeing them! Like the hallucinations are getting jammed up in the space-time continuum and reversed somehow?* Trouble was, as much as he narrated for her what Work and Hoar were doing—Hoar prying his teeth from the golf ball, trying to reinsert them in his bloody gums, Work stealing the ball back and attempting to swallow it whole, spitting it out—he never got the sense she was actually seeing anything. She'd sigh, laugh, and a few times between yawns say things like *Sucks to be him,* and *Really?* and *Which one's which again?* At some point, she'd definitely drifted off and fallen asleep. Now she was sitting beside him, shaking his shoulder, hissing his name. Time had skipped backward or ahead somehow. What had happened? Had anything happened? She was fully clothed, hair combed out and shirt buttoned.

"Wake *up* now, Thomas. My parents are totally going to be home any minute."

"I was asleep."

"I *know*. We'll have to sneak you out the back or something."

"But how"—he yawned—"how long have we been down here?"

She shrugged. "Like an *hour* at least."

"I thought it was longer."

"You ate those pills, duh. No wonder."

"You did, too."

"I had, like, half a one. You ate all the rest."

"True not. There's two left." He rattled the vial for her. "So . . . are they home?"

She tilted her head, listening. "I don't think so." She prodded him with a foot. "Come on, let's get you out of here."

He stood, thumped for a moment at his leg, which also had gone mostly numb, and extended his good hand to pull her up. Held her at arm's length and looked at her straight on. There should be something said about what had happened today. He was sure of it, some kind of pact or acknowledgment, and he was just as sure that he was the one who needed to say it, yet he had no clue what the thing might be—the absolutely right thing. The wrong thing would be so terribly wrong, and yet saying nothing at all might be even more fatal than that.

"Got you a good one there," she said, pointing at his neck. "Sorry."

"What?"

"Hickey."

"Oh." He made a show of trying to see it, and laughed. "The thing is, Jill, I think . . . no, I have to say, I'm totally in love with you." His eyes fizzed and stung as he finished this, unexpectedly, both because of the feelings awakened in him by saying it, whether or not he truly loved her, and because of the risk of devastating embarrassment he'd so casually wandered into. There must be some connection between this and the way he'd felt last night staring in the mirror, wanting to stab or crush his reflection out of existence, but he couldn't quite see what it was. Then he wasn't sure she'd heard him anyway, she'd gone so completely still, and in the interim he became convinced that he needed to undercut his words a little, go back, give things a jokier, easier spin. "For reals, Jills. You're like . . ."

She swatted his shoulder. "You're not in love with me."

"Serious! I'm trying to be serious here. Come on!"

She leaned into him, planted herself with arms circling his ribs so fiercely, he thought he'd never escape. He watched his hands slide up and down her back and move aside her hair, stroke and spin together strands. In the shadow where the waist of her jeans gapped slightly he could just make out the top fringe of her underwear and above that the beginning of the blue-purple stain. Blue butt. *Lots of Korean girls,* she'd said. So he hadn't dreamed it. Or at least not all of it. It had happened.

"Maybe I should, like, camp out here. Spend the night."

"Maybe you want my dad to kill you first."

"Hmm." He pretended to think about it. "*On second thought . . . forget about Camelot. Rather a silly place, really . . .*" They might not have all the movies in the world in common, but they could riff on *The Holy Grail* together pretty well. Sticking her with a scene ending as he had just done left her free to go anywhere in the script—probably the bit with the castle full of young nuns. One of her favorites. "*The peril is much too perilous,*" he said to prompt her, but she was already on another tack, singing "The Ballad of Brave Sir Robin," and skipping ahead to the best, goriest details— smashed head, nostrils ripped, bowels unplugged, bottom burnt off—Thomas joining with her for the final lines of the song and Robin's dismissal of his minstrels:

"*Eh— enough music for now, lads.*"

And like that, released from each other, they turned and headed up the stairs—Jill first, so she was first to see: outside the front picture window, the northern sky torn aside with blue-green smoke and wavering, snaky columns of light.

"Northern Lights!" she said, and crossed quickly to the window.

He went to stand behind her and to one side. Said, "A sailor's reminder there's sunlight still in distant lands . . ."

She glanced at him. "What's that from?"

"The movie. A scene I just finished, actually. Hoar says it when—"

"I love you, too, Thomas. Just so you know. I don't know if you meant it before, but you know . . . I don't care."

He nodded. Waited a moment to be certain of whatever he said next, but before he could think of what it should be, headlights flooded the wall beside them and she pushed him down. "Quick. This way," she said. "Here."

He grabbed up boots, coat, knapsack from the far side of the couch and followed her to the kitchen and out the sliding glass door.

Love and obey: that paradoxical edict from the wedding vows that he and Jane had so ostentatiously (in his parents' view anyway) decided to delete, and had later joked about, semiregularly over the years of their marriage, always meaning, he supposed, to point out to each other just how much they really *didn't,* either one of them, control, obey, or answer to the other—so progressive, so evolved. Later, reflected through the children, it took on other layers of meaning: their unconditional love for the boys never diminished by any disobedient act, yet requiring constant monitoring and rearticulation of all rules, terms, and consequences, so very nearly the exact inverse of the love between Jane and him. When Jane had finalized her plan to leave them, go north, it acquired yet another significance and an accompanying emotional/visual analogue that had felt to him like a giant screw unwinding from his chest, leaving a gaping, raw channel. She'd never obeyed. Not him or anyone. Maybe she'd never loved, either. So was he wrong *not* to have insisted that they obey each other? What was obedience, after all—after nineteen, twenty years of marriage, what could it possibly mean? How did a marriage survive without it? But how obey and still love? Her own grandmother had, notoriously, given her grandfather a letter a few weeks prior to their wedding ceremony in which she asked him, please, to remember to keep control over her. Franklin had never seen the letter but had heard Jane paraphrase it often enough that he felt as if he'd viewed the thing firsthand: the plea to her husband to keep her in control, remember the vows they'd soon take, and manage the *untamable wildness* in her. *Save this letter for such time as you need to invoke the authority I hereby freely grant you in it. I fear you'll need it all too often.* Yet, Jane insisted, her grandmother was always the one in control, managing the family finances, working, running the shop. Free-thinking and well ahead of her time. And, of course, to her knowledge, her grandfather had never had cause to use the so-called *authority* given him in that letter.

It needed a container—that was all he'd ever been able to conclude on the matter. Marriage, love, affection of any kind, it needed some *thing* in which to be contained, reflected, and given form, in the same way people themselves needed some form or structure, however fictitious. Once upon a time, some people had agreed to draw a line around that and call it *obedience*. Politicized, polarizing or not, he still thought it was probably the wrong word, but he had a different perspective now than he'd had twenty years ago on what might have been meant by it. More like a vessel or a seedpod, he supposed. A car. Watch case? Mirror. Anyway, a container. And speeding home to Thomas, he felt *contained* as he hadn't in some time. Held in Moira's attention and given direction by the urge to shape her name over and over in his mind, and to say it out aloud to himself. Also restless and aware that the filaments attaching him to any other human were as tenuous as ever and stretched to the max through the icy dark. Jane would never return from the Arctic. He believed that more fully tonight than he had for some time. Moira might or might not show up at his door. Better to hope that she would; better yet not to expect it.

One of the last times he and Jane had spoken, six, seven months ago now, before they'd agreed to quit their semiregular "talks" and phone updates, she'd told him something he'd often revisited: *It's good you're losing some of your control, John. Your composure, whatever you want to call it, even if it scares the boys sometimes. Good for your soul. I always said. . . . It's like some kind of false veneer or false protective coating with you, isn't it? The way you keep such close wraps on everything you feel and say and do, such command over how you'll choose to react. You think that was ever fun to be around? I mean, there's nothing really wrong with it, I guess . . . just kind of distancing, isn't it?*

Distancing? He'd tried to keep the incredulity in his voice down. *Wow. Did you really say* distancing?

I'm just . . . yes. I don't know. Sometimes I think if you'd maybe let go a little more once in a while, loosened up . . .

Like the time I dislocated Devon's shoulder? You liked that a lot.

Point taken.

Scared the crap out of you. Or with Thomas, that time with the catsup in the hair?

Yes, but I think what I'm talking about here is a little different.

How so? You've never been a fan of the big emotional displays, Jane.

Period. Mine or anyone's. Really, you can't deny . . . twenty years or whatever without ever actually fighting. How else do you think we managed that?

I'm not saying it makes sense, John. I never said that. It's more of a feeling thing. I just . . . I suspect this time apart is as good for you as it is for me. I have to believe. And maybe there's a way you can let back in some of that more immoderate energy of yours, more of that . . . I don't know what you call it. Let it back into your life more anyway, now I'm gone? It'd be good, I think.

Maybe so, he'd said.

That's my hope.

Then it's mine, as well.

Only later, he'd realized she hadn't been talking about *hope* in the sense of suggesting a reconciliation or way forward for them. She'd been describing for him what she wished he'd become, without her. And in doing so, asking him to relinquish the single personality trait of his that had probably done most to keep them together.

Meanwhile, time seemed to have dilated or slipped sideways and backward. Still only 6:42, which made no sense, given how long he thought he and Moira must have sat at Pearle's. Was his car clock frozen? Stalled because of a cold battery? Possibly. He tried to check it against the time on his watch but couldn't manage to push aside his coat and shirtsleeve at exactly the right moment to see. Too, the upper-right corner of his windshield seemed to have been lit with a glow like the sunrise, only paler, more like some kind of neon condensation stuck on the glass. Like aliens had landed. "What the fuck?" he said, swiping a hand at the windshield. Was it somehow 6:42 A.M. and he had managed to lose an entire night? No, wrong part of the sky. He bent lower to see, and realized, Of course. Northern Lights. The crazy elastic ribbons of supercharged particles caught in the Earth's Van Allen belt and streaming along the horizon. Always put him in mind, however incongruously, of sea anemones and underwater currents lit by phosphorescent algae, the chorus to Ringo's "Octopus's Garden" starting up reflexively in his head: *I'd like to be under the sea. . . .* Also some of his earlier,

mushroom-enhanced concert experiences watching the troupes of
young aerial dancers spinning and twisting from vertical ribbons
of colored cloth, doing crazy airborne yoga. The lights tonight were
paler but somehow more radiant than usual. Not for the first time
he wondered just how different they'd look closer to the source,
how much more intense and colorful from Jane's perspective, up
there in the true north. This was the cheap, bargain version, he was
sure—the one that came with at least some hours of winter sunlight.
He pictured the point he'd jogged to that night, at the edge of town
in Inuvik. Threw in Northern Lights, snow, wind, cold . . . no sun.
Decided, no, if he were in Inuvik now, he'd probably venture no
farther than the edge of the driveway.

Turning off the main road and under the overpass, headed north
toward home and past the open field that eventually ran into lots
abutting their backyard, he thought he saw a solitary figure, almost
like a rock cairn, arms upraised to the spires of electronic static, as if
summoning them. *Thomas,* he thought instantly, and just as instantly
dismissed the thought. Couldn't be. Anyway, looking a second and
third time, he was pretty sure it was two people. That, or one large
man pulling something larger behind him; or maybe it was a rock
cairn after all. One he'd never noticed before? Unlikely. What was the
Inuit word for it? He tapped his leg, trying to remember. *Inukshuk.*
Stones placed to resemble a human form, marking the place. Sig-
nifiying, *Someone was here; You are on the right path.* Or, *Here is
meat and fish; here lies the body of so-and-so.* And wasn't that where
Thomas had said Sir John Franklin's remains must be interred, somewhere undiscovered on King William Island, in a concrete cairn? No
one knew for sure. The light continued seeping its weird designs up
the horizon. *What a show,* he thought, turning into their block, and
realizing then that, if he'd wanted to know what time it was, he could
always just check his phone. Of course. Flipped it open and saw not
the clock numbers in the top corner of the phone screen, but the red
square message in the middle alerting him again, as it had the night
before, *"New Text Message! View Now?"* He bumped to the side of
the road and up the driveway. Didn't even put the car in park or turn

the key in the ignition. Clicked *Yes* and waited, eye nerves straining through darkness to make out the pixilated, blocky sans-serif script: *Maybe Tonight lover not sure but do lv door unlocked . . . in case.* He snapped the phone shut. Slotted the gearshift to PARK, stood out of the car, and leaned back inside for his bag, her white hat. The cold outside air smelled of exhaust and hot new metal, sweet as the taste of adrenaline at the back of his throat as he started up the walk, wondering giddily, *Tonight, tonight?*

DESPITE HIS AWESOME NEW IMPERVIOUSNESS to the cold, he didn't want to stay outside. Something at home drew him—food, his notebooks, the possibility of his dad waiting, wondering where in the world he was. He stayed just long enough to see Jill's parents enter the kitchen, first her father, mostly bald, freckled as she was, pudgy, with a fringe of reddish hair. He stood with hands on his hips, and then with the back of a wrist raised to his forehead—classic woe stance, face absolutely stilled by some emotion, puzzlement or horror—eyes narrowing, mouth tightening. *Oh,* Thomas thought. *The hot chocolate. Shoot.* They'd forgotten and never cleaned that up. Then her father was gone. A male voice, higher than he'd anticipated, given his seeming bulk, echoed from inside. Scottish accent? Couldn't be sure—couldn't actually make out any words. Next Jill's mother, exactly in the spot where he and Jill had stood kissing, opening mail. She was slender and pretty—prettier or perkier, anyway, than Jill. Like she was the original, full-color version, the genuine article, Jill the carbon-copy reduction. This was a disturbing-enough comparison on its own—Jill's own *mother*—and led immediately to a full-on recognition of how bad it must be for Jill, always feeling less than and overshadowed, maybe especially because of the birthmark. Birthmarks. Kind of explained all her crying. *Tough luck,* he thought. *Sucks to be you.* But then minutes later when Jill stomped in, sheepish, tragically red-faced, father right behind her, he had to reassess. Actually, facial stain or not, she was the dazzling one. Radiant. He caught her in glimpses coming in and out of the window and once he was sure she was staring right out at him here by the apple tree. Even thought he saw her wink and nod her head. But that was impossible. If she was winking and nodding, it would be at her own reflection. Must be the pills, making him not just impervious to the cold but allowing dream thought to seep up through the optical nerves and seem real. And that was when he knew, in the same way he'd known earlier that day at school, the clock ticking ahead during second period, that his time here was up. He'd been released.

He turned and headed into the empty field bordering their yards, up the incline, breaking through the undergrowth and scrambling over frozen, rocky soil, then turned again and continued along the ridge toward home. He wished he could always be this numb. It was really pretty terrific. Not just the cold but the branches whipping his legs and bare wrists, the ground prodding his sore feet—all of it was dialed down to about one or zero. Barely there at all. Just amazing. He could go anywhere, do anything in this condition. The Northern Lights, wheeling around on his right like the old Spirograph-set designs he'd sometimes drawn as a kid at his grandparent's house— one of his dad's old childhood toys kept there in California and never brought back to Calgary—seemed to be converging in the corners of his eye and coalescing back into the shape of the men, Hoar and Work. He searched the ground for their shadows alongside his own but didn't dare look right at them. That would cause them to vanish for sure. "Guys!" he said. "Can you hear me?" No response. Of course not. What would they want from him anyway, and what could he possibly provide? He reconstructed their likeness in his imagination and matched their shadows with how he would draw them as soon as he was inside again, warm and fed, their actions and facial expressions. He had to remember not to make Hoar anything like Malloy. Darken the edges, imagine a heavy green underpainting, enlarge the nose, angularize everything. The twenty years between the two men would have been almost erased by their time in the Arctic and the ravages of scurvy. Only the color in Hoar's beard might give away his relative youth. *What do you want first? Food or a hot bath? Just to stand over a hot air vent, thawing out awhile?* Their bathwater would blacken with dirt and blood and shit, all the places where blood had congealed and scabs formed around missing toes, reopened old wounds and new suppurating sores probably oozing freely. Little eddies of pinkish red making tornado clouds in the water. A bath would do them no good, really. Yet he had no doubt they'd each want one first. Probably with a jigger of rum and plate of fresh fruit and meat right there on the side of the tub. He'd set Hoar up in the upstairs tub and Work in the downstairs half bath. Work would have to settle for a hot shower for starters, or else wait his turn. And in lieu of new clothes for them: blankets. The thick new felted blankets from the hall closet, one apiece. Then a stew of fresh meat and carrots, potatoes, tomatoes, fresh gallon of milk for them to split. Lemon juice over everything. Side of C supplements. They would love him so much, he'd never be alone again in his life.

Fitzjames and them said we'd never make it on our own, but hang me if we din't somehow walk right all the way back to England, or somewheres else. . . . Don't rightly know.

My teef iv an agony to me now, brofer, can'd fink o nofing elfe. . . .

They must have better docs and sawbones here. Just see them lights everywhere! We'll get you a set a new walies right off. Nice ivory ones with a . . .

The rootf if ftill in! I feelf 'em. Can' do nofing wid falf teef till dey're all de way out. Oh, dat vile egg. Weren't no egg, eifer. I'm fure of it.

Din't taste nothing like one. Too true.

Ead a rock if it tafted like anyfing.

Not with those teeth gone you won't! Work laughed his cruel sibilant *see-see-shoe-shoe* laugh. *Won't eat nothing till you get some falsers.*

Nife hot brofh. Fome noodlef and foft bread . . . I can chew!

Nice hot piece of twadge, too, eh? But isn't there a special place in God's heaven for you dead virgins? Castle full of young nuns, a harem apiece? Hello! What in the world?

Their shadows bumped together on the ground beside Thomas and did not progress any farther. Thomas stopped, too, and did his best to follow where Work seemed to be pointing—not at the Northern Lights but away from them at a smaller pair of lights heading up the main access road toward them. Car headlights. The men were exclaiming to each other, shouting and waving their arms in amazement: *Some kind of travel machine with lights, carriage but no horses anywhere, a ship on the ground but no sails, and how much oil would it take to make that much light shine anyway? Impossible! Amazing! Where are the horses?*

He left them there and cut down the ridge through the underbrush to the picnic table and around the side of the house, up the front walk. No car yet; no Dad. Good. But here they were again, one of the men anyway, detaching from the shadows at the other side of the yard and approaching at an angle, fast, seemingly set on instersecting his path to stop or confront him. He lowered his eyes and gripped the house key between thumb and forefinger, ready, though he was fairly sure he wouldn't make it to the door before being stopped. Like in horror movies where you can see the stalker coming up behind the main character and she starts to run, but you know she doesn't have a chance—still, she has to run, and you have to hope for her. Part of the formula for fear. He heard footsteps crunching over ice, faster, closer, and felt anew the excitement of being face-to-face with the men. Skin prickling. They'd followed! Definitely no escaping it. What would he say? Would he invite them in after all?

"Excuse me, maybe you can help," the man said. He was not one of the men from the ship, after all. No accent.

Thomas looked up.

Someone from present day—a stranger whose car must have died on the main road, or else he was just lost, wandering. New neighbor? Something off or affected about him for sure, like he was trying too hard to seem normal, upstanding and adult, so that instantly you wondered whether or not you were supposed to trust him. His mustache was not the same color as his hair and looked superimposed on his face, and his eyebrows had grown together over the bridge of his nose. Maybe it was the flatness of the eyes and cheeks—made him seem just too handsome and wrongly proportioned, both at once. If you were doing his head on a computer-modeling program, you'd need insanely few polygons for a likeness.

"I'm looking for John Franklin," the man said, and nodded. Cleared his throat. He had on a plaid red-and-white jacket, cowboy boots, no gloves. Something wrong with his hands, too, Thomas noticed. The fingers were bent-seeming and stuck together wrong with what looked like extra knuckles everywhere, and ruined nails.

"He's not here," Thomas said.

"But this *is* his house. Do you expect him anytime soon?"

Thomas shrugged. The more he looked at the man's face, the more it seemed unweird, but then it also became harder to look away. Why was his mustache so much more yellow than the rest of his hair? "I don't. I don't know. Can I give him some kind of message?"

"Sure, you can tell him I was looking for him."

Thomas nodded. "OK. And you are . . ."

"He'll know."

Again, Thomas nodded. "He'll know." As if it made sense. "OK."

The man leaned and made a dry spitting sound, but Thomas didn't see anything come from his mouth. Then he stepped back, tipped an imaginary hat, and went quickly across the yard, boot heels crunching in the ice, up the street, and out of sight.

Thomas was alone again in the semidark, watching his breath cloud and still feeling the house key in his pocket. Moments later, he heard a car door slam and an engine revving. He waited to see if the man would drive by, giving him one more chance to maybe identify him or at least see what kind of car he drove. But no. He felt his blood fizz and settle. What the hell? Maybe he'd dreamed it all. As suddenly as the man had become the singlemost real and weirdly out-of-place thing in the world, he was gone again. Sometimes when Thomas was younger, he used to suppose, given how quiet and private his father was and the number of hours he spent out of the house, that he must be having affairs or involved in some kind of illicit activity, espionage, or drug dealing. Something underground. What else could have kept him away? Poetry? Maybe all that time he'd been right and here at last was his evidence—a message for his father from the underground.

He went the rest of the way up the walk, remembering as he

turned the key in the lock and let himself in that he'd never gotten the mail. Completely forgot. There would be a letter from his mother for sure. But . . . well, given that weird strangers were still wandering around asking for his father, he didn't much feel like going back out for it. Whatever. He'd get it later or tomorrow, or let his dad. Now it was time to get busy. Forget everything. Snack on something quick and head upstairs. Hide away. Draw. Because pretty much everything he'd done to this point must be wrong. He was sure of it. Or, if not wrong, badly in need of a redesign. The men needed to be funny, like wandering zombies, losing blood and teeth wherever they went, heads like rotting watermelons, like seed-blown dandelions, stabbing each other for laughs, gnawing on each other's arms and legs. Clumsy and impervious and indefatigable. Broken, bent fingers. They needed a total do-over.

Still numb but not as chilled, he headed for the washroom. Flipped on lights and was about to lift the toilet seat to piss, when something in his reflection stopped him: on his neck, like a tattoo of a bug or a spider, not quite loonie-size and blackish at the center, lined with pink ridges and serrations. *What the* . . . Remembered Jill's words: *Got you a good one there. . . . Hickey.* That was no hickey. He moved in closer to be sure, breath steaming the glass, colors in his own eyes splitting spirographically, pupils wide as canyons, puffy redness around his lips. The skin had ruptured and underneath was nothing but more crumbling, broken skin. Painlessly putrefying. He reeled back from himself, blackness creeping up in the corners of his sight. Held on to the sink edge. This was not what he'd pictured, not how he'd envisioned it. Too real. He swallowed to control the nausea and looked again. Tore off his shirt for more perspective, to see how it contrasted with the rest of his flesh and to learn if there were any more on him anywhere. Watched the breath swell and lift his rib cage, bones almost showing, the ancient pockmarks around his nipples from chicken pox, mute little fish eyes. He leaned in close again and raised his lips, opening his mouth for a look inside: gums pink and healthy still, but his right incisor . . . no, he was not dreaming this. It had come loose. Wobbly in its roots. If he pushed with his tongue from behind, he could see it surge out of line with the others, a bright pinching pain with that shooting from his cheek up his nose to his eyes and causing them to water. Again he leaned away. That sore would not be covered except with a collared shirt buttoned up all the way. Or a turtleneck. But he rarely wore collared shirts, never buttoned them to the top, and he did not own a turtleneck of any kind. More blackness seeped up in the corners of his sight and he had to lean his head into the sink basin until it passed. "Oh God," he said aloud. "All right. Uncle. I get it. Enough's enough."

Forgetting to pee or even put his shirt back on, he lunged out of the washroom and up the hallway, pausing to reset the thermostat from eleven degrees to twenty-eight, thinking, *Fuck you Dad, heat miser, I'm cold*, and up the stairs to his room, where he collapsed face-first in bed, dead asleep almost before he'd landed.

———

HIS WHOLE FOCUS AND AWARENESS of the world and himself in it had narrowed to his feet, burning, numb to the calves, and the immutable sledgehammer force of the harness shoulder straps cutting in, step after step, hauling the longboat on its sledge over ice and rocks and slush and snow. He was a pair of eyes and ears floating impossibly, imperviously above or through this excruciating assemblage of physical pain and numbness and cold: Franklin's ideal of spiritual transcendence but somehow still not dead yet. Around him the sounds of men breathing, cursing, Armitage to his left, singing again—*Oh the sea, the sea, the open sea, it grew so fresh the ever free*—feet slipping on ice, curses, flashes of cleated boot soles, rope pulled taut, shedding water. From the front, Fitzjames's voice leading them on, apologetic and uncompromising: *Here we go, lads. One, two, three . . . pull. And one, two, three . . . pull. Ready again, lads. One, two, three. . . .* Occasional thudding sounds as one or another man slipped to his knees or fell through a break of softened, half-melted cornmeal ice, bringing down with him the man behind or ahead. Seemed they'd been aimed at the same elliptical crest on the horizon for going on two days now, or maybe it was two hours or two weeks. Impossible to tell with midday forever spinning in place overhead, behind you, in front of you. Always noon. Hammer-blow pain through his shoulders and collarbone, the resistance of the harness; as ever, the sailor ahead of him, crazy old Harry Peglar, singing with Armitage, and another behind them somewhere joining in with their ribald made-up shanty lyrics. Again, Peglar pitched his weight too far to the outside, forcing Hoar to counterpitch, all for another six inches of ground. Eight inches. Another foot. Breathe. Breathe. Rest. Fitzjames's voice, still tired and apologetic in the lead, drawing them on. *Ten more and we break. Here we go. One, two, three . . .* The songs might have helped if they'd ever made enough sense to Hoar that he might join in. Only the call and response parts—*Oh the sea, the sea, the open sea.* The rest of it, an extension of some ongoing joke between the older sailors, topsail master, gunmaster, with their backward talk and stories about tropical beaches, brown-skinned girls, Comfort Cove in Trafalgar, where they'd once been quarantined en masse (Comfort being code for a unique, specific agony known only to them), turtle soup, and favorite dogs. Exhausting even to contemplate, let alone follow.

Suddenly, they were at the top of the ridge and going down, Peglar again lunging ahead of Hoar to the outside but never correcting himself back into the traces. No, they weren't at the top of the ridge, either. The sledge had, for whatever reason, sprung loose behind them, sped forward suddenly as if on waxed runners before grabbing again, stopped as hard as ever and sinking through the snow. Still, Peglar didn't straighten back into the traces and pull; he dangled there, drawing Hoar with him to the side, and the man ahead, as well. Voices rising behind them: *Back in line, sailor. Where do ye think ye're a-goin' anyway. Make it bleedin' hard on the rest of us. . . .* He set his teeth and pulled, jerked on the line, but Peglar would not be shifted. *Man down!* someone called finally, and Hoar fell to his knees, thinking, *But I wasn't down. I'm all right. I'm fine,* until he realized. Peglar. Oh. Old Peglar was down. And no sooner had he realized than Peglar thudded face-first in the snow beside him, inches away, unmoving.

Men circled, Armitage first, followed by Fitzjames, mirror held to Peglar's mouth, and next Gibson, all the older sailors who'd known one another from prior service. But Hoar didn't need to see the mirror to know, didn't need to witness Fitzjames trying and trying again, holding the mirror closer, pinching shut the dead man's nostrils, repositioning himself to get closer, saying, *All right, the joke's done now. It's gone long enough. Ye can stop.* But it was no joke. Peglar was gone. Where he'd been a moment before, alive and singing, pulling the sledge, there was a wet body. Mere seconds was all the difference.

Finally, shaking his head, Fitzjames stood, hands on hips, kicked once at the snow and whirled away before composing himself. In his best imitation of Franklin but lacking Franklin's conviction and natural religiosity, he addressed them: *Men, come now, men. Harry Peglar gave his life in honorable service. No time for a proper burial, but we can return later . . . and now let's pray together.*

Peglar's nose crushed to one side from the fall and his eyes stuck open with that thwarted, upward-looking expression, no beneficence, no divinity, no final delivery into light, broken teeth, cheeks black from scurvy and frostbite. Hoar was unexpectedly affected. Drawn out of himself and possessed of something he didn't understand. Had an idea where its root source must lie—in Franklin; in those days and hours he'd spent brushing lint from Franklin's uniforms, polishing his silver, hearing Franklin calmly intone on the eternal hereafter and earning grace and salvation through Christ—but didn't understand beyond that. He stood and removed his snow glasses as the others had and, in a voice that surprised perhaps him most of all—keening, but not distraught; desperation in check—he began the prayer: *"Oh death, where is thy sting? Oh grave, where is thy victory?"* Narrowed his eyes to slits, blinking away tears from the incessant glaring light, or grief, or both. *"The sting of death is sin. . . .But thanks be to God, which giveth us the victory through our Lord Jesus Christ. . . . and forasmuch as ye know that your labor is not in vain in the Lord. . . ."* As suddenly as he'd begun the prayer, he found he couldn't remember any more of it. If there was more. Maybe that was it. *Here lies Harry Peglar.*

Heard men muttering back, *Amen.*

Amen, he said.

Done.

He glanced again at Peglar and watched as Gibson bent abruptly to extract the booklet of secret backward writing and drawings everyone knew Peglar had kept in his coat pocket, stowing it in his own breast pocket. *Safekeepin',* he said, and winked at the others. *E'd a wisht it.* Nothing was real or right anymore: Here they'd just finished the prayer and already friends were picking the dead man's pockets and winking about it. No one stopped Gibson; no one cared. No more respect for the dead. As Work had said before they'd separated, going on a fortnight now, *Right soon it'll be every man for himself, every man just waiting to find out who dies next. You'll see.* Hoar should put it right. He should stop Gibson. Say, *One day they'll find us! Dead or alive they'll find us and know what you done here. You should have some respect. Put it back.* But looking up too fast and starting after Gibson, he was confronted with a bleached, static expanse of white, through which he could not make out much detail. Armitage's face, a ghost of an arm, Fitzjames approaching, an outline of his own distorted feet, the sledge, the traces. Remembered then to resist the instinct that would surely blind him in full . . . close the eyes, don't open them wider. *Close, close,* he told himself, and breathed slowly, waiting for the seared blood-flower patterns on the insides of his eyelids to abate. Stood still. Slid his snow glasses back on and placed a hand over his eyes, and dropped to a seated position, head between knees, whispering to himself, *Sea, the sea, the open sea, it grew so fresh the ever free,* and waiting for the return of sight.

It all came to the same thing. Older sailors were saying it more and more: With Franklin gone and only the nine officers remaining, Crozier never answering anything in detail, always *Onward, onward, must press on*, spirit in the heels of his boots, anyone could tell, what was left? Why go forward? Why stay? Why do anything? For Hoar, the answer was obvious enough—as obvious as Crozier's grimness and refusal to specify plans was his final vanguard and reserve, beyond which nothing else lay: So long as he had one foot to put in front of the other and energy to do so, *onward* it was. *Because* there was nothing else, not because he hoped any good might come of it. He drove himself upright, hands on knees, and squinted, eyes open. Blinked back the blurred, sun-haloed shadows of black-faced men reclining in ice, waiting, resting, some still within the traces, one gnawing a chunk of hardtack or bone and spitting it back into his palm, trying again, cursing his hunger and lack of teeth, and again licking at the bloody lump of food, shoving it in. Blood in his beard and down his neck. Without chewing, he swallowed and thumped once on his chest, and again, to make it go down. Coughed and leaned, retching. Grabbed handfuls of snow, which he tried to eat as well but mostly spat back out, scrubbing his hand on his leg. Hoar was lucky; he knew it. Preserved by good fortune, a natural adversity to scurvy, maybe, or his stolen extra partial rations of currants and other fresh food from the captain's table all those winter nights, he had his teeth still. Some loose and overgrown by the gums, but all there still, and his joints ached. Bad signs. Stomach always sore and queasy to the root, also bad—but otherwise he was nowhere near as afflicted as most men. *Captain's whore,* they called him sometimes, speaking to one another. *Stole his pearl falsers, and who knows what else besides.* He didn't care. *That's Master Hoar to you, sailor,* he'd reply if any said it to his face, but none did. *I wouldn't steal nothing from Captain Franklin.*

DAYS LATER—HOW MANY? WEEKS?—again partially snow-blinded but pretending full blindness in order not to have to serve or to witness, he sat in ice. Sounds of slurping and contented, barely restrained sighs of relief from men around him. Dead man from *Terror.* Some comfort in that. Dead less than a few hours. Didn't know him, refused to remember a name. Able-bodied Seaman Somebody. The taste was not new, somehow—like much of the fresh game he'd eaten here and at home, bear, marmot, boar—a pungent, metallic blood flavor with rank overtones. At first, he had worried he wouldn't be able to choke it down, but he found, as soon as it was gone from his mouth he craved more. Bitter aftertaste, and too fast his bowl was empty, heat causing his sinuses to flood. *Over here,* he said, bowl raised. *More here. Please.* Licked grease from his lips. Waited for the liquid weight of it in his bowl, misted droplets burning his wrist. *Here,* he called. *More here, please.* All around him lame and weak and snow-blinded men were saying the same, bowls uplifted. *Food here.* He squinted an eye open and again instantly shut it, willing himself not to take in the bloodied, pink snow, trampled around the kettles hung on makeshift spits over burning pieces of disassembled sledge wood; meat strips curing on the bowsprits of the two longboats that would be hauled no farther, others emptied of provisions and turned on their sides to create shelter. Tomorrow, Crozier and any men still able to see or to walk well enough to help in hauling the remaining longboat would leave. *Forty men at most,* he'd said. *The rest of you overwinter here and make it through as best you can. We'll return for you.*

This was their farewell dinner—last fortification and final full-muster mess.

Watch out there, sailor. . . . Straighten yer bowl. He knew the voice. Squinted open an eye to be sure: Thomas Work with a pot and a ladle. Was he so unrecognizable that he no longer warranted a personal greeting after these summer weeks (or was it months?) separately encamped? Or was it just more of the general madness—the fear and hallucinations afflicting them all, distancing them from one another?

Thomas Work.

There you be, then. More for you.

Obliged. God bless you and keep you from harm. He heard something extra splash into the bowl. *I thank you for that, too, Thomas! God loves you, Thomas.*

God's nothing to me anymore.

He was there still. Hoar felt his presence, unmoving before him. Again he opened an eye. Blinked and let both eyes remain open long enough almost to give himself away. Like the others, Work's cheeks and nose had blackened, the gums had grown over his teeth, swelling and disfiguring the lower half of his face, and sores showed around his coat collar, under his beard. Each of his knuckles lay open, pink and scabbed.

Are you with us, then, tomorrow, on the march out, or are you dyin' here with this lot?

I will walk if I can.

Around them other voices raised in protest. *Food here, too. Food here. More. Fill me up, I say.*

Be a fool not to. Crozier knows his way.

So I hear.

He nodded and raised bowl to mouth. Again, the choking first taste of it superseded by hunger pure as hatred. A chunk of something vaguely sausagelike bumping his teeth; he sucked it in and bit down once before swallowing, already longing for more, raising his voice with the others. *More here. Please. More food here.*

GUTTERING ORANGE-BLACK LIGHT on interior ice walls. Sexless, hairless old person, Inuit, in furs, rocking, speaking, smiling, two teeth showing. In her hand a silver plate, a coin, a pen, a boot with brass cleats: *Kabluna means big eyebrows.* Laughing, she points at her eyebrows. *Crazy big black eyebrows. Big white-face man, crazy big eyebrows. We see him around sometimes, sure. "Hey, Crazy Kabluna! How is it going? How is your hunting? How are your women?" It's a joke, because he can't hunt. Can't live alone and he can't live with others. He eats them all. Everything, everyone he meets. He don't fish, either, and don't hunt the seal because he don't know how. Never caches his food. Maybe he don't know about that, either! Won't eat any dovekie or the fishes. We bring him some once. We tell our children, "Go bring him food." And we tell them stories, too, to scare them sometimes, and maybe do some things to make them believe, but mostly they are good children. "Look out, here he comes! Kabluna! He eats everyone in his path! Watch out! He eat you, too!" Some of our women go to him another time with seal and whale blubber, but he say no. Kept one of the women for himself instead. The others, they got away. Some time ago there were many others like him, too, many, many kabluna*

on tall ships—tall kabluna, big eyebrows, black faces. Too many kab-
luna to feed. So after a while, they eat each other, and now there's only
one—Crazy Kabluna. The rest are in his backpack. All chopped up. He
eats them. He wears them on his shoulders and carries them with him
everywhere and some more he drags behind him in the snow, arms
and legs and heads. Sometimes we hear him at night, outside, munch-
ing—crunch, crunch, crunch go the bones—but it's been a while now
and most of us think maybe he's gone south, or else dead. He should be
gone forever! But we can't say for sure. Kabluna! If you're listening . . .
don't come back anymore! OK? Are you listening? We don't want you.
Go away! Shoo! Shoo!

JOLTED AWAKE IN FULL DARKNESS, Thomas was momentarily unable
to place what had wakened him or to piece together his last few
actions before dropping, unconscious, on his bed. Heard the furnace
kick on in the basement, and seconds later warm air rattling a piece
of paper caught in front of the vent. Homework? A drawing from
one of his storyboard books? He'd been dreaming that sound, trying to recollect what caused it or to guess what might be written
on a misplaced piece of paper, but it wasn't what had wakened him.
Pieces of his dreams fell aside, and he remembered: the man in the
front yard—*Looking for John Franklin*—and the reflection of himself in the downstairs bathroom mirror, the men outside exclaiming
over a pair of headlights, Jill with her blue marks everywhere. *Not*
everywhere, duh. With that, the sound that had woken him from his
sleep: a door closing suddenly: downstairs or upstairs? People talking—and, incongruously, words from one of his resource books. The
sea shanty from Harry Peglar's diary, *O the C, the C, the open C, hit*
grew so fresh and ever free . . . O death whare is thy sting . . . remem-
ber Comfort cove and the dyer sad. . . . Couldn't remember which
book he'd seen it reproduced in, but he pictured it exactly now:
words scrawled in a circle, backward, forward, surrounding a drawing of a giant lidless eye, and given the mysterious heading *Lid Bay.*
No one had ever managed to explain. But aside from Crozier's and

Fitzjames's botched and cryptic final notes appended to Gore's much sunnier one and hidden in what might or might not have been Sir Ross's cairn on Victory Point, this was the only written documentation from the Franklin expedition ever recovered: Peglar's notebook, found on the corpse of an unknown seaman with a steward's brush and a silver plate—evidence of lead poison-induced dementia, some said; period-specific parlor-game antics, said others. But why those words now? What time was it anyway, and where was his father? What had woken him?

He rolled upright, shivering, and felt around his sheets for a shirt to put on, overcome suddenly with nausea. Weird, hollowed-out nausea, as if his belly had been blown full of poison gas; it drove every other thought aside. *Water,* he thought, *must drink water,* and he staggered out of the room and across the hall to the washroom, where he turned on the tap for cold and lowered his face in the stream, drinking. Belching, drinking more. And as he drank, he reconstructed further: the pills from Griffin. How many had he eaten? Two to start and another one sometime later. A final half as he'd stood outside Jill's house, watching her and her parents through the glass. That was probably why his stomach felt like this: no food, too many pills. Just thinking about it made him want to puke, but he forced himself to keep drinking. Then staggered down the stairs, cold water soaked into the carpet fibers seeping through his socks to the edges of his feet at every other step. Weird. Why was there water on the stairs? Was it maybe the stalker man? In the kitchen, he went immediately to the fridge and leaned in. Milk. Bread. A moment's hesitation. No it was time: time for the fast to end. Strawberry yogurt. Jam. Stale old rhubarb pie. He carried these things to the counter. Turned on the light by the sink and piled jam on the bread with a spoon and rolled it like a wrap. Gone in two bites. Another. Gone in three bits. It made his eyes sting, that joyous sweet-tart C-soaked flavor. *Ohmygod,* as Jill would say. Here was where he'd been headed all along really: not scurvy, but its logical antithesis—the proof to himself of his own superlative control and mastery of his body, drawing back from the brink of madness and disease at the last minute.

Of course. He mopped milk from his chin with the bottom of his T-shirt and then opened the cupboard beside the coffeemaker to locate the C lozenges. C supplements. "Yes, yes," he said, "I'm doing this," swallowing four 500 mg pills in one mouthful. Thumped his chest where the pills felt to have lodged momentarily. Onto the pie. With ice cream.

But as he carried his steaming plate of microwaved Thrifty apple-rhubarb pie back to the counter where he'd been eating, two things caught his attention. First was the time: 12:44 A.M. So his father had come home and ignored him or chosen to leave him asleep, unfed, facedown in bed. Weird. Or, weirder, he'd never returned at all. But where would he be? The next thing was the letter from his mother, open on the counter beside the sink, pages half-folded back, torn envelope beside it: *Mr. Thomas and Mr. John Franklin, 223 Rattler Way.* This settled the question about his father's whereabouts anyway, and possibly explained why he'd never wakened Thomas: Distraught or distracted by what was in his own portion of the letter, or wishing to protect Thomas from whatever was said, he'd decided to leave Thomas sleeping. Deal with it tomorrow. Thomas stood in the middle of the kitchen, all senses positively attuned, as if he were the brain and central nervous system of the house and feeling through its floors, beams, joists, and walls everything that had happened here and that would happen next; as if his superattunement gave him control of time, which allowed him to foresee and thereby stall all of his next actions indefinitely. If he wanted. If he chose to.

He did not choose to.

He ate the pie. Scraped the plate for every last crumb and smear of ice cream and went to the sink, where he ran it under a stream of water and then turned and began reading. Not in order. The words might have been put down in sequence, but his understanding of them would never be sequential or logical. Without his mother's voice, they would never register with him that way. *Dearest!* she began. *Because of my dreadful habit of hoarding these letters to you, adding a little more and a little more every day, by the time you read this, I'm sure the days will be hours longer, and the ice outside my window.* . . . He skipped ahead. *I hope you'll remember the important thing to keep in mind there with girls is that you must never censor yourself and never hide from them your wildest most wonderful feature which is your IMAGINATION.* . . . Again he skipped down the page. *I could write you pages and pages and swear I'd never gotten it exactly right. Depending on the light—did I mention the glorious return of light?!?!—the angle of sunlight if there is any, what might have appeared translucent ice with a brown undercast of muck or murk could suddenly shift on you, glowing green-blue or blue-green, with a sparkling underlayer of silt. Most beaut-a-licious! I do wish you could see. The oldest pieces of course calving right off the glacier's edge.* . . . *A column today as tall as a house and whipped around the top to the shape of widow's walk or maybe a set of organ pipes, positively stunning. Like the finest fluted* . . . *Next time I'll send pictures. PROMISE.* . . . *Osprey and two eagles. The beavers are asleep with the little beavers in their dens and.* . . . *But what a relief! No bugs!* . . . *ice underwater has its own marble and silver patina quite unlike anything and ice that has set for an eon on a rock wall quite another corked and metal-tinged. How I miss you my boy. You may call at ANY time, you know, except you may not reach me while we're encamped. Number's here.* . . . *Tell your father I.* . . . *Your brother may have mentioned his plans to visit which I.* . . . *It will aid in his studies, I say, as there is so little to do here, most times, beyond read and study and observe.* . . . *One day maybe we'll get farther east, Greenland I hope, where it's said the thaw should begin revealing unnamed heretofore-unmapped islands any day now. Imagine your explorers of old rushing off to name them all! Sir So-and-So's Sound, Lady Bla-Di-Bla's Cove, Heroic Old Man's Island, kabloona, kabloona. So sad if it weren't also the littlest bit exciting, but we shall see.* . . . *Two auk and ptarmigan. Large bear but she turned and ran before we could get in range for a shot of her.* . . . *average temperatures last week consistently 2–3 degrees above normal. Weather permitting, in a few days we leave Tuk for hunting and fishing—seminars with kids and instructors in Inuvik as well, if any will have them, and the ongoing CEAP observations, so I am forever one woman facing two directions*

simultaneously, like your drawing of me which I think I will bring
with me so I can see it every day and think of you. . . . Here's a joke for
you: Why did the polar bear . . .

What drawing? he wondered, and tried to push the thought down.
An assignment from some fourth- or fifth-grade final project on the
Greek gods. He'd chosen Janus, the two-faced, as his subject. Used his
mom to model for the drawing/cover art, and though he'd insisted
it wasn't her, really—only certain details and basic shapes, coloring,
hairstyle—she'd latched onto the finished thing like some kind of
holy talisman, indisputable evidence of his being a child genius (*But*
you GOT me, really, truly . . . that's ME), and, when he brought it
home from school, never relinquished it. Hung it over her desk at
work and bragged about it at any opportunity.

Through the exhilaration of eating, C fast-breaking, and the residual foggy numbness of the pills he glimpsed how he was going to
feel about all of this later on—the lousy, tooth-gnashing, tear-your-
skin-off hatred of everything, the impatience and frustration it was
going to invoke for him; the screaming-little-kid-on-a-rampage
senselessness. Why was she gone? Why had she left them? He
might or might not be able to control any of these feelings, but for
now it was interesting beholding them from afar, like turning a
spyglass around and looking at your feet. *Mom,* he thought. *Who's*
mom? Who cares about you?

He set the letter down and listened. The furnace had gone quiet.
What had changed was an icy presence in the room or just outside it,
sucking away warmth. Not just the cold front, high-pressure Arctic
air mass parked over the top of Alberta or whatever it was out there
but something interior—in him, maybe, or in the house. Dead, radiant cold, like the negative-charged ions emanating from an iceberg,
snowbank, not the icy currents racing around a leaky window case-
ment. Cold like. . . . And then he heard them on the stairs. Their
footsteps creaking down and a high-pitched moaning pinched to a
stop before it said anything. The men had returned or had never left.

Soon after he and Jane had more or less moved in together at the start of his senior year in college and she quit spending any time in her dorm room except the occasional study night, Franklin learned that one of his favorite things was returning from an afternoon of classes to find not Jane in his rented room off campus, but a note from her on his desk or on the communal kitchen table, signed in haste with *x*'s and *o*'s and some offhand remark about seeing him later. Dinner plans. Cryptic reminders to him, limericks or punning updates, references based around a growing cache of personal inside jokes; that feeling of ongoing connectedness with her, and separation, both at the same time, which so pleased him. For a time, he'd saved those notes, the better ones anyway, in an unmarked folder, bottom drawer, left-hand side of his desk. But somewhere along the line, they'd been lost or, just as likely, found by her and discarded. All those days' and mornings' activities cryptically rhymed and remarked upon by her, for him, all that annotation, gone—not that he'd ever likely be able to decipher most of the meanings anymore.

But before that, before the notes, she'd been the girl in the Tyler Alcove whose name he didn't know but whose study habits he'd watched and followed for most of a semester—fall semester, junior year—the better to cross paths with her regularly enough that he'd have an excuse to continue or extend the few conversations they'd begun on study breaks and once on the bus to downtown. Or barring that, just to catch her eye, looking up from a textbook, and to smile in a way he hoped showed affection, deference, and some comradely commiseration . . . or just to stare at her there in the light of the library's cathedral windows, legs outstretched, leg warmers bunched at her ankles, reading, sifting and twisting strands of her hair in her fingertips, nodding off, waking again, taking notes. The light reflected onto her face from the pages of her book seemed to him the embodiment of a live curiosity and focus, a tractor beam of engrossment or attention whose intensity he admired as much as he longed to break into it or cause it to include him. She was a good student. This he learned early. Better, though not necessarily smarter, than he was, and a year younger: music history and mathematics.

Plant sciences. Canadian and no, she'd never spent the night in an igloo. Some of what he learned came from friends of friends, but more and more from her directly, in greetings and conversations, until the handful of days at the end of that semester when they found themselves mostly alone in the Tyler Alcove—other students having finished all exams and vanished—and talking or passing notes at least as much as they were studying. *My ultimate fantasy?* he'd written her their last evening alone together, studying. *Always the same: I walk into my dorm room and she's there under the sheets, asleep or just waiting for me. Probably naked. Not sure about that. Juvenile, right?* He didn't tell her that the fantasy was vivid enough to him sometimes he was unable to stop himself from a trembling and irrationally heart-racing sprint up the dormitory stairs to see if it had come true, if she was really there waiting—as if his haste or general timing might play some role in causing it.

Who? she'd responded. *Who is she?*

He'd cocked his head, and after a moment wrote, *My secret. Can't tell.*

As soon as the semester ended, she was gone. No good-bye. Just gone. Back to Ottawa, he figured—back to her four older siblings and solitary widowed father. Back to her favorite Lebanese bakery and art galleries that beat the Earlham and surrounding area galleries to hell and back. Back to real winters and a multiparty form of government that made sense to her, and real health care. He tried to put her out of his mind. Couldn't. Wrote her dozens of letters, which he didn't send. Started calling her at least as many times. Didn't. Couldn't name what stopped him any better than he could articulate what it was about her, exactly, that compelled his interest. But he was increasingly sure, too, that he'd been gulled, at least a little. Tricked into always telling her more than he'd ever learned and giving away more of himself than he'd gotten back in return, all of which put him at a disadvantage and allowed her all control of what would or would not come next. Start of the final morning's exam period, he'd thought for sure he'd see her there at Runyan, picking up her Baroque music history final; if not then, on the way back out. Pictured them having a send-off lunch, maybe inviting her back to his room, at least a lingering good-bye embrace. Hung around at the exit doors afterward, waiting, watching as the exam period wound down and the few remaining weary students straggled out, exam notebooks full of writing to hand in to proctors, honor-code pledges signed. No Jane. Often, in the weeks that followed, he would remember those final moments of waiting for her: sunlight harsh on the snow outside, eaves dripping, exam proctors eyeing him suspiciously but saying nothing. *OK to wait here a few minutes for a friend?* he'd asked, turning in his own exam notebooks. *Supposed to meet her here. . . .* The embarrassment and dawning certainty that he'd been wronged, stood up somehow. He'd given away too much.

I had to figure out what I thought, and why this was your fantasy. I had to decide a few things, she said the night, just over a month later, he found her in his room under the van Gogh posters and corkboard of images from his summer European sojourn, windows darkened, apparently naked under his sheets. *And I admit, at first I wasn't too keen on it. Kind of risky. What if you changed your mind? What if I couldn't sweet-talk one of your suite mates into letting me in? What if I read you wrong and it wasn't me in the first place? That was your challenge to me, wasn't it—see if I'd take the bait? But why would you do that—or, conversely, why tell me at all, if it wasn't me? It's not your usual macho fantasy, to be sure, and it's not your lost-little-boy-in-the-woods fantasy, either. In fact, I couldn't really tell you what kind of fantasy it is, so I decided finally the only way to find out . . . was just to do it. Take the risk. And I've always liked you a little . . . so, you know, why not? Right? So here I am.*

At first, he hadn't known how to respond. There were his unsent rambling letters to her in a pile at the edge of his desk, facedown and folded in half; he only hoped she hadn't read them. There was his bad breath from having sat too many hours after dinner in the library, studying, hoping to catch a glimpse of her or to cross paths again as easily as they'd done all the previous semester. Also his growing need to urinate, and the distracting noise of funkadelic music from his suite mate's room across the hall.

Only a little, huh?

She nodded, shrugged. Expelled a breath and rolled her eyes. *Yes, John. What do you think I'm doing here? Naked in your bed? Jerk.*

He puffed a breath. *True. Sorry.* He indicated the music with his chin, smiling ruefully. *Sorry about that, too.*

Are you mocking me?

What?

Sorry, sorry, sorry—don't you know that's the Canadian national anthem?

I didn't.

It's me that should be making the apology. End of last semester . . . I should've at least said good-bye.

True. But you didn't owe me anything.

Didn't I, though?

He struggled to recollect any of the tortured logic from his letters and unplaced phone calls to her, one righteous, vindictive sentence from those hours of endlessly looping interior monologue. Could not. *If you say so.*

Come, she said, and held an arm out to him. *This is how it is now. This is right now.*

And through it all, shucking off clothes and slipping in beside her under the sheets, waiting, talking—her yielding heat; the smells and textures he'd anticipated so many weeks now—lay this splinter of worry or grief he couldn't quite name or lay aside: She hadn't said why. She hadn't said, *I'll never disappear like that again.* She'd smiled and sympathized and said she was sorry. So he had to know, from the first moment he lay beside her, that separation was and would always be one of the founding principles of some pact between them. She was with him now; she would not always be. He had to decide this was a given, was all right even, and that he would always let her go, but he'd also always wait for her return, however long.

Heat blasting his face and instantly causing his hairline to prickle with sweat, he stood in the living room doorway now, unopened letter from Jane in hand, and remembered; let this piece of recollection go through him, aspects of it engaging him as vividly as if the bygone versions of himself and Jane were specters visiting from another dimension. The better to understand and anticipate his future a little, he told himself—protect himself, if possible, from whatever it was Jane had to say. Also, he needed to be careful not to base any decision or action with her too entirely on whatever did or did not transpire with Moira tonight, or any other night. These things were all separate and connected only in him—past, present, future—and were not manifestations of some inscrutable design or pattern. Not *fated*. The past was gone: no specters visiting from other dimensions, however persuasively the picture-making part of his brain might struggle to convince him otherwise. He knew this. Knew, too, the danger of using feelings for one woman to offset feelings for another—one to counteract the other. He loved Jane still. Of course. He always would. Yet, it was quite possibly, as Devon had said on the phone the night before, *time to get off the pot*—and if Moira's presence was the thing to help him do that, was that so bad? Regardless, whatever Jane's letter to him now related, he needed to do his best to read it as if there were no Moira. As best as he could, he needed to try to understand Jane as if Moira did not exist.

He tore aside the top of the envelope. Glanced a moment at her words to Thomas, beginning with his name, *Thomas! Dearest!*—the weight in those letters, the ink, and in all the words that followed—before setting that aside and unfolding the slimmer, single sheet of paper addressed to him: a new address and phone number where she could be reached. Balance of money owed her from the house sale still, minus amounts set aside for Devon's and Thomas's school funds, and the amount she was requesting now for her organization. A promise to be in touch more fully soon. That was all. At the bottom, one word from a poem they'd quoted to each other often in their early years, and which had eventually become their ritual sign off: *Without*— And her name: *Jane*.

The full line from the poem went, *Without you, there is no world to speak of*, but he was pretty sure she would no longer be inviting him to think of that. Not inviting him to consider her as having no world without him, or to revisit the old world that had been theirs exclusively. She'd be sticking to custom specifically to avoid hurt feelings.

More heat flooded his temples and prickled his hairline. He had to call her and end things completely. Now. Soon. No point hanging on. Time to close the door and put an end to this miserable, prolonged hanging-on chapter of his life. If he could do it on the spot, if it were as simple as deciding and transferring the decision instantly into action, settlement and lawful agreement, he would do it. He was pretty sure. *Without.* Indeed. "Divorce," he said out loud, just to hear it. "I am getting a divorce." He nodded his head, folded the sheet back into its creases, and whipped it against his fingertips. Too mad. *Don't do anything in anger; you'll only live to regret it.* Wisdom from his own father, of all people, and though he supposed it was true, sometimes . . . maybe sometimes you wanted to stay mad long enough to get something done. He forced back the recollection of Jeremy Malloy—light, springy, pinned to the wall under his forearm and the desire to just bear down harder, harder, until his own rage expired or the boy broke in two. Not that kind of mad. Mad in order to make a little distance between yourself and whatever was wrong. The real problem for him would come with preserving his convictions, remembering tomorrow and the day after and the day after that, and sticking by them. No more Jane. For real. Could he?

He folded the letter in half again. Tucked it into his shirt pocket. Went to the thermostat and hesitated a moment before thumbing the digital dial downward—*twenty-eight! That was like . . . eighty degrees real temperature. What was Thomas thinking!*—past 25 to 21, until he heard the furnace blower disengage and in another few moments all the vents in the house go silent. His fingers smelled of breaded fries and steak grease with chipotle mayonnaise, and in the back of his throat was a lingering beer tang. A smoky smell of charred meat wafted up from inside his shirt collar, and for a moment all his hopefulness and exhilaration from meeting with Moira seemed cheap and foolish. He was exhausted. Nothing would work out right. He went back over their last few moments—the sodium lights on the snow, her face next to his, the longing, his mouth open on her neck. No, it *could* be good for them. Meanwhile, best plan was to get on with the remainder of the evening. He would need to fix something for Thomas, poor wayfaring Thomas, or at least oversee food preparations and cleanup. Stand with him awhile and try to find things to talk about. Draw him out.

But maybe the thing with Thomas was to take a more hands-off approach, à la Moira. Resist always meddling and involving himself, fussing over heat bills and wasted water and toilet paper, lights left on, drawers hanging out, dishes unwashed, dirty socks, bad diet. Just let him be. Let him drift to wherever it was he seemed so intent on going—have his troubles all on his own. Be as compassionate only as the occasion warranted, no more. Sure. He could take a cue from Moira on this tonight and stand back. Fix himself a nice iceberg and spinach salad with fresh raspberry vinaigrette to counteract the steak and fries; Swiss cheese and cubed ham for Thomas on the side— good, quick and easy. Call up to him when it was ready, *Dinner! Letter from your ma for you!* and if he got no reply, bag it back into Ziplocs for him for later. Done.

Reflexively, he traced Thomas's footsteps all the same—best to see where he was, what he was up to anyway. Light left on in the hallway, washroom light, light on in the stairwell; no light shining from his own study doorway down the hall. "Thomas," he called, to be sure. "T?" No answer. Went to the washroom to turn off the light, glimpsing himself in the lavatory mirror as he did—blue button-collar shirt, face flushed from cold or heat or possibly the beer, the haggard planar angularity of his cheeks more and more like his father's every day, though maybe not unhandsomely, he told himself. He bent to pick up a T-shirt of Thomas's left on the bath mat. Hit the lights. Continued upstairs. Knocked once on Thomas's door and entered.

As always, the smell: sweaty, fungal, like the inside of a dirty lunch pail or school locker; like an old sneaker full of orange rinds. Really, there was nothing to compare it with, though all too likely the smell would have an actual single physical source somewhere in the room—pile of ancient unwashed clothes, or plate of molding meat loaf hidden somewhere, cup of sour milk forgotten for months on a shelf. No lights on. In the light thrown from the hallway, he saw him there, naked from the waist up, asleep. "Thomas," he said. Then louder: "Hey, T! Wake up!"

"What's going on?"

He drew nearer. Set the T-shirt on the bed beside Thomas. "Dinner. Put some clothes on. Come on down."

No reply.

"Thomas!"

"What?"

"*Dinner*time." He breathed once in and out. Crossed arms over his chest and stood with his feet spread. "You *feeling* all right there, kiddo?"

"Arrraa . . . no."

"Flu or something?"

Again, no response.

"Thomas! What are the symptoms? You say you aren't feeling well?"

"*Sí, sí . . .*"

"Spanish?" No response. "Hey! Come on." He felt oddly alone and self-conscious—an arm's length from the boy, not much more, and given almost direct sight lines into his psyche and dream life, yet completely unable to access any part of it that might actually help him understand. Amusing, the absurdity (absurdism?) of it and their estrangement from each other. "Hey," he said again. "Thomas!"

"Yes? What is it? "

"You fell back to sleep." And after another silence: "Thomas!"

"OK. I'm up now." He rolled upright, blinking, nodding.

"I'm throwing together some dinner. OK? Nothing much. Just, like, a salad. Ten minutes. You want to eat, come downstairs. Otherwise . . . galley's closing."

"Fair enough." He fell back again and rolled solidly onto his side, tucking back into his pillow. "Galley's closing."

"Also . . . Thomas? There's a letter for you. From your mom."

"Sure." His voice went higher and singsongy. "Be right down."

He was not waking up. Had probably never woken up at any point in the exchange. This was familiar—typical more of Devon than Thomas, though Franklin felt pretty sure he'd seen it once or twice with Thomas, as well—not sleepwalking, just plain refusing to waken. In all likelihood, Thomas was, in fact, on the verge of a flu or other sickness and he would do just as well letting him sleep it off as long as possible. He remembered the heat turned up, the shirt stripped off and left in the washroom—so maybe T had had a fever and broken it . . . possibly taken Advil to cause that. He drew nearer, breathing Thomas's scent, surprisingly not as rank up close—sweet, like dried grass with a tinge of sweat and something else earthy he couldn't place—so evidently there was no direct correlation between the aggregate smells of the room and Thomas's body. Another mystery. He touched two fingers, then a wrist to Thomas's forehead: no heat, cool and dry. Smoothed aside hair and tucked it behind his ear. Delicate ear, outward-leaning like Jane's, tissues thin enough through the middle to glow pinkly translucent in most light—*the ear's pearly flowering,* he'd written her once in a poem, early on, maybe the first he'd ever written for her. *An ear fetishist?* she'd asked then, and he'd assumed this would not be a good thing to admit to, so he'd assured her no. A beautiful ear was a good thing to behold—chalicelike; maybe reflective of an innate intelligence or sensitivity. He wanted to believe so anyway. Sludgy, doughy ears, pancake ears, ears with overgrown flaps, these were unfortunate, sure, but nothing to put you off an attraction. *But is it the first thing you notice?* she'd asked. And he'd told her it was. *Of course. And asses. Bosoms.* His own ears, he supposed, seizing a lobe now, were too furred and square-topped, but otherwise of no interest.

Forget her, he told himself. *Never.*

He stooped and lifted a blanket from the floor. Shook and tossed it over Thomas, causing whatever had been caught in the folds—pens, pencils, a notebook, eraser—to ping and scatter around the room. It was hopeless, really, the boy's room—such chaos. Where would you even begin? He backed out, closing the door softly behind him, and went downstairs.

Moira's hat still rested on the coffee table beside the unopened mail like some alien creature, too plush and white. Why would anyone buy a hat like that anyway, let alone wear it? What was she thinking? Who was she? Yet, on her it had seemed right and of a piece. Glamorous even. He scooped it up and watched his fingers stroke and flatten the fur—Mink? Fox? He couldn't tell—almost disappearing through it, before drawing its brim to his nose and burying his face there to breathe her smell. Withdrew his face and looked around the room, knowing there was much to do here before she showed up. If she showed up. Cleaning, straightening, organizing. A lot to get ready. "Yes," he said, and went upstairs to put the hat somewhere out of sight and change from his work clothes into sweats. Figured he'd clean awhile and then do a half hour on that clunker rowing machine to release. Crank up some music in the headphones and lose himself in a good aerobic purge. Calm the nerves, sweat it out, and ease his passage into whatever was next.

But an hour later, fed up with sorting through the piles of papers and magazines, junk mail, flyers, books left open and facedown, DVD and CD cases missing their discs, he crouched on the sliding padded seat of the rowing machine, arms pumping out and back, legs pushing against an imaginary current, and couldn't focus. Couldn't find a groove. For one thing, the right arm piston seemed to have lost its seal somewhat, so it pulled unevenly and out of sync with the left; also, the rubberized grip material on both sides, from age or disuse, kept shredding in his palms, so the more he rowed, the more he had to stop and regrip, dust his hands together. Resume. It had been much too long, and there was no music he felt inspired by—all of it too old, too familiar to get lost in: Police, Herbie Hancock, Neil Young, Grand Funk. He flung off the headphones and tried to find his own rhythm, out-back, one-two, push-glide, and for a while it was better that way, though boring, and he couldn't shake the persistent feeling that something or someone had entered the house. Kept checking over his shoulder and getting back into it. Someone was watching him. Again he checked over a shoulder. Nothing. Paranoia. Anxiousness about Moira, maybe.

Finally after twenty-two minutes of this stop and start, he quit. Went back to the kitchen on rubbery legs for water, and though he wouldn't admit to himself what he was doing, he knew absolutely: the utility drawer by the side porch door—all the way at the back, the cache of ancient Marlboros in the box of kitchen matches. He was pretty sure, last he'd looked, two or three remained. Well, he'd just check to be sure. . . . Old and stale and nothing to really satisfy the craving, but. . . . Out he went to stand, steaming, in the porch light, smoking, mostly numb to the cold, though he worried his wet shirt might soon freeze to his skin. No Northern Lights visible from this side of the house, only the moon high and small, ringed by a frosty corona. A song he couldn't place played in his head—something from one of the boys, he was pretty sure—the melody or part of a chorus, pieces only. *I don't want to be your ghost.* . . . He flipped away the butt and went back inside, knowing suddenly, as he came up the steps and into the kitchen, what the line was—the key into the poem he'd thought he was hearing the other day at school, weird warm Chinook wind day, before all the business with Thomas and Jeremy Malloy, Moira resurfacing. He went down the hall as if in a trance, snapping his fingers, tearing aside his wet T-shirt and tossing it up the stairs. Stepped through half-unpacked boxes to grab a throw blanket from the couch, tugging it from beneath piles of notebooks and magazines on the cushions and draping it around his shoulders. The word wasn't *sun* after all. Of course. Another trick of the ear: right sound, wrong word. *Son.* Tonight, he swore it, he'd start on their death scene and the final poem of the book—final wave carrying the seal-man and his son into the gunner's sites, one on his back, the other facing forward . . . the puff of smoke, rifle report, seals dropping, diving through the wave too late. . . .

3

PASSAGE/TALLURUTIK

As he'd done when he was a child, Thomas hid in the beam of light thrown from the TV screen and believed himself safe from all harm as long as he stuck in the little circle of blue-green illumination and didn't look outside it—as long as he huddled on the itchy basement carpet remnants and kept his attention on the screen. He started with *Night of the Living Dead* because if zombie sailors were, in fact, wandering around the house—if his imagination had caused some distortion in the space-time continuum, drawing them here to seek him again in Houndstitch, Alberta—then what better way to inoculate himself against their influence and against his own fears than with the mother of all modern zombie flicks? As always, watching, a part of him thrilled with anticipation, seeing the credits roll and the car winding its way through rural central Pennsylvania (so much like southern Alberta in black and white)— zooming toward the camera and careening past it; again, approaching and again zooming by—the creepy music, the turns in the road, entrance sign to the cemetery, all of it just perfect. Unsettling you and preparing you for zombie horror, with nothing but lighting and music to achieve the effect. It sped his heart and sent shock waves to make his fingers twitch and his kneecaps jump; yet, as always, through it all, another part of him stood aside, paying attention to the movie-making trickery—camera work, editing, and perspective. He mumbled along with the dialogue and kept his eyes on the screen, smack in the square, remote control in hand, ready to pause or skip backward or ahead as necessary, fast-forward through the slower scenes, get right to the flames and tire irons through skulls.

Even so, as he watched, he became increasingly aware of shadows gathering in his peripheral vision—deepening and shifting. He couldn't be sure. Didn't want to be sure. Also a naggingly insistent need to urinate. The shadows would most likely have to do with the pills and some way they were still causing light and dark to distort and move unevenly across his field of vision. Also, he'd forgotten about the sore on his neck until something in one of the zombie's makeup work reminded him, and now he badly wanted to see it again. Wanted to stand in the washroom alone with the light on, up close, and give it a thorough inspection—study it and be sure there weren't any others. The tooth that had felt loose to him earlier was still sore and definitely more pliable than any of its neighbors, but that could be anything. Didn't have to be scurvy.

We were miserable living together and I don't imagine we'll be any happier together dead! I'm going upstairs!

"This is silly," he said aloud, and stood. Paused the movie. Still keeping his eyes from the corners of the room, he looked up and across to the doorway. Nothing. No one but himself. "Silly," he said again, and headed up the basement stairs for the washroom, turning on all lights as he went. Not that zombies cared about light. In fact, in some circumstances, light was a hazard, a dinner bell, alerting them to the presence of human life. Fire was good protection, generally. And always, any kind of direct blow to the head was how to take them out. In his mind, he rehearsed some of the ways to pull that off: avoid a full-body embrace; sidestep and use the zombie's own forward momentum to get him off balance, keep him from grabbing onto you; throw him down, and go directly for the head. Stomp on the head. Hit or kick or stab the head. He supposed the scariest thing, generally, was their persistence . . . slow and indefatigable, shuffling after you wherever you went, enduring all body blows and just never giving up. They were as persistent as fear itself—the very embodiment of fear's nightmarish hold on the imagination. "Grow up, go away. Come on. There's no such thing," he said, and flushed, and moved to the mirror to see. Leaned in to examine the teeth first, breath from his nostrils instantly clouding the glass, and tilted his head to the side. It was as he'd remembered, the right upper incisor surging just out of line with its mates. He lifted his lip and probed the gums there with his fingertips to be sure, wincing at the pain. Pressed again and stood back. Yes, redder than pink, sore and swollen. That was new. So he'd done it. Probably. Given himself scurvy.

He lowered his face to the faucet, turned the spigot, and drank. Again stood and leaned to the mirror to see his teeth, and again bent to drink. He focused on the differences in sensation and sensitivity in the various parts of his mouth as he swallowed and, leaving his mouth half-full of water, extracted the last of Griffin's pills from the vial in his pocket. A rectangular orange-pink thing with the letter *M* on one side and a line down the middle—different from the others. Swallowed. Dropped the empty vial in the trash. *Why not?* he thought. *You gotta live life.*

Next he pulled off his shirt and, wiping his mouth with a bare wrist, leaned on the sink to be as close to the mirror as he could get, pinching and stretching the flesh around the sore for a better understanding of whatever was going on there. But this time, he felt less sure of a diagnosis because he realized Jill had, as she'd said, gotten him *a good one,* not just where the flesh appeared to have ruptured but elsewhere on his neck, as well. Like he'd been attacked by vampire bats. Or *was* it all from her? He couldn't be sure. One mark, raspberry-blue and bruiselike just under his collar line, he thought he remembered receiving—remembered a delicious inside-out sensation as she'd gone on and on sucking him, aggregate nerve firings popping all over his body in conjunction with the way her lips and teeth scrubbed the skin. Yes, she'd done that one. The worst was definitely still the one he'd noticed earlier, cratered and crumbling at the center, like a piece of exploded brain matter stuck to his skin. Piece of boiled raisin. That, he was pretty sure, was no hickey. Well . . . regardless, from here on things would only get better. Gradually, steadily, however long it took. Better and better. He pulled his shirt back on. The experiment was done. As of tonight. No more scurvy. If he couldn't draw the men into being just by focusing on them as lines and shadow and light, being as attentive as possible to all actions, then he didn't deserve to draw or film them, period. They'd have to find someone else for the job.

What did Jill see in him anyway? He turned his head one way and the other, trying to imagine whatever it was, but found nothing there to admire. Same old disappointing proportions and too-fine features that were not quite like his father's, not quite like his mother's, not quite male enough, not exactly girlish, either, not grown into themselves and seemingly stuck forever in this half-developed state. Was that all he'd been trying to accomplish with the scurvy? Rush some false transformation for himself—too anxious to wait for the true one, too impatient to let nature broaden the bones, strengthen the angles? He remembered Jill walking to him on her knees, then her bare legs halfway across his lap. Also, just after swallowing the pills, something she'd said that had both puzzled him and strengthened his hopes: *But what if it lowers my willpower and makes me even easier than I already am? Thomas! You have to promise you won't take advantage. . . .* He'd never thought of her refusals as having anything to do with willpower or as marking some internal struggle for and against sex, though, looking back, it almost made sense—how placid and willing she'd become when he first held his hand inside her shirt . . . or that one time he'd managed to slip a hand into her pants, the delirious few moments before she realized, how open to him she'd become and something in her that had shifted, melted under the skin, gone almost out of control. No, she liked it, too. *Next time,* he thought.

Past the cold wet spots on the stairs he went, back up to his bedroom to draw. He needed to see if he could do it—make the men silly or funny, more horrific than tragic anyway. Fun and likable. There were the new colored pens from his mother for Christmas and some fancy drawing tablets from her as well, none of which he'd used yet or even really looked at, because all of his storyboard notebooks were black and white and featured at least as much text as image. Why use good art paper and color for a bunch of words and sketchy pen and pencil drawings? Duh, Mom. But he had a new idea now: fewer words and more pictures of the men—full color close-ups of sores and ripped open flesh; close-ups of mouths, and hands with broken knuckles. The emphasis on garishness offset by comedy, Chaplinesque clumsiness and slapstick grace in all their actions. He lay on the floor, tablet open, and uncapped the first pen to catch his eye from the plastic rainbow panoply: blue. Cyan. And

before he could think to stop himself, he was drawing Jill, starting
with the mark on her face and going from there, the lines and details
tumbling out, blue tones sinking through the paper fibers more or
less inversely to the way they seemed to puff out her flesh in real life.
Again the two of them stood at her living room window, looking
out, and this time instead of just Northern Lights, they saw the men,
as well . . . all the men from *Erebus* and *Terror* in her front yard,
standing around in tattered uniforms and torn fur wraps, Welsh
wigs, waiting.

As he drew, he felt the house tilt under him and begin to spin. This
was not too unusual for him, especially starting into a new notebook, new scene, new vein of material, but he felt it more acutely
than ever before, maybe because of the last pill from Griffin kicking
in, or else the megadoses of vitamin C disorganizing his thoughts,
breaking him up at the cellular level as Peel Sound had never thawed
and broken up for Franklin. The house shifted and leaned creak-
ingly up, rolled to one side, and started moving. South, he thought.
Maybe west. Outside his windows, the tree shadows loomed close
and streamed by. Clouds and more tree shadows, a three-quarter
moon. The floor felt like part of his rib cage and hips now, melded
with him. Floating. From the foundation and lower parts of the
house came a crazy din something like what he remembered having
heard in his seventh-grade drum line every afternoon, the first few
moments of class before the teacher came in the double doors, blowing his whistle, arms upraised to silence them. *Blam rift WAP riddly
riddly riddly riddly BOOM.*

He drew on. The men outside were not interested in him or in
Jill, did not necessarily perceive them, and didn't seem involved in
any of the usual stalkerish zombie antics. Not grimacing and waiting
around menacingly, looking in at them through windows, starved
for their flesh. They seemed caught up in their own drama, which
now appeared to be a series of military exercises—getting into rows
and marching one way and another and back and then reorganiz-
ing themselves according to some inscrutable purpose. Sometimes
it appeared as if they were playing a game of tug-of-war with an

invisible rope, other times like they might be about to scrimmage. Too dark for him to use most of his yellow colors, and all the details of flesh he'd wanted to get—busted hands and faces—needed to be so muddy with shadow that he that couldn't do much with his reds, either. Browns and blacks. Hints of orange. Green-blue waves of color behind them. Interior close-ups of Jill in which it seemed to him the blue mark kept moving around, changing size and shape, sometimes disappearing altogether until he reminded himself (but *was* it the most important thing about her?).

They're trying to decide who's next, she said. *Which man gets killed and cooked next. That's what I think.*

Like a really elaborate sobriety test?

She nodded. *Kind of. That one there is the likeliest candidate, I'd say. See how he's always at the back?*

Back of what?

From this perspective anyway, if they're all like facing in a line together, I think the test is trying to determine which one of them—oh! He dropped it.

Dropped what?

Sure enough, the other men descended grimly on the sailor Jill had singled out, so he was no longer visible, and before long they all stood back again, facing in different directions and not watching what came next. Two sailors remained squatting on the ice beside the one who'd been rushed, then stood and repositioned themselves, kneeling, squatting again, carrying out a series of jerkingly elaborate movements. Cutting him apart, Thomas realized. One man holding, one cutting. Dismembering the sailor who'd done most poorly in whatever that exercise was. It was as neat and efficient as Romero's zombie barbecue pig-out scene was frenzied and atavistic. And try as he might, there was nothing funny about it.

Downstairs, doors continued banging open and closed, cupboard doors, drawers, the foundation screeching and mewling, and then the floor rose up at him—imperceptibly at first, but with a steady insistence he could not ignore or resist.

That one there is my favorite, Jill said, pointing. *He looks so glum and stern, but not like he's going to let it stop him in any way, you know what I mean?*

That's Crozier, he said. He drew Hoar into the background beside him. Tapped his pen up and down and licked a finger to smudge the ink, blackening him further into shadow. *You couldn't meet a sadder guy, probably. Should've been commander, by all rights, but he was Irish. So they made him captain. Saddest thing is, he'd proposed to Franklin's niece, Sophia, right before they left, and she said no way. She was superhot, so everyone was always proposing to her and, but get this . . . she sends him a letter after he'd left, which he would only have gotten if they'd made it through the passage, saying she's reconsidering and might want to say yes after all, when he's home again. True story.*

Jill shrugged. *Anyway, I like him.*

To me, he's too much like my dad.

Then your dad's a hottie.

He scrubbed wet fingers over Crozier's face as well to abrade the outline, elongate and reproportion the features. Footsteps in the hallway approached and receded, and again the floor canted up at him. He tried to hold it back with his wrists. *Oh,* he thought. *This is it. I'm dying. Wow.* Then the notebook was against his face and he was pushing it away, trying to be upright, but he couldn't. He was too unbelievably heavy to move. *Dead,* he thought. *Dying. Who would have thought it'd feel so . . . good. Live life. You gotta live life. What the hell.*

IN HIS DREAM, FRANKLIN was at the steering wheel and flying down a mountain road with Jane at night—Banff or somewhere similarly mountainous. Earlier in the dream, he must have picked her up from the usual scene of their meeting in his dream life: a room of towering gauze curtains, dimly lit, a cross between a new railway depot and hospital waiting room, where she sat on the floor, surrounded by cut-up pieces of paper. She would have expressed her usual muted surprise, tolerance, but no offense at his delight in finding her (*Finally! Jane! You're here!*)—and for the moment seemed willing enough to go with him wherever he said. So, they were driving through the mountains. In addition to pretending he had no desire for her, no designs or will at all, he was also supposed to pretend he didn't notice how obviously something had gone wrong with her—something just fundamentally *off*, like she'd been lobotomized. And the more he pretended not to care or to notice or to have any will, the angrier he got . . . and the more withdrawn and fearful she seemed to grow in the seat beside him, until to shock them both, he turned off the headlights. In the careening darkness, just their voices screaming and then the drop in his stomach as they flew off the road.

He jolted awake. Sat up and glanced at the clock's blurred red numbers: 12:23. So, actually more like 12:12.

In seconds, all he remembered of the dream was the car flying off the road, and Jane in the dimly-lit room, looking up at him in a tank top that showed the full length of her neck and chest. But he knew exactly where the last part of the dream would have come from: one of his worst moments ever, visiting Devon recently and driving back with him in a rental car from Jasper to Edmonton after a day of skiing—stupidly bored and tired, and playing with the headlights' ON/OFF switch for no good reason. Just because. Trying to figure out how to switch between parking lights, automatic lights, fog lights, on and off, turning the dial one way and then the other to no effect, until suddenly the lights went out completely and they were shooting down the mountain in pitch-dark. Devon screamed in the seat beside him, *Turn the fucking lights on, moron!* as Franklin madly toggled the dial back and forth, back and forth, trying to remember the exact pitch of the corner coming up, the concrete embankment, shoulder, staring through the blackness outside the windshield to make out the first detail of what lay ahead. Nothing. No sight at all. He braked and continued toggling the lights, until miraculously they came back on. He'd been doing over 110 kmh. Another two seconds without lights and he'd have killed them both.

That settles it, Dad, Devon said after a few minutes, still breathing hard. Franklin smelled a burst of his soap and antiperspirant as they rounded another corner.

What's that?

I'm piercing my nose and eyebrows and getting any goddamn tat-
toos I feel like. Whether or not it's student loan money. You have no
right *telling me about anything after a stunt like that. You fuck!*

I'd say—

No you can't! You forfeited the right to say anything back there
on the goddamn corner. Holy smokes! For real! What were you even
thinking?

What had he been thinking? He had no answer, then or now. Stupid juvenile impulse. Because the light switch had been there, so he
needed to see what would happen if he turned it . . . also to figure
out what the hieroglyphic light symbols painted around it actually
denoted.

And now he knew, too, aside from the dream, what had wakened him; felt it in the air: cold displaced and seeping up from the
downstairs front doorway—so the front door had stood open a few
moments or was still open. He'd left his bedroom door ajar for just
this purpose, in case Moira showed, so he'd hear or register her
entry right away, or so she'd intuit where to find him in the darkened house. With this knowledge came a recollection of where he'd
left off on the death poem before heading to bed—not any words
or images, only some residual feelings and the general shape of the
thing on the page. Flawed to be sure, but *begun* at last. Finally, an
end in sight. Hours more work ahead pushing the lines to the brink
and feeling his way back again along the blank spaces in his brain
where reason, vanity, and desire ground against one another—the
seismic activity of his psyche never to be fully seen or apprehended.
Where stuff got lost and didn't come back. *Fail.* Or, as the kids
would say, *epic fail.* Because in his experience, there was no other
way to go but straight to the edge of total ruin, a little further even
than that, and finally back again. He whipped aside the comforter,
scrubbed a hand through his hair, pulled on pj pants, and stood.
Went into the hall to listen for her.

"Hello?" he whispered down the stairway. "Moira?"

"John?"

"Right here."

Halfway down, she caught him—hands cold on his bare arms, icy nose on his neck, snowmelt from her boots wetting his bare toes. Her mouth found his and he tasted coffee. Licorice. His own toothpaste and sleep breath. Pushed past her mouth to rest his chin on her shoulder, her cheek cool against his neck, and draw her closer. He heard the stairs creaking under their feet, the rustle of her jacket against him, and smelled outside air. "You made it," he whispered. Felt her nodding. "My God. I hoped, but I didn't expect. How much . . . how did you do it?" In his voice he heard a tremor he hadn't expected. Like being a kid again. But this wasn't the simple terror and exhilaration of new intimacy—wasn't that alone anyway. It was also *knowing*: a woman other than Jane. Knowing what that meant, what it would undo for him. Her hands moved under his T-shirt to his bare rib cage, his hips.

"Warm me up," she whispered.

"Thomas is . . ." He pointed with his chin. "His room's right up there."

She pressed harder against him and forced her tongue through his lips. Allowed him to pull her up a step, then another. Moments longer he acquiesced, letting the weight of her pull him down, fix him in place, turn more and more real and solid against him. More irresistible. Knowing, too, it was a tease and a test: She refused to be directed upward for the simple reason that he'd indicated to her they shouldn't stay here. And why not? How many years now had he waited for just this, and already he was rushing away from it, on to the next thing because . . . why? Why always the rush forward?

He turned and led her the rest of the way, again pointing toward Thomas's room and making a slicing motion with two fingers at his throat, realizing too late she probably wouldn't see well enough to get his meaning. As soon as they were behind the closed door, he'd tell her. Say, *He was out cold earlier tonight. Sick or something. Probably no way we'll wake him up, but just the same. To be safe. I don't know what he'd think. He's a sensitive kid . . . and pretty broken up about Jane.* But watching her shadow shape at the side of his bed, he forgot all about it. "Hang on a second," he said, and went to the nightstand to light the dusty dinner-candle stumps retrieved earlier that evening from the downstairs utility drawer, with matches, for just this possible use. The sulfur and singed paraffin smells put him in mind of countless nights with Jane—different shadows thrown to different walls; same orange-tinged guttering light. Held out a hand for her jacket and laid it on the sweater chest. "Ah, and your hat," he said.

"Hat?"

He lifted it from the dresser to remind her, then placed it atop the coat. Took her hands and drew her to him.

"I'd have forgotten again, for sure. Thank you."

"*De rien.*" He chuckled and lowered his face to her neck. Opened his mouth on her skin. Felt her shift heavily against him.

"Phoque," she said. "Fuck fuck fuck. Mr. Phoque."

"At your service."

"But it's not at all how I'd pictured your room."

"How was that?"

She shrugged. "Or maybe it is."

"What do you mean?"

"I thought more paintings. Books."

"That's downstairs. In the study. It's all a total mess still, sorry. You know, from the move."

"Don't apologize. It's a charming mess anyway," she said. "Kind of . . . a monastic, manly man-cave mess. Like you'd expect hymns or chants in the morning."

"Not quite. Come," he said, and drew her with him onto the bed. Held his palm millimeters above her face, her neck, her hair. "I'm just . . . I'm still trying to make myself comprehend it . . . that you're here really . . ."

She pressed fingers to his lips. Batted his hand away and grabbed a corner of a pillow; moved closer, nose almost touching his. "*Apprehend.* But no more words, John," she said.

He nodded. "Insufficient."

"Traitorous and deceitful. Remember, *Poetry is what he thought but could not say.*"

"Mmmm," he said. He did not remember. One of her poems? No. Someone else's, but whose? He ran a finger from her elbow down her arm to her neck, tracing the curve. "It's been months for me, though, Moira. Years, actually. Three? You'll have to help. Where do I even begin?"

"*Begin*? I object to the terminology. Am I some kind of conquest?"

"Hardly." He pressed himself to her hip. "But we're not exactly on the same page here, are we?"

"You mean in terms of desperation or . . ."

"Maybe. You're still married, for one thing. I'm . . ." He left the sentence unfinished and watched her watching him, realizing he'd stumbled right into the finality he couldn't quite bring himself to say aloud yet: *not.* Not married. Not Jane. Though sure enough his actions were changing that, real time. "Single anyway."

"How little you know, John. Do you not want me?"

He puffed an exhale. "Only enough to eat you alive."

"*Well*, then?"

He dipped his face to her, let her arms enfold him—soap scent, smell of her scalp, her hair in his chin stubble, mouth hungry, slick and warm on his, better than anything he could have dreamed, yet he found there was still no way to focus his desire, no way to rein it in, and no single part of her to fuse with it, exactly, so he kept moving, too fast, he thought, or maybe too slow; cool flesh of her belly on his cheek and again her mouth on his. *Carne, carnal, carnality . . . dominated by flesh . . . meat longing, the oldest knowledge of all,* he thought. As long as he stayed focused on that aspect of it, there was literally not a shred of his consciousness given to any other thing—a relief; a blessed and long-awaited release into nothing but *her.* He watched her sit up to tug her shirt off over her head, unclasp her bra, and then lift her hips to skim away the rest of her clothes, and moments later he kissed down her knees to her open thighs. Lay with his cheek on her leg, hearing the echo of his own circulation, ear caught against her flesh, and raised himself to hold her around the waist. "John. What are you—oh . . ." Familiar bloodlike metallic tang and salt as he opened his mouth on her, adjusting his arms and

settling his weight between them more comfortably, tasting more
and more until she moaned so loudly, hands slapping the mattress
and grabbing at his hair, the sheets, he had to stop for fear of waking up Thomas. He rose and arched over her. "Shh-shh," he said.
She bucked against him as he entered her, forcefully enough that he
couldn't find a rhythm. "Wild thing," he whispered.

"John," she said, and froze. Pushed at his shoulder. "Condom!
John. What are you doing?"

He shook his head. Somehow, in all his plan making, he'd forgotten this one detail. "I'm a married single guy. Come on. Celibate as
. . . until now, celibate as a monk. You think I keep condoms around
here? Anyway, I thought . . . you were always saying there was no
chance you could have more kids?"

Again her hips moved with his and again stopped. "Yes, but you
might give me something."

"Loneliness? That's about the extent of any STDs you'd be in danger of picking up here."

"Or I could."

He stopped.

"Kidding." She rolled from under him, pushed him onto his back,
and straddled him. Tilted her hips forward and back against his,
lifted his hands to her breasts and squeezed her fingers over his.
And long after his pleasure had jolted from him, she went on, reared
back, sweating and rocking, hair whipping her shoulders, grinding, grinding until she was spent. To his surprise (and some relief),
through it all he remained rigid, if unfeeling, inside her.

"That was good, John. God, I must've come at least a dozen times
there at the end."

"Seemed like it."

"If we never made love again, I'd say we could go out fairly glori-
ously on that one."

"*Glorious* would be one word to describe it."

"Washroom?"

"In the hall. Top of the stairs."

She'd seemed so much denser and more iron-willed, resistant or insistent somehow, making love, he was almost surprised seeing her separate from him at the side of the bed, retrieving articles of clothing, and returned to her usual willowy proportions and dimensions. Felt again all his affection for her and reached a hand to touch her. "I'm so glad you're here," he said.

"And I'm so glad you're glad."

His last conscious thoughts had to do with the time: 1:58. So more like 1:47. Late. Early. Four hours more of sleep for him and another day. Maybe he'd call in sick. Sure. He'd be within his rights. He'd taken almost no sick days since coming on board here. But what about Thomas? He'd have to check with him and be sure he knew to catch the bus. If he was well enough. Which meant . . . He blinked his eyes open again. The thing about sex he'd forgotten: It was always just sex in the end. Nothing more, nothing less, stimulus-response-release, nothing transformative. Was he disappointed? The bedroom door opened, light streaking incongruously around her with it, and she slid in beside him, the back of her head under his chin, feet over and under, arms under his and fingers entwined. "Don't let me sleep too long, John, or I'm hooped. Just a few minutes," she said. He grunted. Thought but did not say, *We'll reset that alarm, then. . . . Better set the alarm or we'll sleep straight through. . . . Set the alarm. . . .*

HE WOKE TO MOIRA KISSING HIM and drew her on top again, hands at her waist. The candles had burned down or he'd somehow remembered to blow them out before dropping off, so he mostly didn't see her, only felt the weight of her on him, her mouth against his, and within seconds they were moving slowly in silence together. Darkness in the windows. A bar of orange-gold hallway light from under the bedroom door. Sound of her breath in his ear. Heater clicking on. Outside, wind and what must be ice or snow blew sideways against the windows, *tick-tatting*. The feeling built gradually through him so that when he came, he felt fused to her, and within minutes he was on top, every inch of him pressed to her as fully as possible. "More?" she whispered. He pushed against her to feel the bones of her body against his. Wind gusted at the side of the house and rattled the eaves, a loose gutter somewhere banging, clattering. "Don't finish," she whispered. He lay still, throbbing inside her, arms alongside hers, mouth at her ear. "No, go. Finish. Everything ends." He kissed salt from the corners of her eyes, her mouth, felt her nose damp on his cheek. Afterward, they slept.

Next, he woke with her head on his arm, his crotch still damply stuck to hers, and no feeling through his fingers. "Moira." He shook her shoulder and whipped the fingers of his numbed hand against one another, squeezing his fist open and shut. Propped himself on an elbow and again pulled her shoulder side to side, still trying to pound blood into the feelingless hand. "Hey. Wake up. It's just before six. Moira?"

Sharp intake of breath and she jolted upright, head in hands. "Jesus God. What have I done?"

"It's OK. It's—"

"Oh my God." She patted the bedding for her clothes and stood crookedly at the side of the bed, dressing in haste, snapping elastic in place, kicking feet through pant legs, raking fingers in her hair. "What time did you say it was?"

"It's just about—"

"Dear God, they will have gone already. Another black mark for Moira."

He stared up at her, waiting. "Can I . . ."

"If I leave immediately I might just catch them. Make up some damn excuse." She spun her watch on her wrist, biting her lips, calculating. "No, no. I can't do that, either. I'm . . . busted." She looked beseechingly at him, rubbed her hands together and pressed them to her eyes. Sat again. Leaned for one boot and pulled it on and stopped, collapsing forward with her face in her hands. "So what do I do now, John?" She turned back to him. "I was supposed to meet Jeremy at his father's with his gear for practice. Thursday. Thursday is not Davis's night for Jeremy, typically, but I asked him as a favor, last minute because Rick was held up out of town, so I could come here. But I've got Jeremy's gear *with* me. In the truck. Because I was supposed to fetch him this morning. So even if they figure I overslept and went around the house looking for me or to get his stuff, it's still no good. They'll . . ." she glanced at her watch. "No, they're already at the rink for sure." She used a flat, unhurried tone of voice he might have read as contempt, if not for the words themselves. "It can only look to them as if I have done exactly what I've done. So now what?"

"The truth?"

She nodded. "Please."

"I meant . . . tell them the truth."

Again she nodded. "No, I can, too. I can make up some damn thing. Over at Penny's house or something . . . crossed paths. Draw out the misery a little longer. Where in the hell . . . Oh."

"What's that?"

"Cell phone. I just remembered. I left it in my damn car. For crying out loud."

He put a hand on her shoulder, squeezed and released. "Look. I still say it's the best, simplest way. Whenever possible. The truth."

"Yes, but what would that truth *be*, John?"

He let his hand slide from her. "Well, this. Us. You, me. For one thing . . ."

She drew a breath. "I think there are some things I must tell you." He forced himself not to look away, not to shy from the emotions transforming her face—eyes swollen, skin unevenly flushed, mouth ragged at the edges. "I am not all I seem to be to you, I'm afraid— what I think you'd imagine for me anyway. Not that I'd mind if I were or could be. I'd . . ." She shook her head. "For some time now I've been involved in trying to spring myself one way and another from a marriage so bad and dead, you and I, between the two of us, wouldn't begin to find words for it. But the truth is, I'm not a good person, John. Please. And . . ."

"What are you saying?"

She shook her head. "No. I won't do this, either. Won't do it. What happened here last night, this morning . . . It was good. And I won't say another word to wreck it. Because the truth . . ." Again she shook her head. "You have to trust me on this one, John, but there are things I just can't share with you now—things you should be grateful to have no part of. Later . . . if we can get a little distance down the road, a little space from our respective situations. I don't know. But for now, please believe me, and try to understand." She stood, pulled on her other boot, zipped it, and went to the sweater chest for her jacket. "And count yourself lucky." Slid arms through and turned to face him. Held up the hat, grinning manically and waving it like a flag. "See? I didn't forget," she said, and placed it crookedly on her head. "Now wish the liar luck."

He stood. "Hey," he said. Opened his arms and drew her to him one last time. "I'm glad we had this night, then. And I'm sorry if it causes . . . if it's messed things up for you."

"Not your fault, John."

"Let me walk you out."

Years past, with Devon sneaking out of the house after midnight to rendezvous with friends or, in his last year of high school, slipping away in the early hours to meet up with Charmaine in some park or in her parents' basement, Franklin had learned that the whole parent-as-gatekeeper job was as impossible to enact as it was impossible to dodge or rescind. Bolt and alarm the doors. Threaten and cajole. Plead. Bargain. None of it mattered; none of it did any good. The house was a sieve. Temporarily things might be set right, compromises reached, but in the end it came to the same thing: standing outside his own bedroom door some early morning or in the middle of the night, bleary-eyed and barely awake but knowing, with a shock of adrenaline, the boy had figured out a new way to spring the trap and a new urgency for doing so. Bitten off his own leg and run. Gone. Hours already. Lights left on, a door or window open, smell of cologne in his doorway, empty, unmade bed, nothing more. And though Franklin might wish things otherwise, might hate himself for being in this role of *protector, controller, commander, parent*, he hated even more that he'd failed at it. Again. More even than that, he was plain furious with Devon for running.

But Thomas did not openly fight or run. Consequently, with Devon out of the house for college, Franklin had mostly (and instantly, happily) forgotten these particular alarms and responses—light careening harshly at the corners of his sleep-deprived eyes and the sudden knowledge that something had gone wrong in his off-hours and he was now about to face an outcome he was too late to do anything to fix or stop. The house was a sieve—a sinking ship, a junkyard full of stuff no one wanted anymore, graveyard from which everyone but him, it seemed, longed to escape. If he'd ever truly been the one in charge, it was long past the time he should resign and walk away.

Instinctually, he knew why she must have frozen ahead of him and was now pointing, staring toward Thomas's room.

"Is that . . ." she began.

"Yes," he said. "That'd be Thomas." Looking past her, he saw Thomas, apparently passed out, facedown on the floor. "He does sleepwalk sometimes. Let's just hope . . ." He crossed to Thomas's room, noting as he did the lights left on downstairs as well as upstairs. Wrong. All wrong. A lit-up sieve. He should have known.

September and already the nights were well below freezing, gale winds bringing up black clouds on the northern horizon and bouts of stinging snow and ice. Nothing anymore, but this flat white cusp of world—no trees, no hills, barely any shape to the land. Only rock and snow. Icy, refrozen serrated edges of drifts. Bare slick patches that crunched underfoot or broke open, engulfing him to the knee, slicing at his ankles. Slushy wet snow piled on the back sides of drifts stuck and soaked through the torn bottoms of his boots. Once, breaking through, he'd found himself up to the knees in slushy half-frozen meltwater. Funny, he could still feel it enough to panic, though he wasn't sure whether or not to care. But he did. Enough to pull himself out and trudge on. And two days later, breaking camp, reoutfitting himself in his same wet boots, wet woolens and skins as the day before and the day before that, he'd dared to look. The toes were black and red, nails gone, except the big toe on his right foot, flesh rubbed away between most of them, one little toe bent and twisted back over the others, and though he'd pried it into place again, it wouldn't stay. Dead. Broken. Everything from the ankles down swollen unfamiliarly to the size of his brother's feet, his father's. Well, if they made it through, he'd have to get the toes all cut off, to be sure. Learn to walk with canes. The older sailors said it could be done, but your days at sea were surely finished. A frozen finger or two, easy. But a man who couldn't walk, couldn't climb a ladder or rig a sail, he might as well try to marry a dog as sign on for service again. Life of begging under bridges, or maybe a desk job with the admiralty. And what would she think of him then, a man stuck behind canes, hobbling up and down stairs? A cripple.

Five days he'd been allowed off sledge-hauling duty and still he couldn't easily keep up. East. Why were they headed east now and how much farther? He tried to remember. The plan had been to walk inland, away from the worst of the coastal weather and straight south down King William's Land to Back's Fish River, where, Crozier assured them, they'd find game to shoot. Eskimo to barter away trinkets and silver, guns if necessary, for fresh seal meat, whale, and caribou. But here was the frozen sea before them, crammed with pack ice. If not for the sun, they'd have supposed it a misreading—compasses gone awry from the proximity to magnetic north again. But no . . . it was an unmapped inlet, deeper and wider than any others known on King William's Land, so they circumnavigated, three days now, maybe more, and with every weary step went sideways of their goal . . . east. Every step forward doubling the number of steps toward their destination.

Through the layers of woolen gear, he touched his few remaining possessions. The notebook from Harry Peglar taken off Gibson weeks ago when he died in his sleep. His steward's lint brush. A pen from Jenny, for which he'd long ago run out of ink to write her. And the silver plate stolen from one of the abandoned sledge-hauled longboats, rightfully his—the gift from Franklin. He couldn't say why he kept any of these items anymore except that knowing what they were and why they were on his person reminded him he was alive and had some hope and could still place one foot before the other.

Ahead of him, the men in traces had stopped and broken out, collapsing to either side of the last longboat. Crozier stood to one side of them with another sailor, likely ice master Reid or one of the petty officers, getting another reading on their coordinates. Crozier lifted his spyglass and faced away from the men and spun again, pointing, saying something to Reid.

Hoar seated himself by Work and waited.

"What's he after?" he asked.

Work shrugged and lowered his head on his knees. Turned his face to the side and stared past Hoar. "Seen some tracks a ways back . . . dog sledge and Eskimo. Crozier's hoping they got meat to barter." Still he stared past Hoar. "Half a mile ago now should have been the end of the inlet, by my reckoning. These officers"—he coughed and lowered his voice further—"it's like they been soaked in gin every night and got no wits about 'em anymore. Dizzy stupid they is. We're headed north again soon or my name's not Thomas Work."

"What are you sayin'—north?"

"I'm saying we gone the wrong way."

"Where should we go, then?"

"Straight across."

"The inlet?"

He nodded. "It's no inlet, Edmund; that's your Northwest Passage. *Tallurutik.*"

Still Hoar didn't understand.

"It's an *island*," Work said. "We're on a bloody *island*. King William *Island*. It don't connect with the mainland at all. This right here is the southern coast, and that"—he pointed with his chin to the inlet before them—"is the goddamn passage. Behold the great watery byway—future of English commerce we turned ourselves to walking corpses to find. Just remember you heard it from me first."

Hoar turned. Positioned himself with the sun in his face to be sure, and looked south. Ice. Gravel- and ice-covered rock running down to the frozen shoreline, and beyond that the white humped shapes of pack ice frozen treacherously in place. Glints of water farther on, but no real open leads. Too far to see across, but now at last he understood: not an inlet after all . . . which meant, as Work had said, it was the final missing link, the last unmapped stretch of open water connecting east and west along the top of the North American continent. The passage. Right there.

"Thomas." He searched his inner layers for the silver plate. Handed it to him. "If you make it home, please take this to my mother. In Portsmouth. Like I told you before," he said. "But if you need it to barter. . . ." He shrugged. "God bless you, Thomas, and keep you."

"What are you off about, then?"

"I'm not going with ye's across. I'm done for. Right here, in sight of the passage. I don't think I've got that many hours left me anyway. I'll find my own way." From some of the older sailors who'd gone to the brink and back again, he knew it was an easy-enough death they had to fight against themselves not to succumb to its temptation—*peaceful and restful and by the time ye're done for ye don't even feel the cold so much. You don't feel a thing. Like fallin' asleep in your mother's arms. Like fallin' asleep in your dead mother's arms.* He could just lie out in the open and let the cold take him. "Tell the others I gone to see what's over top of that rise there."

Work stared between his feet. "I won't, either, Edmund. You go now before anyone gets an idea. We got meat for another day or two at the best and there's talk of another. . . . I don't want to be the one cutting you meat-from-bones, let's say, but I will if I have to."

"Godspeed, brother."

He pushed himself upright and walked, singing under his breath. At the top of the ridge, he turned and kept on, the open sea always in his sight. And when he'd gone far enough that the others were out of earshot and hidden behind the ridge, he sat in a crusted drift of snow, propped up and facing south, arms open—a flesh and blood *inukshuk*. He dug in his heels and tipped his head back at the sky to watch the northern stars wheel into view, and sang.

When I was on old England shore,
I like the young sea and more and more,
and ofttimes flew to a sheltering place
like a bird there to seek its mother's case,
and a haven she was and oft to me for I love
I love a young and open sea . . .
oh the sea, the sea the open sea, it grew so fresh the ever free.

YEARS LATER, THOMAS WOULD REMEMBER it as the morning he came back to life. He'd picture his father and the woman in the white hat staring gravely at him as if from a distance, space stretched and telescoped, so they seemed below him somehow yet still looking down. Their expressions of consternation and desperate worry a cause of amusement at first, giving him more of the happy, buzzed, and sloppy-sleepy feelings that had held him down so long, face-first on the floor, dreaming in a pool of blue drool. Incongruously, his father's feet were prodding him and then his hands and the two of them, his father and the woman with the seal-looking white hat, were touching him up and down the torso, saying things to each other, and then he understood. Scurvy symptom number three: old scars reopening. Old chicken pox scars on his chest blistered and bloody, and the cut on his neck, not from Jill after all—now he remembered: It was a rope burn from an incident with Devon years earlier that he'd picked and picked at ceaselessly, never allowing it to scab, until it was an *issue.* Infected. Now reopened and hemorrhagic. *Scurvy,* he wanted to say. Brag, even. *Look at that! I did it.* But he could not be sure he'd actually said any of it, and anyway, they seemed not to understand.

"WHAT DID YOU TAKE?" his father yelled, and this time Thomas was able to hear it, though still as if it were coming from far away. "WHAT ARE YOU ON, THOMAS? ARE YOU SICK?"

Man, I don't know.

They lifted and hauled him to the bathroom, forcing him to walk, and tilted him over the toilet, their fingers in his mouth, prying, one of them holding it open, the other gagging him until all the wonderful food—all the good pie and ice cream and jam and C-soaked deliciousness—came up in a syrupy mess. It flooded his nose and caused his eyes to burn and also brought the world of sound closer again.

"Let's clean him up," his father said, and they were swabbing his face, his neck with a wet facecloth.

"What is wrong with you?" his father said. He had Thomas by the jaw and squeezed painfully, rattled his head from side to side. "What have you done to yourself, please! TELL US. And HOW MUCH?"

"Scu . . ." he tried to say. His tongue was too thick and swollen. Numbed. That was it. Wouldn't curl to the roof of his mouth for the *r* sound. He tried again. "Scurvy."

Now his father seemed irate. Flapping his hands and yelling, yelling, though somehow (thankfully) Thomas was not able to attach most of his words back to their meanings. " . . . old enough now to . . . this sailor crap. . . . Good God! Please tell us. . . ."

He shook his head. Swallowed a mouthful of spit and mucus. Moved his tongue unsurely. "I . . . 'm . . . not kidding."

His father just glared and continued yelling, hopping from foot to foot.

"Devon," Thomas said at last, only it sounded more like *Vevah*. He nodded. Tried again. "Call . . . Devon. He'll . . ."

The seal-hat woman touched his father's shoulder and leaned to whisper something in his ear. This was not someone he'd ever seen before or met. She reminded him of his mother a little, also of lemons—lemon meringue pie with the hat on. He could see why his father would like her, but who? Some kind of on-call Viking nurse? How had his father found her? What was she doing here? "You'll be all right," she said loudly. "Can you understand me?" Together, they walked and carried him to his room again—the door opening too fast, too wide, crashing into the edge of his desk with a sound that made him laugh and want to say *whee*.

WHETHER THERE WAS ANY SENSE trusting Moira's assurances in parting that *all would be well* for Thomas, he decided to wait until first light to call Devon. Hear whatever it was he had to say and then decide whether or not to make the trek to the clinic in Okotoks or Houndstitch, possibly the ER. He wasn't actually sure where would be best. Since coming here, they'd had no medical emergencies, and it wasn't something for which he'd planned or laid in an advance course of action. That had always been Jane's turf—kids' health, knowing where to go, when. And though he'd turned first to Thomas's storyboard notebooks for clues and explanations, anything giving him a window into what had happened and why, the sense of wrongness and violation of T's privacy in perusing those words and drawings, the page upon page of ink-wrinkled squares warping the paper, and dialogue in his crazy all-caps print running from corner to corner, notes and asterisks in the bottom margins, barely a space between words, dizzyingly unreadable, was soon outdone by his realization that there were truly no secrets here anyway—no designs or hints that might let him into whatever had gone wrong. It was just the movie. Thomas's imaginary movie world as solidly real and all-encompassing for him as Franklin's own Sule Skerry, but bound in ice, not water. And more copiously inked. Where Franklin had looked to the ends of his lines, his handsome, stair-stepped, wordless blank spaces sidling down the right sides of pages, to contrast and pull through buried rhymes, enjambments, eye rhymes, subtly opposing thematic tensions, Thomas had poured down more and more ink and pencil lead. Covered the page. Regardless, there was nothing revelatory here; nothing of a personal nature.

He shelved the notebooks as he'd found them and lifted instead the black leather zip pouch of all the boys' old D&D dice—weighty, cryptic things, not meant to be understood by adults. How many? Thirty sets or more—he couldn't count—all manner of shapes, sizes, and colors—red, black, purple, four-sided, six-sided, twelve-sided, and so on—some probably quite expensive, all bearing numbers or mysterious symbols. What had been the spell these dice held over the boys anyway? he wondered—the hours spent together in Thomas's room, nights and weekends, rolling, talking, plotting on graph paper—what was the secret? How did you even read the things? *It's like storytelling, Dad. Kind of build-your-own adventures, with some generic ready-made stuff, and cumulative character points and just shit tons of rules. . . .* Was what had happened to Thomas all part of some more advanced, stranger necromancy Devon had put him up to—some graduated *dungeon master for life* pact or scheme between them? Probably so. *Ask Devon,* Thomas had said.

As light crept over the kitchen windowsill, he called. Leaned elbows on the sink edge and looked outside, waiting as the ring tones pulsed and fluttered in his ear. The snow had stopped, but it looked to be a bleak, windswept day ahead, gray and cold.

On the fourth ring, Devon answered, clearly awakened from sleep. "Dad."

"Wake you?"

Devon puffed an exhale, possibly a yawn. "Little bit, yeah. Late night. It's OK though. I was going to"—here he yawned openly—"sleep till like nine at the latest. Got an exam at eleven. What's going on there?"

"What's going on here." He stood back. Gripped the edge of the sink. Watched the sky in the east brighten a shade redder and more orange. "Gee, I don't exactly know, Devon. That's kind of why I was calling. I was hoping maybe you could tell me."

"Tell you what?"

"This morning, I woke up to find your brother passed out on the floor of his bedroom. We can start there."

"What in hell would I have to do with anything like that? I'm, like, five hundred kilometers away, or did you forget?"

"Yes, well, it's my question, too, *what you could possibly have to do with it.* But the one thing, after my . . . A friend of mine who was here and I, we managed to get Thomas upright and in the bathroom and evacuated of whatever nonsense he swallowed, so he was mostly awake and talking, and Thomas said . . . at least what I *think* he said was, *ask Devon.*"

"Ask me what?"

"Well he seems to think he has scurvy, the best I can make of it, and that you had something do with it."

"Man, oh, man, Dad. I had *nothing* to do with that. Holy fuck." It sounded like something had struck the phone; then Devon's voice returned closer, crisper, and certainly more awake-sounding. "That little pussy. I can't tell you how many times I've been on the brink of blowing his cover or just dropping some good, obvious hints so you could be on the lookout, but . . . man. It's pretty hard to tell from here how serious anything might be, hey? Maybe it's all a bluff; maybe it isn't. Maybe it's a partial bluff. But he's my brother, you know, and he's having a pretty tough go of it lately, so if he comes around with some so-called *top secret experiment* he's doing and needing a little advice about it, what am I supposed to do? I'm not going to rat him out or tell him *no*. But you gotta believe me, too, every *single* time we talk, I tell him to eat some goddamn lemons. Every time. Lemons are *cool*."

Franklin released his hold of the sink edge. Slumped forward, forehead in his palm. "So . . . it's not something you put him up to?"

"*Put him up to*? Are you on glue?"

"OK, OK. It's easy enough for me to misread things, too, you know. If you can believe."

Silence. Breathing on the other end of the line. "How bad, then? . . . What's he got?"

"Like I said, he was passed out on the floor and pretty well delirious. We figured drugs."

"Shit. Let me see. I e-mailed him that check list. Hang on a second."

"Some weird-looking sore on his neck, too. Like a bite or something."

"That's for sure indicated. Here, hang on. . . ." There was a sound of notebook pages turning. "Severe exhaustion and general disorientation, despondence—yes. Corkscrew hairs . . ."

"Corkscrew what?"

"Don't ask. OK, here it is. . . ."

As Devon read aloud, Franklin's attention faded in and out. It was too much to absorb. He watched his hands on the sink edge, furred wrists, hairless curve of knuckles, indentation on the left ring finger almost gone. Saw the ghosted reflection of his face in the sink window looking up, outline smudged and blurry. *Why?* he thought. *How could little T elect to do this to himself?* "'Humans, other primates, bats, guinea pigs, and some fish are among the only animals known to lack the enzymes for synthesizing their own vitamin C–converting glucose to ascorbic acid. . . . Therefore, they can only obtain vitamin C through their diet.'" Again his attention faded and he was remembering Thomas, facedown on the floor. His terror, watching the boy's breaths come and go shallowly, thinking at first that the blue around his lips and mouth might be from poor circulation—something he'd read recently, some bulletin about a rash of teen deaths resulting from prescription painkillers and methadone and this being one of the last, fatal signs—before noticing the pen uncapped on the floor. The blue on the page beside and half underneath him. He'd rolled him to be sure, tapping lightly on the cheeks. Noted the dried blood caked around his nostrils and on his upper lip. What was it Thomas had said the day before yesterday—*that was something else, Dad . . . not related . . . having nosebleeds lately . . . ?*

Devon continued: "'Functionally most relevant for collagen synthesis . . . pathologic manifestations of C deficiency noted in collagen-containing tissues . . . skin, cartilage, dentine . . . so, bleeding gums, blackened overgrown gums. Hemorrhagic sores. Body aches.'" Enough. He turned from his window reflection, crossing arms over his chest. Pictured Moira, on her way down the front steps. Her curt backward wave as she slipped behind the wheel of her Escalade, then rubbing hands together as her engine warmed, blowing him kisses. *You should count yourself lucky.*

"There's more," Devon concluded. "But that's the basic idea. Man, I got this information specifically for the little ratface, to scare sense into him. You should see some of these pictures, Dad."

"Actually, I don't think I have to."

"Right . . ."

"Listen, though." What was he going to say? Words of wisdom and consolation? Who was he fooling. Here he'd failed or been duped and aced out entirely by almost every person he knew or loved. He jingled change in his pocket. "I owe you an apology. . . ."

"You most definitely do *not*. *I* should've said something. I figured if he was still going on about it to where it sounded at all serious, I'd get Mom's opinion—you know, ask her involvement when I visited next month. She's usually the one who can get Thomas's number best. I figured I'd start there."

"You figured right, I'd say. But it was never your job, raising Thomas."

Devon said nothing immediately, but Franklin knew him well enough to picture the slow head shake and the look of concentration creasing and uncreasing his eyebrows as his thoughts shifted from speculative to combative to faintly amused. "True, true, Dad. But you can't exactly do it alone. Speaking of which . . . you mentioned a, uh, *friend* there. I think that was the word you used. At some ungodly early hour of the morning?"

"I did."

"Any more to share on the subject?"

"No."

"Permission to ask a question?"

"One."

"Do we expect to see more of her?"

"That's two questions. But the answer is no, probably not. And yes, it is a *she*."

"Not ambiguous at all, Dad."

"Well, the situation *isn't* ambiguous or complicated, actually. She's married, as am I, more or less."

"A one-night stand?"

"I wouldn't say that, either. Rather the opposite."

"OK. I admit. I'm stumped."

From here, the conversation wound back to Thomas, and Devon's recommended course of action for the present—massive amounts of citrus, C supplements, gooseberry, pomegranate, fresh meat and vegetables; close, constant monitoring; if things looked worse in the next twenty-four to forty-eight hours, get to the hospital. Within a week or two, he should be back to normal. "But keep him away from the notebooks, Dad. The whole thing started because he wanted to make his art more *real* or something—experience it for himself first-hand? I don't know. If it were up to me, I'd burn the things. Little bro'll probably start eating lead filings next."

"Burn what?"

"The story notebook things, whatever he calls them."

"Never."

"Your call."

"Anyway, I should check in with him and quit stealing your precious beauty rest. . . ."

He laughed. "Remember how you used to always call me that—Sleep Stealer? It's payback, at last."

"What?"

"You said if I were ever to have a Native Indian name, that'd be it—Sleep Stealer—because of how I used to get you guys up all hours of the night, sneaking around."

"When did I ever say that?"

"Only like all the *time*, Dad."

"Once, maybe."

"All the time."

WHEN THOMAS WOKE NEXT, the seal-hat woman and his father were gone and he was in his bed, alone, sure of the events that seemed to have come before only because of the scraped rawness at the back of his throat and a faint medicinal taste in his mouth still. Hours must have passed. Midmorning maybe, judging from the light outside his window. The house was silent. *Jill*, he thought. He had to see her soon. Tell her it was done, the experiment, and something else he'd dreamed or decided. What? He didn't remember. Outside, a raven hopped under the cottonwood tree in their side yard, whacking its bill at the snowy ground. So he had not gone to school today. Ah, bliss. He closed his eyes, and when he opened them again, his father was beside him, asleep as well in the papasan chair he must have dragged up from the living room. "Hey," Thomas said, and waited for his father's eyes to open. "Hey, Dad." No response. There was a bowl of soup or chowder on his nightstand, not steaming anymore but smelling strongly enough of tomatoes and curry that he decided it must have been the thing that had awakened him. He rolled upright and moved to the edge of the bed and was about to lift and drink from the bowl, when his father woke up. Blinked at him.

"Chief," he said. He rubbed his eyes. "You're up, then."

Thomas grinned.

"Thought we'd lost you," his father said. The way he said it, Thomas knew they'd never truly been that worried. You didn't say to someone who'd actually gone to the brink and back that you were afraid they'd been *lost*. You asked them things like *Who's the prime minister?* and *How many fingers am I holding up?*

"Nah. I thought about it. But where would I have gone?"

His father's eyes flared and shot wide, and for a second Thomas thought, *Oh no, more yelling,* until he understood. "But *why*, though? Why in the world wouldn't you at least have said something . . . warned me? I mean"—his voice broke, and his eyes moved up and past Thomas to something on the ceiling behind him—"*scurvy . . .*"

"It wasn't that big a deal."

"Wasn't it, though? I'm just. . . . I mean, look at you."

"It's OK, Dad. Really."

From the story myths his mother told, he knew that to resist a radical, evil transformation, you were supposed to grab hold of the person responsible for saving you and hang on—wait for the fairies or demons or wicked elves stalking and surrounding you with their suck-you-under-the-ground evil mojo to finish the paranormal processional and go away again; fold yourself in a black-skinned robe sometimes, or a sack, not to be tempted, and just blindly hang on. Don't look. Let yourself be turned from one thing to another and another—horse, raven, eel, wildcat, seal—until finally the transfigurations were done and you stepped out of darkness: yourself again. He could do that now—collapse at his father's side and hang on. Ask him to please hide them a little longer and stop things from changing. Press his face to those familiar bones and hear the thump and squish of his circulation; try to force back some version of the world they'd had to abandon when she'd abandoned them and gone north. But those were all stories and myths. Not real. No more real anymore than Franklin or Crozier, Work, Hoar, or any of the 128 vanished crewmen of the *Erebus* and *Terror*.

THE WIND WAS BACK. Icy this time, and Franklin stood at his classroom window, hearing it whistle through the eaves and against the window glass, watching the exhaust from the boiler room vent across the quad catch and whip jaggedly before dissipating. The heat blown up at him from the radiator in front of the window was a nice illusion, he thought—nice tenuous protective buffer like the glass he looked through, tenuous *necessary* protective buffer, but the truth was that wind out there. Twenty, thirty minutes you might be able to stand it without full protection before muscles would begin to rigidify and blood stop circulating. Step outside for a cigarette and a walk, you might die. This was the real truth of life on the prairies, and everything else was illusion, theater.

He turned and went back to his desk. Pulled up his chair and opened the bottom left-hand drawer for his lunch—apple, cheese sandwich, Snickers bar. The usual. For a moment, as he had at the start of every meal or snack since the day of the *big discovery,* he had to think of Thomas and to register the very discouraging combination of dread, regret, frustration, and distrust now haloing all food-centered activity for them. Because Franklin had failed so miserably, nearly let his own kid rot his body to pieces, and because, despite this, he still had to more or less entrust the boy to take care of himself. He wouldn't and couldn't stand by every second of the day making sure he didn't find some new, crazy-brilliant way to destroy himself, and making sure he kept up on all his supplements. Wrong and infantilizing. But wrong, too, to ignore what had happened or to ignore his own complicity in how it had evolved.

At first, he thought the man in the doorway must be some kind of apparition—some leftover phantom projection from his morning's work on the poem. He was the seal-man exactly, or his hunter, or both: Slavic-handsome, baby-faced despite graying hair, eyes as earnest as an old-time balladeer's. The mustache was wrong—too blond and ostentatiously swooping or cowboyish, meant to offset the rest of the appearance, Franklin supposed. Somebody's parent here to talk about *issues*, but whose and why? The next round of parent-teacher conferences wasn't for another month or more. All he could think of right off, and with some alarm, was the two Doukhobor Freedomite kids from his senior seminar. So maybe this guy was here to strip and make some kind of silent protest about Franklin's immoral reading list. Liberate Franklin from his worldly goods? Set the file cabinets on fire? No, he'd heard the stories and knew you never got this much warning with Doukhobors: By the time you saw one naked, gasoline in hand, it was already too late. And then he understood. Of course. Davis Malloy. Jeremy Malloy's biological father. The eyes were hypnotically lush and dark. Jeremy's exactly. He was here to settle the score.

"Can I help you?" he asked.

"Depends," the man said. "You John Franklin?"

Consciously or not, wild animal or not, he was ignoring all of Moira's advice on how to deal with him. He looked directly into Malloy's eyes and stood from behind his desk. "Yes, and you must be Davis Malloy," he said.

The man nodded. Did not ask how Franklin happened to know his name. *They've decided you're an abomination and a menace to the school*, she'd said. *His father's way of handling things would be more personal, primal. . . .*

"I am acquainted with your wife. Ex-wife. She'd said you might show up, pay me a visit."

"Moira Francis," the man said. Franklin couldn't read any emotion from the way he said it.

"First off, let me apologize for what happened with your son the other day. It was all"—he considered the best words for it—"so sudden and out of hand, I guess. Out of control. I take full responsibility for my actions there. And Jeremy"—he shook his head—"I know Jeremy was quite upset, but I also thought, by the end of it, he seemed pretty agreeable to the disciplinary consequences, and ready to accept his own role in what had gone down. So."

Malloy shrugged, holding up swollen, twisted fingers, the bones of which did not seem to fit within the skin. Arthritis? "Well, see, that's the thing. No one ever consulted *me* about any of it."

"How's that?"

"No one asked." Some sort of internal tremor was causing Malloy's hair to quiver and Franklin realized that whatever words came next would be the ones he'd stewed on, lost sleep over, rehearsed the last several days. He'd need to be careful how he replied if he wished to avoid a fistfight. "Because as an educator, you, of all people, should know when to leave well enough alone. Boys can settle their own differences and learn from it if we leave them alone. . . ."

"Even if four or five of them at once decide it's fun and games to gang up on one smaller one, beat up on him, give him a nosebleed— you say just go ahead and let that play itself out?"

Malloy smirked and shook his head. Glanced down a moment. "Nah, I'm not saying. Kids have fun, hey? Part of the natural socializing. Some of it's not so nice. Some are in the pack; some aren't. Not saying it's right or fair, just . . . you should know when to leave well enough alone."

And here it was again, the irrational impulse he didn't understand and couldn't control. To hell with avoiding a fight. He came around from behind his desk and went across the room to be within inches of Malloy, close enough to smell the wood smoke in his hair and the cold outside air caught in his jacket.

"If you had an issue with how your son was disciplined, you needed to have shown up for the conference with Vice Principal Legere last week. This isn't some kind of vigilante matter you can take up on your own terms, and frankly, I'm not that interested in how you think I should or shouldn't do my job. I'm going to count to ten, and if you're not out of this room and well on your way down that hall by the end of it, I will call security and have you written up for hostile intrusion. You will not be allowed on this campus again. If you want to talk to me further about anything regarding your son, you can make an appointment with Legere and I'll be glad to continue. Do you understand?"

Still smirking, Malloy took a step back. "Sure thing, *teach*."

"Good," Franklin said, and moved to be within inches of him again. "One."

"You can count—"

"I can and will. Two."

Malloy turned and walked. Hunched his shoulders and seemed to gather his arms around himself. Kept walking. There wouldn't be much left of whatever identity Moira had forged for herself those years ago as his lover and common-law wife, but maybe something—some earliest, liminal version of her young self—might remain. He tried to picture it. Couldn't. Remembered her on the stairs, her peculiar insistence, and wondered which part of that, if anything, might have to do with Davis Malloy. Nothing, probably. He'd never know.

"Three," Franklin called after him. Silly, counting out a grown-up, and yet somehow right. Appropriate—anyway, it seemed to be working. "Four. Five . . ."

Only after he'd turned and gone back to his desk and sat staring at the clock, hearing the wind in the eaves and against the windows again, gusting, whining, did he wonder what in the world he'd done. That close. Davis Malloy could have come unhinged; Franklin would have responded likewise. He couldn't stop picturing Malloy's hands and wondering what it would have been like to fight him. Imagined knuckles breaking, fingers grabbing, pincerlike. Kept pushing the images back and seeing them again, wondering, too, what it might have to do with Jeremy—with who Jeremy was and how Jeremy had mistreated Thomas. Another mystery.

This was not something to tell Jane about, ever probably, and yet he wanted to. It was his first instinct. Call her, hear her voice, tell her the whole thing—Jeremy, Moira, Thomas with his scurvy—make it all real, make it end. "No," he said aloud. And again, "No. Can't." And saying it, though he wasn't there yet, he felt ahead of him, for the first time solidly enough to believe it, the crucial psychic dividing line separating past and future, separating Jane forever from him, and knew he'd soon enough have to step over it. With that, he remembered a poem he'd begun for her years earlier and never finished, one he'd promised for their third or fourth anniversary, half-written and started back into any number of times since, about her chest of socks at the foot of their bed, woolen, cotton, synthetic hose, each a pair chosen by her and worn on specific days of her life. Mated and balled in wads, they comprised a private patchwork, multicolored log of her time on earth—her time with him anyway. Stepped through, walked on, loved or ignored, each given shape by her, marked, and eventually abandoned. He remembered the poem's opening lines with their plays on the words *soul, chest, feet, divine,* and the final couplet he'd always aimed for but never reached, referencing his and Jane's customary sign-off—*Without*—and remembering this, he knew suddenly just how to finish it, leaving the final couplet open and unrhymed. He jotted a few words to remind himself for later—tonight. And when he was done, maybe then he'd call. He wouldn't share the poem, or talk to her about coming home—wouldn't talk much at all, if he could help it. He'd get Thomas on the line and stick around long enough to be sure they were really speaking. The boy needed it. She probably needed it, as well. *You have a mother still,* he'd say, afterward. *You always will. You understand that, right? It's not the same as when you were younger, sure, but she'll always be there, and always want what's best for you. Things could be a lot worse.* Because whatever was next for them, most important would be keeping Thomas in the center and equally connected with both of them. Staying as neutral as possible toward Jane so Thomas didn't have to choose a side. Any residual feelings could go into words . . . more and better. . . .

His thoughts were interrupted by the bell and sounds of hallway traffic outside, locker doors bobbling open and slapping shut again, kids' voices, laughter. Any second now, they'd start pouring in— mild-faced children with savagely cropped and dyed hair, painted fingernails, and torn jeans, some greeting him or nodding in his direction, some not. *S'up, Mr. Franklin? Hey, Mr. Franklin. Hi! Mr. Franklin, do you have our papers yet?* Meanwhile, these last few seconds alone, getting it down in such a way he might be able to access it later, call up the lines and feeling tones, bring it all back.

ACKNOWLEDGMENTS

FOR SUPPORT WHILE WORKING on these pages, thanks to the National Endowment for the Arts, the Washington State Artist Trust; and to the office of grants and research at Eastern Washington University; thanks also to the Vermont Studio Center for a week of solstice solitude and tranquility. Special thanks to everyone at the Squaw Valley Community of Writers, and particularly to Michelle Latiolais.

Thanks to Erika Goldman for thoughtful, insightful criticisms that led me into the homestretch. Hugest, heartfelt thanks to my most trusted, long-time reading/writing friend Ann Joslin Williams for all of her encouragement and for patient, close reading of draft after draft of these pages.

Thanks to John Reischman and all of the Jaybirds for music and inspiration over the years. You guys are the best.

Thanks to my parents, Larry and Alice Spatz for ongoing love, support and advice, and to Tal and Angus Weisenburger who provided more than a few essential character details.

Most thanks of all to my wife Caridwen Irvine-Spatz for support, inspiration, encouragement, research assistance, patience, wisdom, faith, and for building me the rice-hull writing studio wherein just about every page here was written.

FOR A LIMITED TIME
TWO SPECIAL SONGS, EXCLUSIVELY FOR READERS!

Visit www.gregoryspatz.com
Username: inuk
Password: katajjaq

"Lancaster Sound" — This original instrumental by Gregory Spatz features John Reischman and the Jaybirds: John Reischman on mandolin; Jim Nunally on guitar; Nick Hornbuckle on banjo; Trisha Gagnon on bass; Gregory Spatz on fiddle. It was written on a cold winter night in the midst of research about the Franklin crew. In August 1845, sailing from Baffin Bay into Lancaster Sound, Franklin and crew met up with a whaling ship. This was to be their last known encounter with other Europeans...

"Lady Franklin's Lament" features the world-music folk quartet Mighty Squirrel: Caridwen Spatz on fiddle and vocals; David Keenan on National guitar; Nova Devonie on accordion; Gregory Spatz on bouzouki. The melody has its roots in a traditional Irish fiddle tune of the era (1860s), "The Croppy Boy", and the lyrics are from a popular broadside, also from the era.

Lady Jane Franklin, John's wife, was in the public eye almost constantly during the years in which no one knew what had happened to Franklin and his men. She made the most of her public stance as tragically stranded, romantic celebrity, to pressure the Admiralty to send rescue crews after the men, mostly to no avail. Meanwhile, she organized and funded numerous searches for the men, largely paid for out of her own estate. Though she was possibly the best traveled woman in all of Victorian England (having traveled everywhere from Tasmania to British Columbia to Africa), she never actually sailed to the Arctic after Franklin...

"Inuk" is the Inuit word for "man" or "person"

"Katajjaq" is a competitive, Inuit singing style involving vocal overtones (not unlike Tuvan throat singing) and mimicry of animal sounds. Typically, it involves two women standing very close, face-to-face, and singing at each other until one of them loses breath, or concentration, or starts laughing.